Books in this series:

The Dreamer ~ The Beginning (2016)

The Dreamer II ~ The Gathering (2017)

The Dreamer III ~ The People of the Wolves (2018)

The Dreamer IV ~ The Cave of Bones (2019)

Much more to come!

The Dreamer IV

THE CAVE
OF BONES

The Dreamer Book Series

By E. A. Meigs

Dreamer Literary Productions, LLC

2019

For information regarding this novel or permissions
to reproduction selections from this work, please
visit
Dreamer Literary Productions at:
www.dreamerliteraryproductions.com

ISBN: 978-0-9981259-9-2

First Edition

Cover photo by my friend Paula Krugerud
www.PaulaKrugerudPhotography.com

I dedicate this book to my readers:

Thank you for sharing this journey with me.

Fonts used in this novel

Papyrus was created by Chris Costello in 1982.

Garamond was designed by Claude Garamond in the early 1530's.

The Dreamer IV

❧

THE CAVE
OF BONES

The Dreamer IV ~ The Cave of Bones is the fourth in The Dreamer series. This book continues the saga that follows the life of a young Neanderthal man, as told from his perspective. The tale takes place during a time in history when Europe was experiencing brutal climatic changes and man's position on Nature's food chain was indeed perilous. *The Dreamer IV* is written as a stand-alone novel, meaning it is not necessary to have read the preceding volumes to understand the story line. An updated version of the original Introduction is included for those who are new to this time period.

Introduction

This tale takes place approximately 40,000 BCE (Before Common Era), when the last Ice Age was well underway. At the peak of the Great Glacial Maximum, nearly one-third of the earth's surface was hidden beneath a thick layer of ice. A substantial percentage of the planet's moisture was frozen solid, causing the world's oceans to recede and the coastlines to become greatly expanded. At that time the Eurasian landscape consisted of vast, wind-scoured tundra and small pockets of woodland populated by at least two groups of people: the Neanderthal and the Cro-Magnon. These populations probably coexisted in parts of Europe for only a relatively short period of time, geologically speaking. They lived a seasonally nomadic lifestyle, and each hunted the same game. We can only guess at what their lives would have been like: their languages, their social behaviors, their spirituality. Due to the passage of time and the impermanent nature of most materials they would have used in their day-to-day lives, there is little to tell us about their existence besides the tantalizing clues left by their remains, their tools, their art, their burials, and . . . their refuse.

Analyses of fossilized Neanderthal skeletons show that the males averaged five feet, five inches to five feet, six inches. The tallest Neanderthal man found to date was five feet, nine inches. The females were five feet to five feet, one inch. Their bones were about one-third stouter than ours. They were heavily muscled and had tremendous upper-body strength. The Neanderthal had the largest brain size of any known humans. Initial DNA testing showed that they likely had fair coloring: red to auburn hair, green or hazel eyes, and pale, probably freckled skin. Later genetic research on Neanderthal individuals found in different parts of Eurasia revealed that some had brown hair, brown eyes, and dusky skin. It is now considered likely that the Neanderthal had the same variety of skin tones and hair and eye coloring as do modern people.

The Neanderthal roamed the earth for roughly 200,000 years before their trail went cold around 37,000 to 42,000 BCE. That said, the Neanderthal may have persisted to eke out a living for some time afterward. However, since most modern humans outside of sub-Saharan Africa share between one and four percent

Neanderthal DNA, it is almost certain that the Neanderthal are still with us even now, albeit in diluted form.

The Cro-Magnon first appeared in the European fossil record around 42,000 to 47,000 BCE. Over a period of tens of thousands of years they migrated out of Africa, gradually making their way into Eurasia. They were anatomically constructed more or less the same as most modern men and women. Cro-Magnon men averaged about five feet, nine inches in height, but it is thought that some taller individuals may have been upwards of six feet, five inches. Like the Neanderthal, their brains were also bigger than those of today's people. They are believed to have had dark coloring: dark brown to black hair, brown eyes, and tan or olive-toned skin. (Blond hair and blue eyes are a relatively new development in modern humans, having first appeared about 6,000 to 12,000 years ago, long after the pinnacle of the Ice Age, but possibly coinciding with the end of that last glacial period.)

* * *

It is my humble opinion that after so many years of existence in a world that often presented extreme challenges, these intelligent beings would have been at the top of their game in leveraging the available resources to ensure their own comfort and the continuation of their species. Some indications suggest that early man was potentially much more advanced than is generally credited (more on this topic in the author's note at the end of the book), and it is my guess that we will continue to be surprised by what is revealed when ongoing and future anthropological studies peel back layers of time as we search for ourselves within the lives of our ancestors.

* * *

An animal index is presented at the end of this novel for the convenience of those unfamiliar with the animals of Ice Age Europe. It gives basic information about most of the creatures mentioned in this book. It might be useful to know, for example, that a wisent is a European bison, and that the animal to which North Americans refer as a moose is called an elk in Europe.

* * *

This is a work of fiction and it is not intended to hold up to scientific scrutiny. I merely seek to tell a story that is set amid this ancient backdrop. I have peopled it with those whose lives — when broken down to their most basic elements — would not have been so different from ours: sharing care and concern for loved ones, enduring all life's hardships, and reveling in serendipitous moments of love, beauty, and joy when they grace us with their presence.

Mammoth cow coaxing her calf to cross the river

Chapter One

It is raining. A young woman sits on the damp earth, lashed at her wrists and tied to a tree. I am stunned at the sight of the forlorn figure, wet to the skin and dark hair obscuring her face. She speaks one word, "Run!"

It was uttered so vehemently that I was startled to wakefulness. I sat up and cast a glance around the little room, lighted by the feeble flames of a dying fire. My dog Raena, surrounded by six of her half-grown pups, lifted her head to gaze at me quizzically. I silently motioned that she could lie down and relax. My mate Morning Star, however, was stirred from her sleep by my movements.

"Tris, what is it?" she asked. "Were you having a Dream?"

I knew that she was speaking of my visions, which were strikingly different from normal dreams.

"Yes," I replied, resettling into the warmth of the cozy cocoon that was our bed. "But it was nothing to worry about. I am sorry I woke you."

Morning Star wrapped her arms around me and embraced me tightly.

"I have found that your Dreams are seldom *nothing to worry about*," she murmured dubiously as she nuzzled me and kissed my ear.

I did not want Morning Star to be concerned, so I usually tried to make light of my Dreams, but by now she knew better. We had known one another all our lives and had been paired for several years, so there was little Morning Star did not already know about me.

I had begun to experience extraordinarily vivid Dreams just a few short moons before Morning Star and I were joined. In fact, it was that first Dream which had led to that happy occasion. Before then I had despaired that our union would ever come to pass. I had loved Morning Star from the time I was a boy, but as I grew older I gradually came to believe that she was beyond my grasp.

We were of two peoples: my kin were Old Ones, those whom many considered to be primitive and lowly. Morning Star's family were of The People from the East. Old Ones tended to be slightly shorter and much stockier than The People, who were generally gracile in build. My clan had pale, freckled skin, green eyes, and curling red hair, while The People had straight black hair, dark skin, and brown eyes. Mixed pairings were said to have taken place, but at that time I had no personal knowledge of any such an event.

All the same, when that first Dream had foretold of a savage cave bear attack on my Puh and uncle, I was compelled to seek out Morning Star's father, Black Wolf, who was also Puh's closest friend. Black Wolf had solemnly listened to my description of the Dream, and then he had eagerly agreed to accompany me on the quest to locate Puh and my uncle. As it turned out, we were too late for my uncle, but we did indeed save Puh. Then it was Black Wolf who needed to be extricated from a deadly trap. When I was on hand to deliver him from a sure death, in his gratitude he graciously offered me the right to be paired with his daughter. Every time I bemoaned the unpleasant or even frightening things my Dreams sometimes showed me, I recalled that without them I would not have Morning Star or our two children.

* * *

We arose soon after sunrise, and Morning Star began to prepare our morning meal. Both children were still asleep. Seven-moons-old Pony had awakened earlier, but she was nursed and soon went back to sleep and now she dozed peacefully. Our oldest, Fox, who was a little over one and a half winters old, was a sound sleeper and had slept all through Pony's brief squall and subsequent feeding.

After rekindling the fire, I threw our nearly empty household water bag over my shoulder and toted it down to the nearby stream that kept us supplied with potable water. It was a mild spring morning: the sun's rays highlighted the early morning mists and the great dewdrops that glistened on the end of each fattened bud. It pleased me to see the signs of the earth's reawakening after a long and dreary winter.

Great Gran was already at the burbling stream, and she smiled a gap-toothed grin when she saw my approach. Gran was a Dreamer, too. It was said that I inherited my ability to Dream through her. Although Gran's hair was whitened and she did not walk far anymore, she still had an acute intellect.

"Pleasant day to you, Gran," I greeted her. "Why do you carry that heavy bag? Let me fill it for you."

"Oh, Tris! I have been hauling water bags to and from this stream for most of my sixty-six winters!" Gran shook her head as I took the bag and began to fill it for her.

"I know," I acknowledged, "but you have earned a respite from such chores. The water is cold . . . you must be freezing! Come stand on the bank."

Gran was in a chipper mood. She stepped out of the swirling water and laughed silently as we Old Ones do, but did as she was asked.

"How old are you now?" Gran suddenly questioned me.

I paused from filling the water bag to look at Gran and noted that she was observing me closely.

"I will be twenty winters old this next winter." I replied. "Why do you ask?" My mother had sometimes mentioned that my birth had taken place in the spring, so the twentieth anniversary of my birth had probably already occurred, but we measured our age by how many winters we had survived. The water bag was now full. "I will carry your bag home for you," I told her.

As I gingerly placed it onto my shoulder, it wriggled as though it were a living thing. I waded my way to the edge of the stream where I joined Gran.

"Many thanks," Gran nodded to me. "I thought you might have reached your twenties by now. You have always been mature for your age, but for some reason, this morning, you look particularly serious . . . introspective, even. Does something trouble you?"

I was not aware that I was any different than usual. But then Gran knew me better than I knew myself. I took a moment to think.

"I am a little concerned about leaving Morning Star and the children for the duration of the journey to Gray Elk's," I admitted. "But the sooner we deliver those puppies, the better. Even Raena is becoming fed up with them. I do not know what else we can do with the pups other than bring them to Black Wolf's dog-trading cousin."

"Is Morning Star pregnant again?" Gran inquired. She knew that I hated to leave Morning Star for any length of time, especially when she was carrying a baby.

"Not that I am aware," I shook my head. "Although I suppose she could be."

"Morning Star has two small children, both of whom are still nursing," Gran pointed out. "I doubt she will conceive until Fox is weaned. That might be another six moons or more."

"I guess that is true," I admitted.

"You sound disappointed."

"Although I know that Morning Star will cope with whatever life throws at her with good grace and good humor, I also know that her hands are full right now," I said to Gran. "I should not wish for her to be with child again so soon, but I cannot help it. Fox and Pony bring us such joy. Each new baby could only make us that much happier."

"New life is a joyous thing," Great Gran agreed. "But never fear. The years will pass and the children will come and then you will wonder how it all happened so fast."

"I know you are right, Gran. I will try to be patient."

"It is rather morbid, but I have always wondered," Gran began, "if some people felt the need to have lots of children in case of loss, to insure that at least some of them will survive to adulthood."

I stared at Gran, feeling a sudden stab of pain pierce my heart. Great Gran had the advantage of perspective gained by one who had reached extreme old age; she had outlived all her children and most of her grandchildren, of which my Puh was one of the few survivors. Did I have this underlying fear of losing some of my children? It was unthinkable, but how many of my siblings had not lived to maturity? Two died in infancy and my brother Dak was killed at the start of his fifteenth winter, when he should have reached manhood. It was a sobering thought.

I accompanied Gran to the family household which had been my home up until the time I was paired with Morning Star. As I hung the water bag in its usual spot, the youngest of my many sisters came out to greet me. Her cheerful smile broke my melancholy mood.

"Tris, where is Fox?" three winters old Mi wanted to know, holding her arms aloft in hopes that I would pick her up. She was a plump, sweet-natured child who was always willing to snuggle. Like all my family, Mi was red-haired and freckled. She appeared as though she might take after our late mother. Muh had come from a clan of exceptionally tall people who also had deep red hair. Mi was already almost as tall as her five-winters-old sister, and her hair was a rich, dark red. I myself had inherited the height of Muh's clan, but otherwise I resembled my Puh with his pale red-gold hair and light green eyes.

"Fox was still asleep when I left home, but it is early yet; perhaps you can play with him later," I said as I lifted her off her feet for a brief cuddle.

I did not stay long. I said farewell to Mi and Great Gran, and then retraced my steps to the stream to refill my own water bag,

As I returned home with my sloshing liquid burden, I was forced to simultaneously dodge Raena and her pups as they met me outside our home. The winsome creatures welcomed me as though I had been away for an entire moon.

"Come now, let me through!" I said lightheartedly as I stepped carefully to avoid accidentally treading on any paws.

I suspended our water bag from the notched branch that protruded from the wall and then bent to kiss Morning Star's cheek as she finalized our breakfast preparations. Both Pony and Fox were awake now. Fox was sitting up on his bed. He smiled and said *Puh-Puh* when he saw me. The dogs had accompanied me indoors, but Fox determinedly forced his toddling way through the canines to join me.

Morning Star sighed as she, too, waded through the many dogs to retrieve Pony so that she might feed her a breakfast of mashed tubers.

"Although I do not like to think of you going away, I will be glad when these puppies have been taken to Cousin Gray Elk," Morning Star stated. "Has Da said when he would like to leave?"

"Yes. I know he would like to go soon. I believe he has been waiting for the weather to improve before we embark on the journey. I will speak to your Da and my Puh about it today," I replied. "Since we were fortunate to bring in a couple of deer over the past few days, you should all have plenty of meat while we are gone, but I will need to restock the firewood and tinder so you will have enough to last a half-moon or so."

"Is that how long you think it will take to go there and back?"

I nodded.

"At most. We will stay with Gray Elk for only a day or two." I paused and smiled at Morning Star. "I do not like to think of going away from you, either. And our little ones!"

Fox had already devoured his meal, and now he squirmed as Morning Star began to wipe down his face with a dampened scrap of hide.

"Muh-Muh!" Fox protested. "Ugh!"

Unlike our sturdy, ruddy-haired, fair-skinned Fox, who took after me, Pony resembled her mother; she was dainty and black-haired, with a darker complexion. When it was her turn to be washed, she squalled mightily.

"There, there," Morning Star cooed to her as Fox looked on sympathetically.

"Nee no like, Muh-Muh," Fox observed. Fox could not yet say Pony, so he called his little sister *Nee.*

Raena also appeared to feel compassion for Pony's plight, and she came up and licked the baby's face to comfort her with her long pink tongue. Morning Star did not appreciate Raena's gesture. She pushed the dog away, gently but firmly. In doing so, Raena backed into a large shell bowl in which Morning Star was soaking precious grains for a future meal, upsetting the bowl and spilling the half-swelled grains onto the grass floor mats.

"Oh!" cried Morning Star as the puppies all descended upon the grains, eating them with rapt enthusiasm even though they could not be terribly palatable in their present state. "Oh, Tris! Stop them!"

Raena looked both confused and guilty, as though she knew she had caused Morning Star's consternation, but did not understand exactly what she had done to incur her wrath. I pulled the pups away from the upended bowl, but they had eaten every last morsel.

"I will take the dogs from here. I will go see Puh," I said hastily, shoving the pups toward the doorway. "Come on, Raena," I called, knowing the pups would follow her.

"Take Fox with you," Morning Star said as she placed Fox in my arms. "Go with your Puh-Puh," she told him, giving him a kiss on the cheek. Then she tiptoed up to kiss my lips. "Thank you, Tris."

"Anything to please you, my sweet," I smiled as I returned her kiss. "Enjoy your peace and quiet."

Morning Star pointedly turned to look at Pony.

"Hmmm, I am not so sure about peace and quiet, but we shall see!" She grinned as well.

* * *

I had just started down the trail to the family compound where the rest of our combined families lived when my sister Ru came panting as she trotted up the path with our younger sisters Twie, Saree, and Mi close at her heels. Fifteen winters old Ru was my oldest surviving sibling. She had been paired last winter and was now five moons pregnant with her first child and already sporting a large bump. Like Mi, she also had our mother's dark red hair.

Reader reviews from The Dreamer saga

The Dreamer- the Beginning is a captivating tale, giving a convincing and passionate voice to a young man from humankind's early history. It is well researched and based on scientific study, lending additional credence to a very creative story involving a time in our history that is very much shrouded in mystery and conjecture.~ N. I. Bourdeau

As an avid reader I am always excited to step out of the box and read something different, The Dreamer Series delivers! A delightful journey set during the last Ice Age brings to life a Neanderthal family; their lifestyle, daily struggles to survive, love and loss. The author delivers a story set in prehistoric times described so well, so vividly it leaves the reader wanting more! Write faster, we want more! Donna R. Fox

Fascinating saga of the times and life amid a Neanderthal family as seen from the perspective of a man with a special gift and a love of his family. It's just like being there; you become involved with their trials and joys. The dreams give you a glimpse of future dangers and events, leading you through an engrossing journey. ~ C. H. Beusee

This is not the usual type of book that I read but I was fascinated and could not put it down. The author did so much research that it felt like I was reading a true story of a family and how they lived during that time! I wish the author could write faster so I could get my hands on those next ones...keep them coming!~ L. B. Collins

This is a unique and interesting read. I couldn't put it down–almost missed my flight! ~ J. Simmons

Just like The Dreamer – The Beginning, once I started reading Dreamer II – The Gathering I could not put it down. It is so interesting with a great personal story line. And I love all the historical information. After reading the first two books of this series I cannot wait to get the third one! Keep it up! – Patti Stribling Lauer

I read this book and thoroughly enjoyed it...so exciting that you can't put it down. Kept me on the edge of my seat. Great writing. ~ J. Stuller

I've read the whole Clan of the Cave Bear series by Jean Auel, and I was bummed when it ended; you got the ancients going again in totally different happenings and people's! I will probably read all three again. Can't wait for book four! ~ John G. Smith

Before Ru could speak, ten-winters-old Twie blurted out, "Tris, strange men have arrived!"

"*Strange men?*" I repeated.

"Yes," Ru gasped a little as she caught her breath, holding onto her bulging stomach. "They are men of The People. They asked for Black Wolf, but he is not here. He, Puh, Ria, Ty, and my Bror are wandering around in the forest somewhere, looking at the trees so they can discuss which ones might make the best bows."

I nodded with understanding. Our Puh's new mate, Ria, owned a weapon that was previously unknown to us. It was made for her by her now-deceased former mate, and no one was quite sure how to replicate it. My brother Ty, even at the age of fourteen winters, was by far the most skilled woodworker of all of us, and he was very keen to try to recreate Ria's bow. He had told us about the resilient qualities the wood must have to shoot the tiny spears into the air without cracking or snapping in two.

Fox was attempting to wriggle from my grasp and jabbering at my youngest sisters Mi and Saree. He leaned toward them and held his arms out in his eagerness to be let down so he could play with them.

"Sit tight, Fox," I said gently to him. "Where are the strangers, now? Did you leave them at the compound, or did they go in search of Black Wolf?"

"We left them at the compound," Ru replied. "When we explained that Black Wolf was not home just now, one of them asked for you. So I ran up here to get you."

"They did not ask for Little Fawn?" I persisted.

Little Fawn was Black Wolf's mate. The two lived in a perpetual state of rancor, but they were doting parents to their offspring, and their dedication to those children was probably all that kept them together.

"No," Ru shook her head, "which is just as well, since Little Fawn and the children have gone out in search of new spring greens."

I was very curious as to who these men might be. There were not many men of The People who knew where to find our remote woodland homes. As I hastened my step down the path, Twie jogged to keep pace with me.

"Tris," she began, "may I carry Fox? Let me carry Fox . . . I will be careful . . . I promise!"

I halted just long enough to place Fox in her waiting arms. Even though Fox was a robust toddler, Twie was a big girl for her years, and she was old enough to have spent a lot of time tending her younger siblings.

"Many thanks, Tris!" Twie grinned.

"When may I carry Fox?" five-winters-old Saree piped up. "I am big enough, too!"

"Me, too!" Mi chimed in, "I carry Fox, too!"

I had resumed walking but turned to look at the little girls, Saree toting her ever-present doll, the poor bedraggled Hork, tucked casually under one arm, and

Mi clutching her "baby," a smooth stone she had adopted and wrapped in a pelt.

"You two may take turns holding Fox on your lap — if he will sit still long enough — later on today," I told them.

I listened to them chattering about who would hold Fox first, but as I entered the compound, my attention was focused on the small group of men who stood conversing near the fire pit. Great Gran and the resident dogs were there with them. I could see that Gran was calmly answering their questions and plying the men with food and water.

The gathering turned to face me as the throng of dogs, including Puh's pup Ochs whom he had taken in from Raena's litter, and Black Wolf's furry menagerie began to bark at our arrival. I instantly recognized one of the men. I had met Slow Bear several times over the last few years. He was attached to The People from the East's Head Elder's household; in fact, he was probably the most important man on the Head Elder's staff.

"Pleasant day to you, Slow Bear," I greeted him. "How good it is to see you!"

Slow Bear smiled broadly and stepped forward to grasp my forearms in the traditional way of The People. Slow Bear was a tall, stocky man of a somewhat advanced age, but he glowed with vigor and good health.

"Tris! It is good to see you, as well!" Slow Bear responded. "I have come with my companions Crow Feather and Roe Buck to speak with Black Wolf."

I vaguely knew the other men, but I doubt I had ever spoken to them. They were slightly younger than Slow Bear and seemed to defer to him, allowing Slow Bear to speak for them. Our happy reunion was suddenly clouded by the thought that they must have come on an important mission indeed to have traveled all this way to see Black Wolf.

"Would you like to make yourselves comfortable by the hearth while we talk?" I invited, gesturing toward the area around the fire pit, which was padded with woven grass mats. Gran was already bringing out a variety of pelts and laying them on top of the matting to further cushion us from the hard-packed earth. "Many thanks, Gran," I nodded to her.

The men also nodded to Gran and gratefully lowered themselves to the ground.

"On our way here we spent many days passing through lands that had burned. How fortunate that your homes were spared," Slow Bear said.

"Yes," I agreed, "the fire happened after a violent thunderstorm last summer. Puh had enough foresight to realize that if he burned out an area ahead of the fire, it would have no fuel and thus it would be stopped. Also, rain helped to put the fire out too."

Slow Bear and his companions exchanged glances, looking as though they were impressed with this novel strategy.

"I do not know your father well; he is a quiet man who does not let on much, but he is very astute," Slow Bear told me. He hesitated a moment and then continued on. "I am sure you must be wondering why we have journeyed all this way to visit Black Wolf."

"I hope you have not had trouble," I said.

"The Elder wishes to see Black Wolf," Slow Bear, seeming unsure of how much he should divulge. He then whispered to me, "Is it safe to speak? Should we go somewhere more private?"

I looked about us. The dogs were the only beings in evidence. Gran had taken all the children indoors, leaving us alone. Slow Bear's eyes frequently wandered toward the gaping opening to Black Wolf's home. Unlike my petite mate, her parents were extraordinarily tall, and the unusual height of the doorway clearly indicated that it must be Black Wolf's dwelling. I immediately caught his drift.

"I know that Ru told you that Black Wolf is not home at present. His family have also left for the time being as they forage for greens," I informed Slow Bear.

Slow Bear smiled with relief. He had good reason to be concerned. Black Wolf had been romantically involved with Willow Woman, the Head Elder, for several years and this was not something that was openly discussed. All the same, Willow Woman had given birth to a baby boy last fall and it was possible that the only person who did not know Black Wolf was the child's father was Black Wolf's mate, Little Fawn. She was capable of great ire, and only a fool provoked it lightly.

"Willow Woman has been ill. She is asking Black Wolf to join her as soon as he is able. We had hoped to bring him back with us," Slow Bear said.

"I see." I furrowed my brow in thought. This might delay our departure for some time.

"What is it?" Slow Bear asked, having perceived my moment of reflection.

"We were planning to go to Black Wolf's cousin Gray Elk in a day or so," I answered. "But if Willow Woman has been ailing, I am sure that Black Wolf will want to go to her."

Black Wolf's liaison with Willow Woman was a mystery to me. While I could not deny that she had not been good to my people and that she was an exceedingly intelligent, warm, and generous person, she was also quite unusual. She was the first person I had ever seen who was tattooed. In fact, not only was she tattooed, but all her visible skin was covered with lines and markings. Additionally, she was strikingly large, but not in the same way as Black Wolf's statuesque mate Little Fawn. Willow Woman was not only well over the height of an average man, but she was probably equal to the weight of any two men. She had a forceful personality and an intimidating presence. Most men would likely consider any sort of intimate contact with her to be a daunting prospect. But Black Wolf was not most men. He adored her, and she him.

Slow Bear smiled and nodded. He was also well aware of their mutual devotion.

"Perhaps you may be able to combine the errands. You would not have to deviate too far from your planned route to see Willow Woman. She is already at her summer lodgings. We left her winter home for the Fen of Falls nearly a moon ago. Willow Woman has not been the same since her arrival. She does not complain, but the long journey was hard on her. She would not let anyone else carry the baby. He is heavy. Willow Woman's recovery from the birth was a long one, and she should not be toting him across great distances. Nevertheless, I could not persuade her to do otherwise."

I well understood that helpless feeling. I myself had had little success in trying to change Morning Star's mind when it was set on something. And especially when it came to our children, she had definite opinions.

"Are you deeply concerned?" I asked.

Slow Bear did not answer right away. He stared at his hands in his lap, his face betraying the look of a man lost in thought.

"I believe . . ." he began, "I believe that she will eventually regain her health, but I also think that Black Wolf's presence would do much to lift her spirits. She has not seen him since last fall's Gathering, and I am guessing that she is pining for him."

Before I could respond, the multitude of dogs and puppies began to bark, their tails wagging furiously. We stood to greet whoever was approaching. I fervently hoped it would not yet be Little Fawn and her children. As luck would have it, it was not.

"Slow Bear!" Black Wolf called out happily has he strode into the clearing at the center of the compound.

Black Wolf's darkly handsome features lit up when he saw our guests. He sometimes complained that his feet hurt him, but at this moment he was so pleased that he had a bounce to his gait. This caused the many stiff braids that sprouted out the sides of his head to jounce exaggeratedly with each step. Some jokingly referred to his novel hairstyle as his "spider hat," since it gave him the appearance of wearing a huge spider on the top of his head, but due to his great size only those who were closest to him ever mentioned the phrase *spider hat* to his face.

It was good to see Black Wolf smiling. This was a welcome departure from what had become his habitually haggard appearance lately. Up until a year ago, I had thought that Black Wolf was impervious to time. Black Wolf was older than my Puh, but his hair had remained the color of charred wood and his countenance was unlined. Now his eyes were hollow, and creases had begun to appear on his lean face, and a few white hairs were gradually sprinkled amongst the black, much like stars in a nighttime sky. However, the sight of our visitors suddenly banished this formerly careworn appearance.

"Pleasant day to you, Black Wolf," Slow Bear replied, looking up at Black Wolf. Although Slow Bear was a tall man, the top of his head scarcely reached Black Wolf's shoulder. Slow Bear was equally happy to see Black Wolf, and they grasped forearms.

"And to you, as well," Black Wolf returned.

Puh and the others soon joined the group, crowding around the fire pit and exchanging greetings. Most knew one another. Only my brother Ty did not know the visitors. Ty tended to be somewhat introverted with strangers, but he smiled shyly and, when asked, eagerly showed our guests the long sections of saplings he toted and noted their flexible properties.

"So, you plan to construct new bows?" Slow Bear grinned at Ty. "I would like to see the results! Ria's bow and little spears have always fascinated me."

Puh's mate Ria grinned back at Slow Bear and the other men. Ria was a small woman, with a thin but strong build. She was decidedly plain, however she had a sunny disposition that made up for what she lacked in appearance. Ria's bow and quiver of arrows were slung over her shoulder, but she too was also keen to show off what she carried.

"I will be thrilled to finally have a replacement bow should this one break. But see our new child!" Ria presented her ten-moon-old infant, who looked rather large for his age in comparison with his diminutive mother, despite the fact that he had been born well before his time and had been a mere mite of thing at his birth. "This is our little Mror."

Puh also smiled proudly. Putting a leathery hand on Ria's shoulder, he kissed her cheek and then kissed the top of the baby's curly head. Baby Mror giggled and drooled in response.

"He is certainly a fine child," Slow Bear said approvingly.

Roe Buck and Crow Feather also came forward to see the baby and let him grasp their proffered fingers, cooing to him gently.

Black Wolf seemed impatient with all the idle talk. He sidled closer to Slow Bear.

"What news?" Black Wolf inquired. "Is Willow nearby? I have not seen her in many moons, and I am beside myself to hear of her."

Slow Bear suddenly became solemn.

"I am afraid she is less than her usual . . . um . . . stalwart self. She sent us here to ask you to go to her," Slow Bear informed him.

"Of course," Black Wolf was suddenly apprehensive. "But is she all right? Does Gray Owl worry for her?"

Gray Owl was Willow Woman's healer.

"As I said," Slow Bear began, "she is somewhat diminished. Gray Owl has not confided in me, nor has Willow Woman. She only asks for you."

"I will be ready to leave at first light," Black Wolf promised.

"I understand that you were preparing to leave for the home of your cousin, the dog breeder," Slow Bear went on. "Willow Woman is at her summer lodgings, so it is possible to still venture up to see your cousin after your time with her."

Black Wolf smiled slightly.

"Yes, that was our plan. But we will have quite a few dogs in our company."

"No matter," Slow Bear assured him. "Willow Woman does not mind dogs."

Just then, our canines set up barking again. This time they announced the arrival of Little Fawn and her offspring. Little Fawn looked at Slow Bear and company curiously. Her satchel was overflowing with an assortment of spring greens. Little Fawn walked toward us, holding the hand of her youngest child, Dewdrop, whose free hand sported a number of wilted and bedraggled sprigs. As they reached us, three-winters-old Dewdrop wriggled loose from her mother's grasp and she ran to her father, where she clung to his leg and looked up at the strangers with round, dark eyes.

Slow Bear and his friends gaped at Little Fawn, shocked. It was likely that they had never seen a woman of her height. Little Fawn towered over them. She wore her long hair in four neat braids, and her long buckskin gown had obviously been assembled with great care. All in all, she and her children glowed with good health and a prosperity that spoke well of Black Wolf's skills as a provider and Little Fawn's as a homemaker. For a moment, her long horse-like face appeared stern as she stared at the men, but then she remembered herself and smiled engagingly to put them at ease.

"Why, who do we have here?" she asked cheerfully. "We do not often receive visitors. I am

Little Fawn, Black Wolf's mate. Welcome! These are our younger children. Our eldest, Morning Star, is no doubt at home, tending to her little ones. She is paired with Tris, you know."

Little Fawn adored her grandchildren and seldom missed an opportunity to spend time with them. She then presented her own family, beginning with her daughter, fifteen-winters-old Petal, who was tall like her parents and had a long face much like her mother's; and then her two sons, ten- and twelve-winters-old Hawk and Swift River; and eight-winters-old Sky, followed finally by Dewdrop. The men smiled at the children and seemed quite pleased to make their acquaintance. I then realized that they came from a household in which the only young occupant was Black Oak, the infant of Willow Woman and Black Wolf. Slow Bear and his friends were all old enough to be the parents of adults, and I could imagine that they were fondly remembering their own years of raising a growing family. Little Fawn continued to chat with the newcomers. If she was curious as to why we were graced with their company, she did not betray it. But Slow Bear must have felt obliged to explain their unexpected arrival.

"We have come here to speak with Black Wolf. The Head Elder has requested that he come — um — on important matters. We have been tasked with bringing him back with us," Slow Bear said.

Black Wolf looked as though he wanted to be anywhere but here. His eyes cast around the area wildly, as though seeking an escape route. When Little Fawn gazed at him for his response, he averted his glance. She waited expectantly until Black Wolf, sensing that some words from him were required, finally cleared his throat.

"Yes, well, we are leaving to go to Gray Elk's tomorrow, anyway, so we will just make a slight detour and then we will continue to Gray Elk's." Black Wolf hazarded a gander at Little Fawn to see how she took this news. Little Fawn was silent a moment as she digested the information.

"We will await your return," she said coldly, and then she gave everyone else a forced smile and added, "pleasant day to you all." With that, she turned on her heel and entered her home.

Chapter Two

There was an uncomfortable pause in the conversation. Most everyone was well aware of the perpetual state of antagonism between Black Wolf and Little Fawn, and it was also known to quite a few that Black Wolf was deeply involved with Willow Woman. The adults tried to pretend that nothing was wrong, but the children stared after Little Fawn, confused and upset. Large tears appeared at the corners of Dewdrop's eyes and she began to tug at Black Wolf's tunic for his attention. Black Wolf hefted the child into an embrace.

"Why do you cry?" Black Wolf asked as he cuddled her.

"Da-Da, you go away?" Dewdrop inquired.

"Only for a while," Black Wolf promised, kissing her and wiping the tears from her cheeks. "Sometimes I have to go away but I always come back."

Bror, my sister Ru's mate, then nudged me.

"If you are going to be traveling as soon as tomorrow morning, you will need to bring quite a bit of wood up the hill for Morning Star and your little ones," Bror predicted. "I would be happy to help you."

I smiled gratefully for Bror's foresight and willingness to help.

"Many thanks, Bror," I said to him. "Your assistance would be most welcome."

"Let us get started," Bror advised. "Then we will be done by the time our evening meal is ready. And we will have worked up a good appetite while we are at it."

"My appetite seldom fails me," I admitted with a grin.

Bror and I nodded our farewells to the others, and we walked toward our communal wood cache, a short distance from the compound. Raena and her pups accompanied us and settled themselves around the little clearing left by the hewn trees.

As Bror and I started to sort through the split wood and rough log lengths, Bror began to speak again. "How long do you think it will take to make the journey to Gray Elk's and back, considering that now you will be forced to make a detour to the Fen of Falls?"

"I do not know," I shrugged. "I guess that will depend on how long Black Wolf intends to stay with Willow Woman and how ill she is. Besides, I am sure that he is also looking forward to seeing little Oak."

"Yes, I imagine that is so." Bror tossed a few chunks of wood into a separate pile that we would later transport up the hill to my home. "We can haul enough wood for the next few days or so for now. I will make sure that Morning Star does not run out of firewood while you are away. Ru and I will check on her frequently."

"Many thanks, Bror," I clapped a hand on Bror's muscular shoulder to show my earnestness. Old Ones were usually heavily built, but Bror was even more robust than most.

Bror and Ru lived in an earth-bermed home ten or twelve strides from the place where Morning Star and I dwelt; they were our closest neighbors. Bror and I were also cousins, and I considered him to be one of my best friends. Bror had patiently wooed my sister Ru for several years before finally winning her affections the previous winter. It was only last year when I found that some cultures took exception to the idea of being paired with a cousin. Our people did not especially seek out a cousin, but if a cousin was the only person available or the only person who had captured your heart, there was no compunction against the union, either. This was fortunate for Bror, since his courtship had been a long and nearly futile one. Ru had almost been swept away by the brash charms of a dark and daring visitor, and we feared that this man might succeed in his attempt to tame Ru's heart. But then in the end, Bror's persistence and many fine qualities sealed their fate.

"You will take care on the trail?" Bror questioned.

I knew what he meant. When we had last traversed the path that led to the Fen of Falls, particularly the sections that ran beside the White River

— a seething torrent of water if ever I have seen one — the conditions were slippery, and I fell into the river. I survived my mad dash through the boulder-strewn waterway only thanks to a compassionate woolly mammoth cow that had mercifully rescued me from a bloody and waterlogged death.

"Yes, indeed. I will not count on being rescued from those waters a second time. I still can barely comprehend the first!" I told him.

"Comprehend or not, it was a lucky thing. After you took that tumble I did not think I would ever see you again." Bror threw a few more slabs of wood at our growing heap. "Shall we take a load up the hill?"

I nodded. There would be many, many trips back and forth, so we might as well get started. And some of the wood still needed to be split into kindling.

Morning Star was alerted to our arrival when Raena and the herd of puppies accompanied us home. Fox was still visiting with his little aunts. Morning Star peered out the doorway, carrying Pony, who whined sleepily and rubbed at her eyes. It seemed that Pony always fussed at this time of the day, and again later, just as we readied for our evening repast. Most times we ate this meal with the entire family. Even though everyone might have their various chores or embark on any number of errands during the day, each evening we gathered around the fire and shared food and tales of our day's adventures.

I then realized that Morning Star did not know about Slow Bear's visit, or the news that I would have to stay away for a longer period of time.

"I will go in and speak to Morning Star for a moment. I will rejoin you at the wood pile," I said as I set down my armload of wood.

"All right," Bror nodded, also placing his wood on the ground.

I turned and stepped inside our little dwelling, the dogs following me faithfully.

"Slow Bear has arrived with a few other men," I told Morning Star, reckoning that I should break it to her slowly.

"Oh?" she responded. "Is he one of those men attached to that woman's household?"

Morning Star knew of Willow Woman and her father's relationship with her, and she had heard me speak of Slow Bear many times.

"Yes, he is," I answered. "Slow Bear has come to speak to your father. It seems he has been summoned. We have been asked to make a stop on our way to Gray Elk's."

Morning Star took a moment to soothe the baby, but a look of dismay had crossed her lovely features.

"This will mean that our trip will be extended. I do not like it, but I do not have much choice in the matter," I added.

Bror then stuck his head inside the doorway for a moment and grinned at us.

"Pleasant day to you, Morning Star!" he said cheerfully. "Pardon this intrusion. I just wanted to tell Tris that I will be back shortly with a load of tinder. I have plenty to spare at home and I would be very sorry to see you run out while Tris is away."

"Thank you, Bror," Morning Star said to Bror and me, managing a smile. "And thank you both for bringing up the wood."

"We will bring up more. After Tris leaves I will stop in now and then to make sure you are well-stocked," Bror promised.

"Thank you, Bror; you are very kind," Morning Star replied.

Bror left us to retrieve the tinder.

"I know you do not have much say in the matter, but oh! It is bad enough when that woman takes Da away from his family, but now she requires that you stay longer from your family as well!" Morning Star fumed. Pony seemed to sense her mother's angst, and she began to cry.

I did not know how to respond, except to embrace her and kiss her forehead as the baby continued to wail loudly.

"I do not like to cause you unhappiness," I finally stated.

"I know," Morning Star said with a sigh.

I did my best to comfort Morning Star, but I could not stay for long. I had to finish bringing the wood up the hill with Bror. Morning Star was readying to leave, anyway, so she could assist with the meal preparations as she always did, leaving Pony in the care of her aunts. Both Morning Star and I were the eldest children of our respective families, so we each had numerous younger siblings who were quite willing to watch over our little ones at times such as these.

Bror soon returned with the tinder, and after it was stowed in our storage chamber we retraced steps down the path to the wood pile we had made and shouldered more cut logs. After we transported all the sorted wood, we scarcely had time to split the logs into smaller chunks and kindling before Morning Star came up the hill to remind us of the impending meal.

"The food will soon be ready," Morning Star announced. "I am just going to take a few moments to do a little quick tidying while the children are elsewhere. Tris, will you bring some of our shell bowls with you when we join the others for dinner?"

"Yes," I replied. "Just show me which ones you would like to take."

I guessed that this meant our families were hosting a feast given in the honor of Slow Bear and his companions and that we were running short on bowls.

Bror and I were both liberally covered in bits of bark and wood splinters, so we stopped at the stream to wash away the debris and sweat that had accumulated during our day's work. As we scrubbed away the grime, I was making mental notes about my axes and the worn state of the heads. It was necessary to rework or replace the heads frequently since the procurement of firewood was one of our most common chores. I kept several axes for use in rotation, so that each one varied a little at any one time in sharpness and the tightness of its hafting. Right now, especially since Bror had been using one of my axes while he was helping me, all of them needed attention. But it would have to wait until my return. By then, it would be early summer and we would be cutting and splitting the trees we had already downed this spring, stockpiling firewood against the coming winter, when the biting cold and fierce winds made it not only less pleasant work, but also more dangerous.

"I will tend to your axes before your return," Bror spoke, evidently thinking along the same lines as I. "One of your mauls lost a big chip out of it today; it looks as though it may crack, too. I will see to that, as well."

"Many thanks, Bror, but will you not have plenty to occupy your time while we are gone? I fear you take on too much," I told him.

"I may ask your brother to assist me," Bror said with a grin. "I expect he can make a new maul . . . and a better one . . . before I could even cut the wood to size."

"What am I to do? Make a new maul?" Ty had come up from behind us, carrying Fox, and he overheard us.

"One of my mauls is looking the worse for wear," I replied.

Ty nodded.

"This little one says he wants his Muh-Muh. But yes, I can help with that. I know where I can find the perfect tree branch to make into a maul." Ty placed Fox in my arms and then smiled shyly. "Bror, I am glad you are staying home while the others leave. Usually I am the only male — well, semi-adult male here during that time. I will be very pleased to have your company."

"My brother Dor knows of what you speak," Bror acknowledged. "It is the onus of every second son who is left behind while all the other men go off on their errands. And as one who has had to endure many, many of those, I am more than willing to sit this one out. Besides, I get to stay home with my new mate." Bror grinned broadly. "What could be better than that?"

"Staying at home with my not-so-new mate," I piped up. "And my children. But it is my dog that gave birth to all those puppies, so I am the one who must take them to Gray Elk's."

* * *

My not-so-new mate watched Fox and me come in through the doorway. I set down Fox and then slowly dropped my armload of axes and mauls, which fell clattering to the floor. When my hands were free of encumbrance, I enthusiastically embraced and kissed Morning Star.

"You have bits of bark and wood caught in your hair," Morning Star told me. "Would you go back outside and see if you can rid yourself of them?"

That was not quite the greeting I was hoping for, but I smiled sheepishly and went back outdoors, where I bent over at the waist and attempted to brush away all the bits of debris caught in my hair. Fox wandered out as well, and he solemnly watched me. I then brushed at my clothing, as well.

"What do you think, my little Fox?" I asked him, "Is your Puh-Puh clean now?"

Fox looked up at me, and sensing my light mood, he smiled.

"Puh-Puh clean!" he repeated.

I hoped he was right. I snatched him up off his feet and playfully kissed and snuggled him as he giggled and squirmed. I carried Fox indoors and awaited the coming judgment on my state of tidiness — or the lack thereof.

Morning Star had just finished putting away my axes and mauls in our storage room and she then stopped what was doing and turned to me, gazing at my now brushed-off form.

Suddenly, her shoulders slumped.

"I am sorry, Tris," Morning Star began, "you do not have to stand there looking like a boy who has been caught doing something naughty. It is just that there are times when you come home and leave a trail of mud behind you or throw your things down carelessly and all I can think of is that I just finished picking up after the children and you have undone all my work."

Fox still wriggled, so I set him down and he ambled over to amuse himself with his toy animals.

"I am sorry," I said to Morning Star, feeling chagrined. "I did not realize. Why did you not tell me sooner?"

Morning Star gently wrapped her arms around me, stretching up to kiss my cheek.

"I know you did not realize," she told me. "Do not take my words to heart. I should not have spoken. You are a good mate and I am lucky to have you. I did not want to tell you because so many times when you return home from a hunt and you are so tired; you may be bloodied because a thrashing deer caught your arm with his antler and cut you, or you may be limping and bleeding at the knee because you have been kicked by a sharp hoof. And I know you face many dangers you do not want to tell me about and cause me to worry. You do so much and risk so much to keep us warm and fed — how can I complain about a little mess? I am just irritable about your upcoming journey. And worst of all, I hear myself sounding like my mother. I think it was Mama's incessant harping at Da that drove him away. But then, Da's refusal to allow Mama any independence frustrated her to no end." Morning Star paused, deep in thought. "I do not want us to end up like my mother and father. So do not pay me any mind. And most of all, remember that I love you."

"As I love you," I responded, kissing her.

* * *

Our evening meal was more festive than usual, thanks to our guests. I was pleased to show off Morning Star and my little ones to Slow Bear, Roe Buck, and Crow Feather, and gratified to hear the praise they heaped on my sweet mate and our two children. Morning Star was dressed in her best garment for the occasion, the same dress she had worn at our pairing ceremony. Now that she was older and had borne two babies, the gown fit her a little more snugly through the breast and hips, but in my mind, that only made her all the more attractive. I could not help staring at Morning Star. Even now, with a baby pulling at her hair and a toddler clinging to her leg as she scolded him to take his finger from his nose, Morning Star was still the most beautiful woman I had ever known.

"Will you be ready to leave in the morning?" Puh asked, disrupting my reverie.

"Um . . . yes," I answered. "No doubt you have heard that we are to make a detour to the Fen of Falls?"

"Yes," Puh nodded. As always, Puh was serene. "Ria and I packed for the journey this afternoon. Bror and Ru have agreed to look after Ochs for us."

"Poor Ochs will miss his siblings," Ria added. "But, I think Ru will spoil him while we are away. She does so dote upon dogs! And Ochs reminds me a bit of her old dog, Rooph." Ria paused a moment before going on. "Little Fawn has hardly shown her face this afternoon. I wonder if she is ill."

"Sick at heart," Puh said quietly.

"Yes," Ria nodded. "Not that I blame her. Even though she and Black Wolf are constantly at odds, I think I understand how she feels."

"What do you mean?" Puh suddenly looked concerned.

"Oh, I do not mean you and me!" Ria hastened to assure Puh, "I mean my former mate, Bakkae. I was with him for many years before he passed, and while I did love him, I did not always like him. I think it is the same for Little Fawn."

This was news to me. Not only that Ria had not liked her prior mate, but that there was such a thing as loving someone but not liking him. It seemed a perplexing contradiction. My mind simply could not grasp the concept.

* * *

Our meal was consumed with rapt enthusiasm. I sat between Morning Star and Great Gran, holding Fox in my lap as I ate, feeding him tidbits at the same time. Fox was a good eater; he was still nursing, but not as often, and sometimes it was only for comfort as opposed to a need to gain sustenance. He was soon distracted by his little aunts, and he trotted off to play with them.

"Twie, do not go too far!" Morning Star warned. "And do not let Fox out of your sight!"

"Yes, Morning Star," Twie replied. "I will hold his hand at all times!"

Good luck with that undertaking! I thought to myself. Our little Fox was so active that I doubted Twie would be able to hold him close for long.

"Fox, you must hold onto me at all times or I will have to bring you back to your Muh-Muh and Puh-Puh," Twie said as she took Fox by the wrist and led him away.

Morning Star traded glances with me.

"Your little sister is growing up!" Morning Star noted. "She will be a good mother."

"She has two little sisters, a young half-brother, and now your two babies at hand," Gran said. "By the time she has children she will have had plenty of practice! But even without that, she is a natural mother. She has a rapport with children that cannot be taught."

"I did not know there was anything to learn," I admitted. "I thought that all women were natural mothers."

Gran shook her head.

"Most are, but not all. And yes, a lot of parenting is a learning process. You must be finding that out by now," Gran teased.

Morning Star had turned to talk to her sister Petal, so I took this moment to speak privately to Gran. "Gran, do you ever Dream about strangers?"

Gran peered into my face for a moment, as though trying to read something deeper from my countenance.

"Sometimes," she said slowly. "Why do you ask?"

"I had a Dream . . . a woman was bound at her hands, and she was tied to a tree like a dog you are trying to keep from running away," I explained. "I could not see her face, but I know I do not know her."

"How do you know that?" Gran inquired.

"She was a brown-haired woman. I have never seen a woman with brown hair before," I answered.

"Was there any more to the Dream, other than just seeing her there?" Gran questioned.

"It was raining. She was wet. I think she said the word *run*. Then I awoke."

Gran's brow furrowed in thought.

"It could be an *ancient memory*," Gran began. "Sometimes those Dreams visit only fleetingly and show us something from the distant past. There is usually some tie between that person or experience and you. I wonder who she might be . . . I will think on that."

"Tie between us?" I was momentarily bewildered. "You mean that we are related somehow?"

"Possibly," Gran nodded, "like you and your Puh. You two are bound in a way that transcends the things of the real world and enters the Dream world. Both worlds are real, but the Dream world can show us different aspects of each place. Sometimes it is an ancient memory, sometimes the Dreams brings us to our loved ones when they need us, and sometimes they give us a glimpse of the future. We can only wait for their visits and attempt to interpret what the Dream is trying to convey to us."

My first Dream suddenly replayed itself in my mind. A vicious animal burst through the tall grasses and underbrush; it moved so quickly that I could not see anything but a gaping mouth full of large teeth and a rush of dark fur. I had been terrified at the vision.

"Gran, when I had my first Dream I saw the bear, but not Puh. I sensed Puh but I could not see him." I was momentarily at a loss for words. "How can I sense a person I cannot see?"

"Ah, I have spent much time thinking on that recently. I have come to believe that it is because you are seeing events through their eyes." Gran must have seen my look of wonder. "As I said, you and your Puh are deeply connected. That was not the only time when you have seen things through his eyes, was it?"

"No, there were other times . . . if that was what was happening. But how did you know?" I asked.

"Because I have seen things through your father's eyes, as well. When he was caught in the bear trap awaiting rescue, I saw the circle of nighttime sky overhead. I saw the northern lights undulating across the stars. I saw a lioness circling the edge of the pit, looking down at him all the while and trying to decide if she could leap down and make the kill. I did not know what I was seeing at the time, but not long ago I was speaking with your Puh about those Dreams and he recognized the images right away. For many years I have wondered how it was that I would know I was Dreaming about someone but not see them. Now I know."

"So, you mean that when I Dreamt of this woman, that maybe someone else is seeing her, not me?" I asked.

"That is one possibility," Gran replied. "Have you ever sensed anyone else in a Dream except your Puh?"

I shook my head.

"Only Puh."

"Hmmm." Gran was pensive. "In all my years, I have only sensed three people. My mate Goren, your Puh, and you." Gran smiled. "If you are Dreaming of this woman, she must be truly special."

"Who is special?" Morning Star was no longer talking to Petal and had turned back to us.

"I do not know," I answered, still bewildered by Great Gran's explanations. "I told Gran about an odd Dream I had last night. I do not know the person in the Dream. It was very odd," I said again.

"As I said before, it may be an ancient memory," Gran pointed out. "Maybe it will come back some night and show you more of the scene and you will recognize something . . . a person, a place. If you do, tell me. If it happened long ago, perhaps I will know something about it. Sometimes these ancient memories appear without any apparent reason, and not always at night."

"Do you mean during the day?" I asked incredulously.

"Yes," Gran started. "For instance, sometimes you just know something, but you do not know how it is that you know it. That is an ancient memory too — a lesson that someone connected to you learned and handed down through his or her progeny to pass on knowledge and protect them against the same dangers. Sometimes it is called *instinct*. But it is an ancient memory."

I still was not sure that I really understood, but I had faith in Gran's store of knowledge. If she said it was so, it must be so.

* * *

I was rather bleary-eyed when the rising sun announced that it was time to rouse myself from our bed. Morning Star and I had had very little sleep throughout the night as we tried to make up for what would surely be a prolonged absence. All the same, it was a contented sort of exhaustion. I wondered at the prudence of starting a long trip in this state, but I was sure I could manage in spite of my fatigue.

I noted that Morning Star seemed preoccupied as she began to prepare the morning meal — more preoccupied than usual, that is. Very often her attention was diverted by an awakening baby or a dog underfoot, but this day she was uncharacteristically clumsy and forgetful. At first I chalked it up to sleepiness, given that we had not slept much, but then I saw glimmers of tears in Morning Star's eyes.

I moved closer to her as she bustled about the room and caught Morning Star in my arms.

"What is it?" I asked softly, wiping away her tears.

Morning Star was silent a moment, but she held me tightly.

"I do not like to start complaining again, but I hate for you to leave," she said finally.

"I do not want to go," I admitted regretfully. "I wish I did not have to be away from you and our little ones. I will return as soon as possible."

"I know you will," Morning Star sighed and rested her head against my chest, while I stroked her hair. "Mama wants me to come down the hill and stay with her, but there are three of us now, and Mama and Da's house is already crowded. I would rather stay in my own home. Besides, we will have Raena, and Ru and Bror will be close by; the children and I will be fine." She hesitated before going on, "It is just that I always miss you so. And I worry. I do not like to bother you with my small troubles, but I scarcely sleep while you are gone, and when I do sleep, I am plagued with awful nightmares. It gives me a real appreciation of what you must endure with your Dreams, because you know that they are real. At least mine are only born of my fears for you . . . I could not bear to lose you."

Morning Star looked up at me, with fresh tears glinting at the corners of her eyes. I could never stand her tears, and I felt my own eyes well up. I kissed her long and deeply.

"I will be back," I promised Morning Star. "And soon afterward, we will leave for the shore and spend a carefree summer at the ocean. Just remember that . . . remember how wonderful that summer was when we were there two years ago."

Summers at the beach were not completely carefree, what with hunting seals and fishing, but they were a comparatively easy existence when you considered what we survived each winter.

"Yes, I will remember that, but all I care is that you come home to me . . . and come home without looking as though you have been thrown off a cliff, for a change!" Morning Star finished with fire in her voice.

"But there was just that one time . . . ." I began.

"Then there was the time you came home covered in blood!" Morning Star countered.

"But it was not my blood . . . ." I pointed out, hoping she would find consolation in that fact.

"If you keep up your habit of finding calamity every time you go out venturing you will come to look like your Puh!" Morning Star went on.

"My Puh has the appearance of a man who has lived hard, but I do not flinch from such a fate. Besides," I said with a grin, "I remember you once told my Puh he was a fine-looking man."

"Oh, you remember everything!" Morning Star grinned back. "Yes I did, and he is . . . although he is a bit lean for my taste; lean and scarred. But one can still see that he was once quite a handsome man. You, my dear mate — however — I do not want my beloved to be that way. I want you to be robust and as untouched by injury as possible. And before I forget, I have made new inserts for your boots. I saw that your old ones were quite worn out, so I cut new ones to shape yesterday." Morning Star retrieved the new inserts from our storage room to show me her handiwork. "Sit down," she ordered, "I will tie your boots on."

I did as I was instructed and waited patiently while Morning Star fussed at my boots. Even in the dim firelight she could see that some of the previous day's dirt still adhered to the soles. She took my boots to the entryway, lifted the hide flap and smacked the boots against each other outside. A cool draft wafted into the room, making the fire dance and sparks fly. When she discovered that my boot liners were in equally bad shape, she also shook those outside the door.

"My boots were still damp when I removed them last night," I said apologetically. "I guess the mud must have clung to them."

"And everything else, too," Morning Star noted. "How do you get grass and even bits of tree bark inside your boots?"

I could only shrug in response. The tree bark must have filtered into my boots when Bror and I were splitting wood, but the grass? I had no idea. My dear mate now kneeled in front of me as she assembled my boots and then motioned for me to lift first one foot, then the other as she slid the boots over my feet and then laced them securely to my lower legs, making sure to first tuck my leggings into each boot.

"There," she said with satisfaction. But then her worried look returned again. "You will be careful to keep your feet warm and dry, will you not? And if it becomes hot, be sure to stay in the shade if you take your tunic off. Your skin sunburns so easily . . . ."

"Yes, I know," I assured her. "I will be very careful."

Just then we both heard Black Wolf hallooing outside. He must have become impatient as he waited for me to join them so that we could embark on our journey. Black Wolf then stuck his head inside our doorway, soon followed by the rest of him.

"Pleasant day to you both!" Black Wolf smiled broadly at us, standing with his head tilted awkwardly to one side since he was too tall to stand upright in our home.

"Da! The children are still asleep!" Morning Star chided him.

Black Wolf looked abashed, but only for a moment.

"I will keep my voice down," he said a little more quietly. "But I am here for Tris. We must go now."

"Pleasant day to you, Black Wolf," I greeted him. "I will be ready to leave shortly. I am packed; I just need to kiss Fox and Pony — even if they are asleep — and take my leave of Morning Star."

I rose to my feet and went over to the children's alcove off the main room. Both were snuggled comfortably in the beds. They looked so beautiful and so peaceful. I gently kissed their foreheads. Fox rubbed at the spot as though to wipe it away, but he did not awaken. I then turned to Morning Star as she stood there looking so unhappy. I tried to smile at her, and she tried to smile back. Wrapping my arms around her, I pulled her close, embracing her as tightly as I dared.

"I love you, my sweet," I told her. "I will be back. As quickly as possible." I kissed her.

"I love you, my dear Tris," Morning Star replied. "Please, *please* be careful! I love you!"

"I love you," I said again, reaching for my pack and putting my arms through its straps. I then placed my rolled wisent cloak over my left shoulder and took up my best spear.

Morning Star looked stricken now that the time to go was imminent. I hugged and kissed her one more time. "I will be back," I repeated.

"I will be waiting," Morning Star answered.

Chapter Three

Black Wolf was in high spirits as we set off down the trail, but my heart was heavy as I trudged under the slowly brightening skies. Although Raena was left at home so Morning Star and the children would have the dog's protection and company, her pups trotted along with us quite happily. They were excited at this new adventure, and they appeared eager to explore more of the world around them. Since I had known that this trip would be in our future, I had started taking the pups out without their mother for some while, in hopes that when the time came they would not balk at leaving her behind. It seemed their training was successful.

I had been to Willow Woman's summer lodgings and Gray Elk's mountain abode, and although both places were exotic compared with my woodland home, they held no mysteries for me. This was just a long trek I would have to see through, and I anxiously awaited its end.

Puh and Ria strode along easily under their loads. Puh was burdened with a heavy pack, as he carried most of their gear since the baby, Mror, rode in a sling at his mother's back. Like his parents, Mror was stoic and good-natured. Mror often snoozed during our outings, but this morning he was wide awake and looked around with interest. If a bird caught his eye or a hare darted across our path he pointed and called out, but mostly he was silent.

I missed Morning Star and the children already. I wondered what they were doing now; the little ones must have arisen and would be looking for their breakfast. Morning Star's mother, Little Fawn, came over almost every day at this time, and she was probably helping Morning Star to feed and amuse Fox and Pony.

I was unhappy to hear about Morning Star's nightmares. She had never mentioned them before. My own Dreams sometimes left me shaken and wary. I could only imagine that Morning Star's dreams would be equally disturbing. It pained me to know that she suffered from them on my account.

Additionally, it concerned me that Morning Star feared we might become like her parents. I did not think this was likely, but it worried me that she thought so. I understood her recent criticisms grew out of living in a cramped space with so many dogs, the demands of caring for a household, two small children and — apparently — a messy mate. And now I realized that Morning Star was also coping with her previously unspoken worries for me, particularly while I would be away from her on this trip.

It was not long before my companions' conversation distracted me from my state of preoccupation.

"How is the hunting since last year's wildfire tore through the area?" Crow Feather asked. "We saw much damage and wondered how well the animal populations were recovering."

"Some of the animals have returned," Black Wolf stated, "but they are nowhere near as numerous as before. We could usually count on bringing home a deer every few days or so, but now it is more apt to be a few deer every moon."

"Is that enough to feed your combined families?" Slow Bear questioned.

"If we compensate by bringing in other animals as well," Puh replied. "We have done pretty well supplementing our stores with the migrating fowl that have been winging through this spring. Ria is a remarkable shot with her bow and arrows; she has brought down many ducks, geese, and swans." Puh looked at Ria with pride, and she responded by smiling up at him.

"And thankfully, we started the winter with ample stores," Black Wolf pointed out. "Thanks in part to our guests of the previous year. Those Wolf-men were certainly proficient hunters. If the fire had not killed so many prey animals, I am sure they would have instead fallen to those Wolf-men."

The Wolf-men were from another far-flung clan, The People of the Wolves, and they had stayed many moons with us. We had liked those adventurous men a great deal and we were sorry to see them go. Their leader, Karno, was the dark and daring man who had hoped to be paired with my sister Ru, but his considerable set of skills did not include those of a suitor. In the end he went home without her, much to our relief.

All the same, I missed the Wolf-men. I fervently hoped that one day we would see them again. In addition to being fine hunters, they also busied themselves with creating small gifts for the children, mostly in the form of carved toy animals. The Wolf-men had introduced us to music, as well, when they played their rhythmic, chanting songs every evening.

Before then, the only songs I had ever heard were those Black Wolf sang when we were on the trail. His theory was that his full-throated tunes kept predators at bay. Black Wolf's voice was a powerful instrument indeed; it was quite deep, and it carried some distance, much like bellowing stags during the rut. In fact, if it were not for our continued conversation, I suspected that Black Wolf would have been indulging in a song right now.

"The fire was unfortunate, but at least it did not touch your homes. And with luck, the wildlife will come back to its former state of profusion before too long," Slow Bear said. "I remember Karno and the two injured friends he brought with him to the Fen of Falls.

What delightful fellows they were! I suppose they have gone home by now."

"Their home was very far away," I joined in. "Karno told me that it took them two years to journey here. That means that they would still be traveling home, maybe a quarter of the way into their trek at this time. I only hope that they are well. It was a hard winter."

"Yes," Slow Bear agreed, "a hard winter indeed. We went through more firewood than I can ever recall. And speaking of wood, when I left, there was already discussion about moving this fall's Gathering to a new location where there will be more firewood. It is becoming too difficult to keep everyone warm and fed at the old location."

"You must be concerned to know so much potential firewood was consumed by that wildfire," Crow Feather spoke up. "What a shame so much valuable fuel was destroyed."

"That is true," Black Wolf began, "but thankfully the wood to the south and east of our compound was left untouched by fire. A lot of trees on all sides of us were downed by a very bad storm a few summers ago. So the trees had been lying on the ground for about a year by the time the fire happened, and they had become fairly dry and probably exacerbated the wildfire. We have been making use of as many of those trees as we can, even some of the bigger ones that we wouldn't normally tackle with our poor axes. We hate to waste the wood, even if it means constantly breaking our axes in an attempt to chop through the trunks. We make handful upon handful of woodchips, though. When dried, they make wonderful tinder, and sometimes we use them for smoking meat. But afterward I feel half-dead from day after day of working on just one enormous tree."

"Well," Slow Bear began with a laugh, "at least you can have your revenge on the tree when you burn it and enjoy the warmth from that wood next winter!"

"I think it has its revenge on me, first." Black Wolf replied.

"How so?" asked Roe Buck. "What could the tree possibly do to you?"

"It causes me days of aching muscles and joints in return for all the suffering I heap upon it thanks to the hideous hacking it receives as a result of my labors," Black Wolf told him. "But part of that is because I become too impatient. I start hammering on the trunk with the axe trying to bite straight through instead of properly slicing at an angle and letting the axe do its work. Then when my hands and joints start to hurt I realize that I am not making better progress this way. It is ironic that the seemingly most direct cut is not the fastest way to hew wood."

"Ironic, yes," Slow Bear agreed.

Puh, Black Wolf, and I had already discussed our firewood situation at length, so my mind began to wander once again. It was still cool while the sun hid behind dense gray clouds. The damp ground on the trail gave way beneath our feet, creating perfect imprints of each step.   I knew that the dampness would eventually seep in through my boots, even though the soles and seams were treated with birch tar to help waterproof them, and also to make them wear longer. I was grateful for Morning Star's foresight in making the new boot inserts. These provided a little extra cushioning between my feet and the ground and did much to add to my comfort.

My thoughts drifted back to Morning Star. I counted myself as incredibly lucky to have her. I completely adored her; and best of all, she adored me as well. I had thought that we were perfectly happy up until our talk revealed Morning Star's reservations about us and her nightmares. I was frustrated that I was not with her so I could reassure that all was well; she need never worry that we might end up like her parents.

"Tris?" Slow Bear said.

I had been staring at the ground as I marched along, but now I started and looked up abruptly.

"Yes?" I responded.

"You must have been very deep in thought; you did not hear me," Slow Bear chuckled. "I asked you what those things are around your dogs' necks. When I was patting some of the pups yesterday I noticed that their necklaces had quite an aroma."

"I do not know what is in them. Morning Star makes the collars for the dogs," I explained. "She soaks long strips of hides in some sort of strong tea . . . it smells rather minty . . . and then she sews them into tubes, which she fills with various herbs, and then ties them around the dogs' necks. My Muh used to make them for our dog, as well. The collars help to keep fleas and ticks at bay."

"Very clever," Crow Feather said. "I suppose those collars must make it much more pleasant to share your home with a dog."

The puppies suddenly stopped in their tracks and, heads raised, sniffed the air. We stopped as well, gazing alertly about us and listening carefully. Then I heard it. A low, despairing groan. It did not seem as though it could be an utterance from a human.

"It sounds as though there is a wounded animal up ahead," Puh stated, beginning to walk forward once more. "It must be bad off, since it no doubt has listened to our approach for some time and either does not care about us or is too injured to move away to a safe distance."

Most animals did not desire human company and did their best to avoid us if it was at all possible. If this animal had heard our conversation as we neared and had not run away, it must be in dire straits indeed.

The moans gradually grew louder as we drew nearer to the unfortunate creature. The trail remained muddy, and although the burned forest around us showed signs of recovery, the sodden spring landscape had been largely devoid of all but the smallest animals thus far into our trip. Although we had noted deer tracks, Mror's hare was the largest thing we had seen as of yet.

Finally we came upon the poor beast. I could smell it even before I could see it. The pup's hackles rose and they began to growl. It was a brown bear, a boar perhaps only a year or so old. It was quite thin and molting great patches of winter wool. It must have been lying there for some time, because its flanks were encrusted with its own feces. The young boar looked as though it had been attacked by another bear; perhaps its post-hibernation hunger had driven it to seek sustenance at another bear's kill and the other bear had declined to share its bounty. In any case, this poor bruin lay on its side in the mud, wheezing and lamenting its wretched state.

We stood by without fear; it was too far gone to do us any harm, and besides, it was too small to be truly worrisome, even if it had been well. Standing on its hind legs, this bear would hardly have reached my shoulder. I looked into its eyes and saw that they were glazed with pain. Its wounds were weeping blood, and an apparent bite to its neck had opened up its windpipe, causing the bear to make a sucking-whistling noise with each breath.

"How terrible to hover between life and death like this," I said, feeling sympathy for the poor brute. "I will dispatch this pitiful animal and end his suffering."

As I stepped forward, the bear watched me. It did not move, except to shift one of its forelegs a little, and to continue its incessant wheezing. The bear and I held each other's gaze for a moment. I then realized that I might need to turn over the bear a little so I could strike it directly in the heart. Puh seemed to come to the same realization at the same moment.

"We will need to make his chest accessible," Puh said, removing his pack and pulling out a length of rope. "We will have to move fast," Puh said to me, "so the bear is caused as little discomfort as possible. He is lifting his paw now and then; I will try to get the rope under his paw then next time he moves it and then I will turn him enough for you to lance his chest."

"All right," I said, nodding in agreement.

Puh stood at the bear's back, holding an end of the rope in each hand as he waited for the paw to rise. As soon as the foreleg muscles twitched to raise the paw, he tossed the loop of rope over it and quickly drew back, just enough that the bear's chest was exposed.

I darted in with my spear and the bear's last groan was cut off with a gasping bark, and then it was still.

We were all quiet as we stood over its battered carcass.

"Join your ancestors, little bear," I murmured, breaking the silence. I then turned and stabbed my bloodied spearhead into the wet ground several times until it was clean.

* * *

There was no use trying to save any of the bear's meat, as it would be nearly impossible to keep it from being contaminated by the bear's excrement. Besides, we really could not spare the time needed to butcher the animal, so we recommenced our trek.

The sun was high in the sky by now, though still obscured behind clouds. Winter should have been over at this time, but that cold season seemed reluctant to relinquish its hold over the lands. Yet, there was no doubt that spring was here. The snow had melted away and the buds on some of the trees and brush were nearly ready to open. Early flowers were in bloom, and the sight of them was cheering. It was funny how something so small and insignificant would seem so important. Maybe that was because those fragile petals were some of the first of the season's new plant life. Whatever the reason, it gave us hope that grander things were yet to come.

When the day was drawing to a close, we chose a level spot near the side of the path by a grove of blackened trees.

We set up our lean-tos in a semicircle, building a sputtering fire in the center of the configuration. The overall dampness made it difficult to get a fire lighted. Additionally, the amount of available deadwood was scant. Finally, we were able to scavenge just enough to warm us as the sun went down and temperatures abruptly dropped.

Puh, Ria, and little Mror soon left us to retire to their shelter. The baby had been so quiet throughout most of the trip that we had hardly known he was with us, but he had begun to doze, so it was time to put him to bed.

The rest of us lounged by the fire, talking and still nibbling on our rations of dried foods. I was very hungry, but I did not dare eat too much. Although I was carrying as much dried meat as I could and Black Wolf was also toting some extra food for me, it had to be enough to feed both myself and the dogs until we reached Gray Elk. Of course, there was a chance we might find some game between here and there which would extend my rations, but I could not count on it. I really hoped that it would not be necessary to halt our journey so that we could hunt, since that might delay our return home by several days.

When our foraged wood was reduced to little more than coals and ash, the rest of us went to bed as well. For once, I was very grateful for the company of all the pups. They snuggled up against me and I had the luxury of using not only my wisent cloak for warmth, but a live blanket of dogs.

The rest of the journey was fairly uneventful. We saw a herd of deer as it dashed across the trail in front of us and the pups wanted to chase after them, but I called them back.

"Your puppies are amazingly obedient," Slow Bear observed. "I wonder that the impulses of their wolf ancestors does not compel them to follow their instincts, regardless of what their human tells them to do."

"They may have their instincts," Black Wolf started, "but they know who feeds them and like most animals, they are slaves to their stomachs!"

After we passed through the area affected by fire we saw more deer, plus tracks of several elk, dainty lynx paw prints, and the huge tracks of a large bear where it had crossed the path sometime in the recent past. I wondered if this was the animal that had maimed the little bear. It was good to finally reach normal woodlands again and leave the desolate, blackened, muddy forest behind.

* * *

The last few days of our trek took place alongside the frothing waters of the White River from which I had been rescued by the cow mammoth the previous summer. We also passed near the place where Ria had lived for most of her adult life. I saw her look down the trail that veered off toward her former home, but although she appeared thoughtful, she did not remark on it.

On the fifth day we came to the Fen of Falls. Black Wolf had been so eager to at last reach our destination that he was perpetually on edge throughout the trip. Generally, Black Wolf's feet would have him in considerable pain after a trek of this duration, but he had not complained once. He had hurried us along, urging us forward if any one of us straggled. I was willing to make good time as well, as I was anxious to complete this mission and go back home.

I smiled at the thought of home and family. Maybe Morning Star would have news for me upon our return. Perhaps she was pregnant. I told myself not to be too optimistic. Great Gran had pointed out that it was unlikely that Morning Star would conceive for as long as she was nursing two little ones. But Fox was not nursing as much as he had been when he was younger, so just maybe . . . but then I sighed. I knew I should not be impatient for another child. I still wondered if Gran was right — was I subconsciously trying to beget as many children as possible in the event that we might lose some? I pushed the awful thought from my mind.

We knew we were approaching the Fen of Falls while we were still some way off as the sound of thundering water filled the air. The White River was by far the fastest-moving river I had ever seen; the falls roared, and to stand near them was to feel the earth tremble beneath your feet.

Willow Woman's summer home was situated a short distance from the falls, and as soon as it was in sight, Black Wolf ran the rest of the way to her door, bypassing a man standing at the outdoor hearth without so much as a glance. I, on the other hand, saw that the man at the hearth was cooking a vast array of foods, and I immediately began to salivate. I was famished, and I hoped that we would be invited to partake in some of these victuals. The pups also hovered nearby, sniffing the air and looking at the food with hunger apparent on their faces.

We did not want to follow Black Wolf into Willow Woman's large home, a long, narrow construction of wood, stone, and mud, and disrupt what would surely be a tender reunion, so we waited outside with the man at the fire, whom I recognized from our visit the previous year.

Slow Bear and his companions also paused to exchange pleasantries about their trip with White Cloud, the man tending the food.

"Pleasant day to you, White Cloud," I greeted him, speaking loudly to be heard over the falls. "I am sorry to bring all these dogs. We are on our way to bring them to Black Wolf's cousin, Gray Elk. I hope they will not be an inconvenience. You have not yet met my father. This is my Puh, Tor, and his mate, Ria . . . and their baby, Mror."

White Cloud smiled broadly at us and he turned to grasp our forearms and welcome us.

"Pleasant day to you, Tris!" White Cloud exclaimed. Then he turned to Puh and Ria. "Pleasant day to you both. Do make yourselves at home. You all must be very hungry after such a long journey. The food will soon be done. I believe you may start on those ducks whenever you would like. They are stuffed with herbs, tubers, and leeks, and they should be ready about now. The elk roasts will take a little longer."

White Cloud began to remove the spitted ducks from their places over the fire pit, where they dripped fatty juices that fell hissing onto the hot coals, and passed the fowl to us. We quickly set down our packs and assorted impedimenta so we could free ourselves to eat in comfort. Puh and Ria shared a duck, I shared one with Slow Bear, and likewise, Crow Feather and Roe Buck shared one. The puppies began to whine, so I hastily dug into my pack for slabs of dried meat and gave one to each dog.

The skies had been full of migrating fowl for some time, so we had been consuming many ducks of late, but White Cloud's birds were the best I had ever eaten. Succulent and studded with herbs and crispy slivers of onions, they were quickly devoured.

Since no one had been expecting a large group of people to arrive that afternoon, it was necessary to bring out more food to add to what was already cooking. But White Cloud , like all of Willow Woman's staff, handled everything with good-natured competence. Most of the household occupants came out to join us for the meal. Even Black Wolf and Willow Woman's seven-moons-old infant, Black Oak, was brought out to visit with us. I had yet to see this child. Oak had the black hair and dark skin of The People. He was also quite large, but that was hardly a surprise, considering that both his parents were quite tall, and Willow Woman had the physique of a bear that had feasted on salmon all season in preparation for a long winter's hibernation. The little boy was cheerful and friendly, and he was obviously doted on.

We were so absorbed in consuming our repast and the engaging conversation that accompanied it, it did not occur to me until later when we had been shown our rooms that Black Wolf and Willow Woman had not made an appearance at any time during the evening.

Chapter Four

The mammoths are pacing back and forth, trumpeting with alarm and rumbles issuing from deep in their throats. The smaller mammoths run about in aimless confusion as their elders try to herd them toward the center of the group. The matriarch lifts her head and her eyes meet mine . . .

I bolted awake. The pups raised their heads in the dim morning light, and the two closest to me nuzzled and licked my face comfortingly.

"I awoke you, I know," I said as I petted them. "You are good puppies. Someone will be very lucky to have you."

It was cool, so I dressed and took up my spear before going outdoors with the dogs where we could find a place to relieve our bladders. White Cloud was already at the fire pit, spreading out a bed of shimmering red coals over which he would make breakfast. The puppies had learned that White Cloud was the Keeper of the Food, so they sat down in a rough circle around him as he worked, in hopes some stray scraps would come their way.

"Pleasant day to you, White Cloud," I said. "I am sorry about the dogs. They are eternally hungry." For a fleeting moment, it crossed my mind that the same could be said about me. "Is there anything I can do to assist you?"

"Pleasant day to you, Tris," White Cloud returned. "You may help me set up the spits, if you would like. We are having fresh fish for breakfast. They will cook quickly, but then I have a good many to prepare, so I am just going to keep the spits full until all the fish have been roasted."

White Cloud pointed to baskets of gutted fish. I could see that this was going to be quite a project.

"Of course," I replied.

Working together, we strung four whole fish on each spit and placed it over the coals. When all the spits' frames were full, we went back to the first spit and turned it halfway around so the other side could cook. We adjusted each spit likewise, taking care not to dislodge the fish from the spits. Even in the cool morning air, the fish roasted quite fast. When this batch of fish was done, we then stripped the spits of the cooked fish and repeated the process.

As soon as the fish had cooled a little, White Cloud and I were each helping ourselves to the tender flesh as we continued to work, and tossing bits to the pups here and there, as well.

The rest of the household, residents and visitors alike, gradually joined us. The day was warming up nicely and the wind was mercifully light.

I was surprised at Willow Woman's appearance when she and Black Wolf finally exited the structure, and it was not just because she was an unusual-looking person. Her normally glowing dusky complexion had become dull and wan. Willow Woman's dignified but energetic waddle was now slow, and although she was still very large, she had lost quite a bit of weight.

All the same, Willow Woman smiled as she saw me and she came toward me with arms extended.

"Tris!" Willow Woman exclaimed, throwing her arms around me. Considering her weakened condition, she still had a powerful embrace. "How good it is to see you! You are well? Your family is well?"

"It is good to see you, too," I said to her. "Yes, my family is indeed well. Many thanks for remembering them. Morning Star is in good health, our son Fox is getting big, and we have a lovely daughter now. Her name is Pony. We met little Oak last evening. He is a delightful boy."

Willow Woman beamed at the praise for her boy.

"He is asleep just now," Willow Woman explained. "The darling awoke early this morning for his feeding, but now he is dozing again. Slow Bear insisted I come out for my own breakfast, and he promised to bring Oak to me as soon as he awakens again."

"Yes, you must have a good meal," Black Wolf said to Willow Woman. "I want to see the color come back to your cheeks."

"Is it not enough that you have brought a smile back to my face? Now I must have good color, too?" Willow Woman teased him. "Never fear, your presence has done much to ease my malaise."

She smiled up at Black Wolf and touched his bearded face as he grinned down at her.

"As you have eased mine," Black Wolf returned.

This was an acute departure from the gruff Black Wolf I was accustomed to. I knew he was capable of great love; I had seen it in the way he treated his children, grandchildren, and friends. But his attachment to Willow Woman was turning him into a definite romantic. Nonetheless, I was happy for him. While I wished Black Wolf could have found this happiness with Little Fawn, if that was not possible, at least he had found it somewhere.

I knew that monogamy was not strictly practiced. Life was far too uncertain, so many decided that since they never knew when they would meet with death or disaster, they would seldom pass up an opportunity to lie with a potential lover. From what I knew of Black Wolf, he had embraced this notion wholeheartedly up until now. Last year Black Wolf had confided in me that Little Fawn had not allowed him to touch her in a very long time. It seemed ironic that Black Wolf's illicit liaison with Willow Woman would finally make a faithful man out of him.

The meal was a merry one. If not for missing my own mate and children, I would have enjoyed this gathering completely.

* * *

It seemed our stay was to be brief. That evening, Black Wolf took Puh, Ria, and me aside.

"I have a proposition for all of you," Black Wolf stated. "I know you are eager to take the pups to Gray Elk, so why do you not leave me here while you continue on to Gray Elk's, deposit the pups there, and then stop back here on your way home and I will accompany you the rest of the way? That will give me more time with Willow and Oak, and you will not have to waste time here."

Black Wolf looked into our faces anxiously, awaiting our replies. I exchanged glances with Puh and Ria. I thought it was an excellent plan.

"I think it is a good idea," I said. "I would like to go before the puppies wear out their welcome. They do not mean to be trouble, but I would not like to abuse our hosts' hospitality. Besides, I would welcome any means to shorten this trip. I very much want to go home."

"I think it is a good idea as well," Puh nodded. "We can leave first thing in the morning, if everyone is agreeable."

"I am ready to go anytime you are, my love," Ria told him with a smile.

"Good! Then it is settled! I will tell Willow; she will want to know so she can plan a special evening meal before you leave," Black Wolf remarked, seeming quite pleased.

I was struck by his comment about Willow Woman wishing to put together a special meal. Every meal was prepared with care, and the food was served in great amounts. I felt as though I had done nothing but eat since our arrival, but I was not complaining. I had been very hungry for days while we were traveling, and it felt good to at last have a full stomach.

*   *   *

The mammoths are still pacing back and forth. I can hear them calling out to one another, almost as though they are talking amongst themselves.

I awoke with a start, as I often do when I am Dreaming. Something about their vividness always startled me from my sleep before they went on for too long. That was one of the perplexing aspects of the Dreams. Many times I had thought that if I could stay asleep longer, I might be able to learn what the Dream was trying to tell me. As it was now, those fleeting images were frustratingly brief.

I rose to my feet, took up my spear, and paused in the doorway, stopping there to watch and listen for any other living things that might also be awake at this time of day. Unseen birds were singing cheerfully in the dawn's cool air. A few of the pups roused themselves to join me. In the semidarkness, I could see their alert eyes scanning the nearby woodlands and ears shifting as they sought to intercept any stray sounds.

One of the pups suddenly woofed softly. Another followed with a suspicious bark as well. They and I both heard the approach of a two-legged being. It was White Cloud, who was bringing out an armload of tinder and wood to restart the fire in the outdoor fire pit. The silly pups now wagged their tails at the sight of him. They were always eager to meet anyone who could be a potential playmate. Or better yet, anyone who might be carrying food. White Cloud evidently heard the pups' low barks.

"Pleasant day to you," he said. "Breakfast will not be ready for a while, but I can offer you some water and dried fruits and meats while you wait."

"Many thanks," I told him. "There is no hurry. Is there anything I can do to help you?"

"You are good to offer your assistance once again," he answered. "If you are still willing after I get the fire going, I would be happy to have an extra hand or two."

"It just so happens that I have a hand or two that can be ready whenever you please," I told him.

White Cloud grinned in response and then returned his attention to the fire pit, gently stirring the heaped coals. I could see a faint red glow from where I stood, but no active flames. He began to carefully place little bits of tinder over the coals, so as not to smother them. Soon, little flames leapt up and more tinder was added, bigger pieces this time. White Cloud blew on the growing fire from time to time, continually adding more and larger fuel until the fire was going well enough that he could walk away to retrieve more wood.

The fire was now strong, and it provided a circle of light to the area beside the house. I decided that this would be a good time to take the dogs to a place where both they and I could relieve our bladders. Next, we stopped on the bank of the White River, where I cautiously dipped my hands into the water to wash them, and wash the last vestiges of sleep from my face. The pups wanted a drink, so they lapped from the rushing waters, backing away carefully once their thirst was slaked.

Then I rejoined White Cloud, the dogs still at my heels.

"What may I do to assist you?" I asked.

"Would you mind toting some more wood to the fire?" he answered, indicating a large pile of firewood near the rear of Willow Woman's substantial house.

"Of course," I nodded and left to collect an armload of wood.

I noticed that the dogs seemed reluctant to leave White Cloud. Even though no food had been brought out yet, they knew that he was the person who produced a wide array of delectables, and they were hesitant to let him out of their sight. But then some sense of loyalty or perhaps curiosity won over and they trotted after me. I stacked my arms with as much wood as I could carry and retraced my steps to the fire pit, where I set it down.

"Thank you, Tris," White Cloud said as he reached for several small chunks of wood and set them up as a tripod over one of his piles of burning tinder. White Cloud then moved to the next piles of tinder and repeated the process. This fire pit was large, so it was prudent to start several small fires within it, gradually building them up until finally there was just one big roaring blaze.

I made a few more trips to the wood pile and back and then we sat back to tend the fire as we waited for it to burn down to coals.

"I am so very glad that Slow Bear and the others were able to find Black Wolf and bring him back with them," White Cloud began. "I mean, I am sure she is very happy to see you and your kin as well, but she was so very ill . . . I was worried . . . however, as soon as Black Wolf arrived her spirits were immediately lifted, and she seems much improved."

"May I ask what ailed her?" I inquired.

White Cloud shrugged.

"I am not a healer, so I do not know much about these things. I can only say that she was not herself." White Cloud shrugged again. "Willow Woman is not one to complain — in fact, I have never heard her complain, even when she had just cause. I can only guess that it is possible that her illness was a complication of giving birth, since it was shortly after then that it set in."

We were both silent a moment. I was only too aware of the perils of childbirth: my own mother had passed away as the result of a miscarriage. I swallowed hard, as memories of my Muh returned to me. She had been a tall and graceful woman, loving and placid in nature, and so very beautiful. I was somewhat aghast when Puh fell in love with Ria, who was a small, scrappy woman, so different from my beloved Muh. But I had to admit, Puh and Ria were indeed devoted to each other. All in all, I think Muh would have approved. Her love for Puh had run so deep, I believe she would not have wanted him to spend the rest of his life the way he was in the interim between her passing and the time when he met Ria. Puh was so devastated; it was as though he were trapped in a quagmire of living death. Ria gave him back his life and brought joy to his heart once again.

"I am glad that Willow Woman seems improved. I hope she makes a full recovery," I said earnestly.

"Me, as well," White Cloud agreed. "I know you must be impatient to deliver your dogs and go home, but it would be nice if you all could stay a while. That would allow Black Wolf to make sure she is taking care of herself until she regains her strength."

"Yes, I am anxious to get back to my family," I admitted, "but I have come to consider Willow Woman to be my friend. Last evening, Black Wolf spoke to Puh, Ria, and me about going on to Gray Elk's without him, and then returning to accompany him home after we have dropped off the dogs. So we will leave this morning."

"Oh! Well that explains why Willow Woman asked me to make this day's breakfast an extra hearty meal. I believe she wished that you all be well-fueled for your long journey." White Cloud paused. "I will do my best to come up with a collection of foods that should sustain you for a while. It is still early in the season . . . so many foods are not available yet. But I do have some elk meat left. And perhaps Spotted Turtle will bring me some fish this morning. I am partial to fish for breakfast, are they not just the thing? Such a delicate flavor, and so juicy! I will slice the elk meat very thin so it will cook quickly. I am sure you will want to leave as soon as the sun is well risen."

"Yes, while I always enjoy my stay here, it is my hope we can set out as early as possible," I replied, nodding my agreement.

* * *

A few of the other household staff soon began to come out to attend their various chores. The pups rose to their feet and watched them come and go from the dwelling, but they soon lay back down again when they saw no action that piqued either their curiosity or alarm.

White Cloud's fire now contained a good amount of coals.

"I am going to gather up some foodstuffs," he announced. "I will return shortly. Mind the fire, will you?"

"Of course," I said as he left.

Then Roe Buck approached with a number of unlit torches, which he began to erect in various positions around the fire pit. We greeted one another in a friendly manner. I could see that new torches were probably placed in the posts that held them at measured distances around the clearing at the front of the house every day, probably every morning and as the sun set every evening. The huge fir trees that shaded this compound kept the area wonderfully cool even on the warmest summer days, but they blocked out a lot of sunlight as well. I stood to offer Roe Buck my assistance; after all, the fire did not require any attention at this point.

Roe Buck smiled when he saw my intention, and I nodded as I took the torches from his grasp and held onto them until he was ready to situate each one.

The pups then began to bark softly, tails wagging. I followed their line of sight and saw that Puh was walking toward us.

"Pleasant day to you," I wished him.

"And to you," Puh responded. "And you as well, Roe Buck."

"Yes, it does bode to be a very pleasant day, indeed!" Roe Buck agreed. "The sun appears to be strong. Perhaps that will encourage the trees to begin to leaf out."

I glanced up at the canopy created by the branches of the fir trees overhead. Although the smoke from the fire was filtering through the web of tree limbs, I could see that the early morning sky beyond was turning a bright shade of pink. Roe Buck then took the last torch from me and immersed it in the flames of the fire to light it. He used this torch to ignite the others and finally installed it in the notched pole.

"Ria is feeding the baby," Puh announced. "She will soon join us. We are already packed."

"I can be ready to leave right after we eat our morning meal," I said. "Have you spoken to Black Wolf yet today?"

"No, I have not seen Black Wolf yet." Puh shook his head. "The household is still quiet; I would guess that most are still asleep."

The truth was, I would likely still be asleep, too, if it had not been for my Dream awakening me while the night was just fading into morning. I then realized that I should feed the pups.

"I had better give the pups something to eat before we leave," I said to Puh, starting to walk back to the room where all my gear was located.

"Wait," Roe Buck stopped me, "do not use up your precious dried stores just yet. We have plenty of food scraps that the dogs would enjoy. Wait here!"

He did not pause for my response but quickly turned and trotted away.

"Many thanks, Roe Buck," I called out to his retreating form.

"Well, pups, it would appear that you are going to get a good breakfast before we hit the trail," I said as I bent down to stroke a few of the puppies.

I was grateful for Roe Buck's offer, but I was eager to do something, to be in motion. Feeding the dogs, helping one of Willow Woman's staff, anything to use my pent-up energy. I was eager to get going so we could finally deposit the pups with Gray Elk and then go home. The dogs seemed to sense my uneasiness. They stuck close by and watched me carefully, as though they anticipated that something was about to happen.

I thought on how much I missed my family and how I could not wait to return to them. I could not imagine enduring as Black Wolf did, long absences from the woman he loved and their infant child.

"I do not envy Black Wolf," I admitted. "It would tear me apart if I had to live away from Morning Star and the children. I understand why Ria insists on accompanying you everywhere. If Morning Star and the little ones were able to make the trek I would wish to have them with me, as well."

Puh smiled at this.

"I was a little taken aback at first when Ria proclaimed her intention to continue to hunt, even after Mror was born, but she is able to carry him in the sling and she is only walking and shooting her arrows, so Ria makes it work. We have not spoken of it, but when Mror becomes too big to carry, she may have to forgo hunting. We are fortunate that he is a quiet baby, but a small child cannot remain still long enough for us to find game — plus, there is the constant worry that a predator will find him and snatch him up while we are occupied with other matters. It simply will not be safe to bring him with us anymore. I suppose Ria could leave him with Ru or someone while we are gone, but I do not know that she would want to be away from him for so long. She adores that baby. But although I do not wish to be separated from them either, if it means keeping them safe, that is what matters."

* * *

Our morning meal left us all well-sated. Willow Woman and Black Wolf came out in time to eat with us and see us off. We had only a few moments to talk with Black Wolf in private before our departure.

"We will back in five or six days," Puh said to Black Wolf. "Will you be ready to leave for home shortly after that?"

"Ready? No," Black Wolf answered. He had the appearance of a man who was somewhat troubled. "I will never be ready. But yes, I will leave with you after that time."

"Do you think Willow Woman will be recovered from her illness by then?" I thought she already seemed to be much improved.

"I hope so." Black Wolf smiled weakly. "But I fear that she is not confident about her own health. This illness has shaken her mentally as well as physically. This is the first time in her life that she has suffered any sort of serious ailment. She had a long talk with me last night about what she wanted me to do if anything . . . anything happened to her."

"*Happened to her?*" I repeated.

"She wants me to take her place as Head Elder until our son is old enough to assume his role," Black Wolf divulged with a great anguish apparent in his voice. "She says that I am the only person she trusts to do this, both to take on the responsibility of the role and then to give it up so that Oak may one day realize his destiny. Also, should this scenario come to pass, I must complete his training. I have assured Willow that I will do as she asks, but that it will not be necessary. I told her that she will regain her health and live on for many, many years." Black Wolf paused and then continued, "I am counting on it."

* * *

When at last we were ready to depart, almost the entire household turned out to see us off. Little Oak was not present; he must have still been asleep at that early hour. As usual, Willow Woman gave me a warm and heartfelt embrace, but when she came to my Puh, I was surprised to see her take him by the forearms, in the way of The People, and regard him silently for a moment. She and Puh had not had much contact with one another. I doubt if they had ever said more than a few words to each other.

"Black Wolf has told me much about you, Tor," Willow Woman finally said. "I hope the future provides an opportunity to know you better. But if fate has other plans for me, however, it pleases me to know that Black Wolf has such a good friend as he has in you."

Puh's expression softened at her words.

"We will return before long. Perhaps we may talk a little then," Puh said to Willow Woman.

Willow Woman grinned mischievously.

"Do not hurry back too quickly, because I know you will take my Black Wolf away with you soon after your return." Willow Woman then faced Ria, and bent down to give her and baby Mror a gentle hug. "Take good care of yourself and your sweet baby," she said. "Our boys are almost the same age. Maybe they will grow up to be friends."

"I would like that," Ria said, nodding vigorously.

"So would I," Willow Woman stated.

"I will accompany you to the head of the path," Black Wolf announced.

"Many thanks to you all for your hospitality," Puh spoke to the group.

"Yes, many thanks," I said, waving farewell.

"Many thanks!" Ria added.

Little Mror saw my wave and he too, waved a floppy hand at our hosts.

"Safe journey!" Willow Woman called out after us as we started to walk away, the others echoing her sentiments.

The puppies danced around our feet as Black Wolf walked between Puh and me, with a long, strong arm around each of our shoulders.

"How is your pack riding, Tris?" Black Wolf asked. He had given me the stash of extra dried meats he had been carrying for the pups, and it was now crammed into my pack on top of everything else I toted, and it was exceedingly full.

"It rides very well," I assured him. "The pups will eat quite a bit of the meat between now and the time we reach your cousin's home, so I will not have to worry about carrying its bulk for too long."

Black Wolf thumped my shoulder approvingly with his hand.

"Well, here is the path. Give my regards to Gray Elk, Buttercup, and any others who may be in residence when you arrive."

"We will, indeed," Puh promised.

"And be safe," Black Wolf admonished us. "Remember the lions of last summer."

"I remember," I assured him.

Those lions had put up a good fight over a woolly rhino that we had just killed.

"Even though I was not there," Puh began, "I have probably met with many of their relatives in the past. We will take care, my friend. Besides, I have a feeling that the lions will be far more interested in the new wisent calves that will be trotting around at this time of year. We will be sure to keep as much distance as possible between us and the herds."

"Good thinking," Black Wolf said, moving to give Ria a quick hug and then raising a hand as we stepped onto the trail, "I will see you soon!"

"Farewell, Black Wolf!" Ria waved as well.

"Yes, soon," I replied.

Puh gave Black Wolf a brief nod in response.

And then we began to walk forward with purposeful strides.

* * *

It took us two days of fast hiking to trek to Grey Elk's mountainside home. We saw no lions, but then, lions were seldom seen unless they were charging out of the tall grasses or undergrowth, where they had been patiently lying in wait to attack their prey. We did occasionally note their tracks, however, along with the tracks of many other animals.

We came across a sizable herd of mammoths almost as soon as we reached the open grasslands. They were quite a distance away, but I did observe that one of the mammoths suddenly stopped in place and watched us with avid interest. I supposed it was silly to even ponder, but I wondered if she might have been the mammoth that had rescued me from the raging waters of the river last year. Mammoths consume prodigious amounts of grasses, roots, bark, and foliage, and they strip an area fairly quickly, forcing the herd to move from place to place to keep their voracious appetites satisfied. I liked to think it was possible that I might come across that mammoth now and then as each of us traveled on our separate errands.

Later on, a sow bear and her three tiny cubs were encountered as they drank from the far side of a small swampy pond. The sow stared at us apprehensively, probably as much concerned about the half-grown puppies as it was about us. They quickly disappeared into the nearby brush.

As Puh had said, the wisents were present, and most of the cows were either bulging with an expected calf or shepherding their new babies along. Meat on the hoof positively abounded here. It was unfortunate that we were not on a hunt.

* * *

The last day of our journey consisted of steep climbing up the lower reaches of the mountain. Even the dogs seemed to find this leg of the trip tiresome. We stopped periodically to rest and finally arrived at Gray Elk's cavernous dwelling around midday.

Gray Elk was already standing at the entrance to his grand home, ready to welcome us. He smiled broadly and shushed the several dogs that stood by and barked enthusiastically.

"Greetings!" Gray Elk cried out. "Tor, Tris, how wonderful of you to come here! And you have brought a bunch of dogs with you as well! And who is this?"

Gray Elk grasped each of us by the forearms, and stopped at Ria.

"This is my mate, Ria," Puh said, introducing her to Gray Elk, "and our son, Mror."

A series of emotions passed over Gray Elk's face, going from beaming happiness, to a poignant sadness.

"Ah . . . Mror. Such a good name. After your brother Mror, no doubt. He was a fine man. I miss him still." Gray Elk shook his head. "Mror was the best Keeper of Stories I have ever known. I have heard that his oldest son, Bror, now tells the stories."

"Yes, he was named for my honored brother. And yes, Bror will tell stories when asked. Bror is now paired with my eldest daughter, Ru. They are expecting their first child this fall," Puh informed Gray Elk.

"Well, that is good news! And this is a fine little fellow," Gray Elk said, peering around Ria at baby Mror, who was grinning and drooling as he rode on his mother's back. "But let us not stand here in the entry. Let us go inside and talk by the fire."

I still had vivid memories of this place: a great cavern with numerous halls and rooms, but at its center was an enormous chamber in which they kept their indoor fireplace. We followed Gray Elk through the various passageways, all lighted with lamps that were interspersed between the enormous skulls and antlers of giant deer, elk, and even some huge red deer. These were the remains of animals that had been harvested over the many years that generations of Gray Elk's family had lived here. The huge skulls seemed to stare down at us through their empty eye sockets, watching the procession of people pass them by.

The cavern's floor sloped upward at first, but then it began a gentle decline as the passageways twisted and turned. It seemed to me that during my last visit the hallways had been dazzlingly lighted with a profusion of lamps, but this time, the lamps were few and it took my eyes a moment to adjust to the darkness. Finally we arrived at the great chamber. Almost immediately, Gray Elk's mate, Buttercup, emerged from an adjoining room. Like Gray Elk, she knew Puh well. She went straight to Puh and embraced him.

"Tor! How good to see you! How is your family? I was so grieved to hear about Awna. Although I never met her, I heard that she was lovely and so devoted, too," Buttercup said sadly. "I had hoped that one day you would bring Awna with you to visit us."

"Many thanks, Buttercup," Puh said quietly. "Yes, Awna was a lovely woman, and she is much missed by all. I too am sorry that you did not have an opportunity to meet her. But I am grateful to say that my family is well. I am paired with Ria, now, and we have a fine boy."

Puh presented Ria and then lifted Mror out of his sling and proudly showed off his newest child. Buttercup and Ria exchanged hellos, but Buttercup was evidently enchanted with the baby.

"Oh, he is a fine boy! May I hold him? I have a few grandchildren, but unfortunately, we lost the youngest one when he passed unexpectedly suddenly last year. Such a sad time. Poor little thing was never well from the time he was born." Buttercup paused and sighed. "Such a sad time," she said again. "We fear we have lost our sons Sky Fire and Running Buck. They have been gone many moons now."

"Buttercup, that is indeed sad news," Puh said, placing an arm around Buttercup. "I am so sorry to hear it. Losing a child, whether an adult or a youngster, is the worst thing we can face."

Ria and I added in our sympathies, too. As a fellow parent, I could not imagine her grief. Again, this brought back Gran's speculation about the need to produce numerous children. I still could not bear to think on it.

"May I hold him?" poor Buttercup asked again, blinking back tears.

Puh nodded and Buttercup gingerly took little Mror from Puh and snuggled him close. "Oh, he is heavy!" Buttercup said with a little smile. "And he is a sweet little boy!"

"He is an armful," Ria agreed. "But Mror is such a good baby. He is almost always happy, and such a good sleeper, too."

I thought to myself that baby Mror did not have anything to be unhappy about. He was always carried; I wondered at what age his feet would first touch the ground. Mror chuckled readily, eyes shining with merriment. In another year or so he would learn to modulate his voice, and to laugh and cry silently. We Old Ones strive to make as little noise as possible. We believe that human sounds betrays our presence as much to our prey as to potential predators. But in the meantime, Mror's was adored by a large family and his every whim was catered to.

As Buttercup and Ria stood side by side, Buttercup rocking Mror back and forth in her arms and cooing at him, I had a moment to observe her. I had not seen her in two years. I thought she seemed to have aged noticeably during that relatively short time.

She was a tall, slender woman with mid-back length graying hair and an attractive face. But her braided hair had far more white sprinkled through it, and her face was more lined than it was when I had last stopped here. Gray Elk, too, seemed somewhat diminished. Before, he had had a look of a man who was well-fed, but now he was thin, and his hair was limp and stringy. After hearing about the loss of their sons and a grandchild, I could understand their appearances.

Buttercup then glanced up at me and I felt a little self-conscious to be caught staring at her.

"Oh, Tris, I did not mean to ignore you," she said apologetically, trying to sound cheerful. "I was just so excited to see the baby."

"It is understandable," I told her. "Mror manages to charm almost everyone."

"He does indeed!" Buttercup smiled, causing Mror to grin broadly at her. "How is your family, Tris? I understand you have a little one now?"

"Morning Star and I have two little ones. A toddling boy named Fox and a baby girl named Pony, but Fox cannot say 'Pony' so he calls his little sister *Nee*. And you? You are well?"

Buttercup's smile faded and she quickly traded glances with Gray Elk.

"Thankfully, Buttercup and I have been well," Gray Elk answered for her. "But not only did we lose one of our grandchildren to a fever and our two sons after they left to deliver several young dogs to their new owners last fall, but we lost many dogs as well." Grey

Elk sighed, "Our son's mates and their children still live with us, but now we are down to only two healthy men, our daughter's mates, who do all the hunting and the wood procurement that we need to survive. In fact, they left us yesterday in hopes of bringing in some fresh meat. These few dogs are all I have left. I see that you have brought . . . let me see . . . one-two-three-four-five-six half-grown pups with you. Are you hoping to trade for them?"

"My dog Raena, the one Black Wolf gave me when we were here two years ago, had these pups last winter." I replied. "I would like to give them to you. They are smart, good-natured dogs; I hoped you could find homes for them."

Gray Elk's face lit up at this news. He knelt and called the pups to him.

"Yes, these are good dogs," he agreed. "They come when called and sit so nicely." He stroked their heads as he looked each one over. "But I would like to give you something for them. I am so glad you brought them here. Some people, if they found themselves with extra dogs, would simply eat them."

"Eat them?!" I exclaimed, horrified. "How could anyone eat a dog? A dog is like a member of the family."

"Well, I would agree with you, but sometimes they do." Gray Elk shook his head, but then he added, "There must be something I can give you for the dogs."

"Really, Gray Elk, it will be payment enough to know you will find each of them a good home," I told him.

"Well, perhaps there will be something I can do for you in the future . . . just keep that in mind," Gray Elk said, smiling at me. "How pleasant it is to have you all drop in like this! We have had an immense amount of snow this winter, and the weather has gone back and forth between cold and wet all spring. We have had heavy snows and then heavy rains and then it freezes again and snows again. Ack! We can hardly keep track of what season it is out there!"

"Yes, this is certainly a wonderful surprise! Make yourselves comfortable around the fire while I see to the preparations for our evening meal," Buttercup said, passing Mror to Ria and gesturing toward the fireplace. "Thank you for letting me hold your baby. I may pester you again to snuggle him more, later."

"Whenever you would like," Ria said, smiling in response.

"Many thanks, Buttercup," Puh added, nodding to her as he ushered Ria and Mror across the room to the huge fire pit situated under a gaping chimney hole in the ceiling.

I accompanied them, followed by the trail of dogs, and we all sat down on the layers of matting heaped with pelts by the glow of the flames. Gray Elk joined us, and we enjoyed an afternoon of quietly subdued conversation.

Buttercup supervised her daughters and her son's mates as they brought out various foods to be cooked over a section of the fireplace where seething red coals were spread out so that the meats might cook over them, and tubers were roasted amongst them. The repast was tasty and hot, but I guessed that Gray Elk and Buttercup were embarrassed that the meal was not up to their usual standards. I had had some very fine victuals here in the past, but it seemed that their stores were vastly depleted at this time. I felt guilty to be eating up some of their precious food, so I ate lightly. I noted that Puh and Ria did as well.

The other household members joined us for the evening meal. There were four children in addition to the young women. They brought with them an air of sadness that even the pups seemed to sense. The puppies nuzzled them with their snouts and attempted to lick their hands and faces, as if to bring solace.

After dinner, Puh, Ria, and their baby were shown to a room where they could bed down for the night. I was offered a room as well, since there were many vacant spaces in this huge cave, but I opted for the warmth of the fire. Unfurling my cloak, I laid it over me and settled down to sleep with the pups.

Chapter Five

The ground was shaking. It was enough to awaken me from a sound sleep. At first I thought I was dreaming, but then I realized that the quaking was real. It lasted only a few moments and then it was over. The pups whined and cowered by me, some of them actually trying to climb into my lap for comfort.

The fire was still alight, but just barely. I heard the muffled and confused voices of the other people residing in Gray Elk's home: the trembling earth had roused them, as well. I gently poked the dying fire and carefully added a few small sticks to bring it back to life. I was still building up the fire when everyone came out of their rooms to discuss what might have happened.

Gray Elk and Buttercup brought out a torch and they began to light a few lamps to brighten the great chamber, but then Gray Elk suddenly stopped in his tracks.

"Doro! Zepper! Wassie! Venner!" he called to his dogs, who had been skulking in the room's shadows, but now were made visible by the lighted lamps. "Why are you in here? Normally, they sleep at the entrance to the cave because they are unaccustomed to the warmth of the inner rooms," Gray Elk explained to us.

The dogs gathered round him, eyes wild with terror and tails between their legs. Like my pups, they whined piteously.

"What has happened to so upset the dogs?" Buttercup asked. Then she turned to the younger women. "Put the children back to bed. There is no reason to keep them up."

"But Grandma, what was that shaking?" one of the boys inquired anxiously.

"Maybe a herd of mammoths has passed by," Buttercup replied quickly. "Go back to your beds now. It is over. I am sure everything is fine."

"Mammoths? Up here?" he persisted.

"To bed!" Buttercup pointed to his room.

After the children were led away, Buttercup turned to us.

"What *was* that?" she questioned.

"I have never felt anything quite like that before," Puh responded, "It was almost as though part of the mountain came down. But it does remind me a little of when my brother Mror was killed. We started a landslide to bury him in the ravine where he was pinned under the bear in the trap. The falling earth and tumbling boulders caused vibrations something like this."

We were silent a moment as we absorbed this disturbing information and then, as a group, began to walk toward the cave's entrance, Gray Elk carrying his torch and Puh and I toting our spears. Gray Elk and Buttercup continued to light a few lamps here and there as we made our way up the passageways. The rest of us followed their smoky trail until we came to a stop just short of the entryway, which was now blocked with a wall of snow.

Puh and I moved to the front of the procession, apparently both thinking the same thing. The snow sloped downward from the roof of the entryway, so we climbed up a few steps and then plunged the butts of our spears into the snow and worked them in a circular motion to widen the holes. After removing our spears we peered into the openings with the aid of a torch and saw nothing but more snow at the far end.

"Well, the layer of snow is at least as deep as a man is tall," Puh stated.

"Yes," Gray Elk agreed, "I believe that the snow has come inside the entrance quite some distance. It was lucky that my dogs must have heard or felt the avalanche coming and run away before they were buried. No wonder they were so frightened."

"My pups seemed to sense it as well," I added. "We will need to start digging our way out or we will all be trapped."

"And we will need access to fresh air, as well," Puh pointed out. "Does this cave have another exit?"

"No," Gray Elk shook his head.

"What can we use to remove the snow?" I asked.

"Come with me," Gray Elk responded.

Again, as a group, we retreated back into the bowels of the cave until Gray Elk halted at a room. He went in ahead of us and then motioned for us to join him. It appeared to be a storage room for anything that had no place in any other part of their home. Stacks of frayed and broken baskets lined one wall. Cracked spears and broken tools were leaned against another wall. Busted-out snowshoes and worn boots were tossed in a heap in a corner by a pile of animal hide scraps. But there was also a collection of giant deer antlers. We often made these into shovels by breaking off the long tines and sharpening the leading edge so that it cut into snow well. The antler shovels could be used on dirt, too, but one had to dig with care, as they were brittle and prone to cracking.

"We seldom need to dig anything other than occasional leeks, onions, tubers, and things like that, and we use broken spears as digging sticks for that chore . . . the fire-hardened wood holds up well for the task," Gray Elk told us. "Our snow is usually light and fluffy, so we either sweep it aside or remove it from our entryway by scooping it into baskets and then dump it outdoors."

"What about the giant deer antlers?" Puh asked. "Would you be willing to let Tris and me knock off the tines so we can make shovels out of them?"

Gray Elk looked thoughtful.

"These antlers have been stowed here for many years; so there's no reason not to use them. But are they not unwieldy?" he questioned.

"I guess they are rather large, but Tris and I are used to shoveling with them. Unlike you, we must dig our homes out of the hillside, and the last few winters we have received more snow than usual, so we have had quite a lot of practice," Puh said. "We will just need to score the antler tines with a sharp flint and then knock them off with a hammer stone. We will not have time to make any of the usual refinements, however."

"All right," Gray Elk said, nodding in agreement. "I can help score the tines. Let us retrieve the proper tools and set to work."

We worked quickly, fueled by the food and drink that Buttercup and the other women prepared, as we had a lot of heavy work ahead of us.

"How fortunate it is that the avalanche did not occur while any of us were outside," Buttercup pointed out.

"Yes," Gray Elk agreed. "But now we must clear an opening in the entryway to bring in fresh air. I have heard that when people have no access to new air, they go to sleep and they do not wake up."

"And the fire in the lamps and fireplace all need air, too," Puh added.

"What about the chimney?" Ria inquired. "When we walked through the great chamber, I could still see smoke going up toward the ceiling, although it was too dark to see whether or not was actually exiting the chimney hole."

"The ceiling is very high there, so a certain amount of smoke could pool up at the ceiling and probably go unnoticed," Gray Elk said thoughtfully.

"But the draft would be cut off. Would the smoke not start to simply drift around the upper reaches of the room?" Ria asked.

"I suppose that is so. Perhaps we should be looking at the chimney before we begin to clear the entryway," Gray Elk stood from where he knelt at the enormous giant deer antler, and he hastily began to walk back to the main room.

Puh and I also temporarily abandoned the antlers and accompanied the others back to the fireplace, where we all gazed up at the ceiling.

"It is still too dark to see much up there," Buttercup said disappointedly. "I wonder how long it is until morning. As soon as it is daylight we should be able to see sunlight through the chimney hole."

"There were still small flames in the fireplace when I first awoke, so I would think that it would have been at least halfway through the night by then," I said, calculating how quickly the fire was apt to burn down. "And now, I would guess that morning is not too far off."

Ria still stared upward, walking back and forth around the fireplace, trying to see the chimney hole from the best vantage point. She suddenly placed little

Mror in Puh's arms and walked determinedly toward one of the cavern walls.

"What are you doing, my love?" Puh questioned her.

"I have an idea," she replied, beginning to climb up the stone face of the wall to one of the naturally occurring shelves in the rock upon which rested a huge giant deer skull that sported some of the biggest antlers I had ever seen.

"I gathered that," Puh spoke apprehensively. "But what is it you hope to do up there?"

"To begin with, I will ascertain if the chimney is in fact open," Ria said, pausing as she assessed the next stage of her climbing route. "It is much warmer up here than it is down by the floor."

"Is it smoky?" Puh asked.

"Not yet," Ria replied, resuming her assent.

I then noticed drops of water splattering amidst the blaze in the fireplace.

"There may be melting snow coming in through the chimney hole," I stated.

Ria's coughs floated down to us.

"Now it is smoky," she announced. "It is rather dark up here . . . I think there is a small hole that is allowing some of the smoke to escape, but it needs to be enlarged."

I immediately began to climb up after her, spear in one hand. This was a tricky proposition, one-handed, especially when I reached the ledge with the giant deer skull. I needed to get over the huge set of antlers without toppling down off the rock shelf. My boots, which consisted of several layers of hide and fur between my feet and the soles, did not exactly give me good traction.

I glanced down for a moment and saw the others below, staring up anxiously, all except little Mror, who had fallen back to sleep in Puh's arms. Looking up again, I carefully chose my next steps and handholds and proceeded onward.

I was relieved to reach Ria and join her on a narrow outcrop near the chimney hole. The smoke made my eyes sting and I began to cough as well. Ria pointed at the opening.

"Do you see the stars through the smoke?"

"Yes," I nodded. "I will try to use my spear's shaft to widen the hole. It is almost completely closed off."

I leaned out as much as I dared and jabbed my spear upward into the gaping chasm in the stone that created the chimney. Clumps of dislodged snow rained down on the fireplace, causing the fire to smoke even more. By now everyone was coughing, and Puh left the chamber to put the sleeping baby back to bed, but he soon returned.

At last the opening was considerably enlarged.

"It would be better if we could move some of the snow away from the chimney hole on the outside," Ria pointed out.

"Yes," I agreed, "if we can manage to get out there."

"Push me up through the hole," Ria said, gazing at me expectantly.

I balked.

"How will you shift the snow? It may be hard-packed," I told her. "Perhaps I should do it."

"You will never fit through that opening," Ria insisted. "Just give me a boost and lend me your spear. I will use it to break up the snow into chunks that I can move out of the way."

I glanced down at our companions again. They could not hear our conversation from where they stood.

"All right," I finally agreed. "But do be careful! After I lift you up and you can get started, maybe you could knock some more snow away from the chimney hole and then I will see if I can find a way to climb out, too, so I can help you."

Ria nodded and waited once more for me to raise her up to the opening in the roof. I was not sure what would be the most dignified way to thrust my father's mate through the hole, but finally I decided I would first place her on my right shoulder and then, with my hand under her bottom, thrust her upward in hopes she could scramble the rest of the way by herself. This was accomplished with only a small kick to my head in the process, when Ria tried to propel herself through the opening.

"Sorry, Tris!" Ria called down to me. "Did I hurt you?"

"I am fine," I assured her. "Fortunately, I have a hard head."

I passed my spear up to her so she could start chopping at the snow, which now fell down in greater amounts.

"What is going on up there?" Puh asked.

Ria and I had been working in the deep shadows by the ceiling, and those on the floor were unable to see us.

"Ria is outside of the chimney, trying to clear the snow away. As soon as she widens the hole far enough, I will join her," I answered.

"What?" Puh exclaimed. "I am coming up!"

Puh began to ascend the wall. He was carrying his spear, so he too had to carefully skirt the same giant deer skull and antlers. But he was a strong and agile man and he soon joined me.

"Ria, my love, what does it look like up there?" Puh inquired, shouting through the chimney hole.

"It is fortunate that the setting moon is reflecting off the snow, because the sun is still below the horizon . . . but I think it will rise before long," Ria answered.

More snow came down.

"I think I can squeeze through now," Puh said to me. "Give me a hand."

Puh did not need to be pushed through the opening as I had Ria, but I did hold his spear for him, and helped to steady him as he hefted himself into the air. Puh then leaned back over the chimney hole, coughing on the continuing flow of smoke, and held out his hand for his spear.

It was not long before the opening was large enough for me to climb through. I eagerly pushed myself through and was startled when I stood upright on the mountainside. Much of the craggy landscape was obliterated in the pristine white drifts. We were extremely lucky that there were massive rocky outcrops just a little way above the chimney that had sheltered the opening from the worst of the avalanche.

The air was frigid, and our breaths came in gasping clouds. I took just a moment to observe the sky brightening to the east. The stars were slowly fading, and a pale moon hung low in the sky.

"Let me take over," I said, reaching for my spear, which Ria was still putting to good use.

Ria nodded and placed it in my hands.

None of us was dressed for being outdoors, and although Puh and I were somewhat warmed by our work, Ria began to shiver.

"You will be chilled through and through, my love. Go back inside," Puh suggested gently.

Ria hugged herself and hopped in placed, but suddenly she stood stock-still as something caught her eye.

"Tor!" Ria's eyes were wide, and she pointed behind us.

Puh and I wheeled just in time to see a snow leopard charging forward from the rocky outcrops, lowering its body the last few steps as it readied to pounce on Puh. Puh and I quickly poised our spears defensively, adopting the usual one-foot-forward, one-foot-back stance, which allowed us to brace our legs for an impending strike. However, when Puh stepped back, the snow beneath his feet gave way and he disappeared into the smoking chimney hole.

"Tor!" Ria cried out again.

"Puh!" I shouted, at the same time turning to fend off the snow leopard.

The snow leopard bounded off, leaping gracefully over the chimney opening, but stood there, about ten or twelve paces away, growling and glowering at Ria and me. I glanced down and saw that Puh's spear was wedged across the gap, and Puh's hands were still holding onto the weapon, which flexed under the burden of his weight.

Ria tugged at my spear.

"Give it to me!" she said desperately. "I will deal with the leopard! Help your father!"

I saw the sense of this immediately. I let loose my spear and Ria took it from me without hesitation.

"Help your father!" she repeated, and eyes narrowing, she turned toward the snow leopard.

My spear looked ridiculously huge in Ria's hands, but I trusted her to wield it effectively. I knelt at the rim of the chimney, and took a deep breath before I thrust my face over the opening. My eyes began to water instantly as the hot, smoky air hit my face, but I could see that Puh was determinedly hanging on, the fire in the fireplace burning brightly directly below him.

"Puh," I said as I lay down on my stomach in the snow and then kicked my toes into the snow's crust at my feet to help anchor me.

Puh looked up.

"I think my spear is about to snap," Puh said.

"I know." I reached down and locked my hands around Puh's wrists. "Let go of the spear and latch onto me. I will pull you up."

Puh nodded.

"Ready?" he asked.

"Yes," I replied.

Puh quickly transferred his grip from the spear to my wrists. Now that his weight was no longer hanging off the shaft, it sprang into the air, much like Ria's bow when it releases an arrow, and fell down into the fireplace. I drew Puh up higher, so that we were face to face. One hand at a time, Puh let go of my wrists and grasped my shoulders, pulling himself along until he was at last free of the crevice.

At that moment, a blur of movement caught my eyes as the snow leopard charged us once more. Two prone targets must have been too much temptation for the animal, and it was nearly upon us when Ria intercepted it. She caught it squarely in the center of its chest. The animal yowled with pain, but managed to free itself from the lance. It growled again, and spat at us as it withdrew, evidently, deciding that it had met its match. The snow leopard left a trail of blood as it retreated down the mountainside.

I rose to my feet as Ria hastily passed my spear back to me. She threw herself at Puh, who still reclined in the snow. She embraced him tightly, sobbing silently, but wholeheartedly. Her tears left pink trails down her face, where they washed away the soot which coated her visage.

Puh comforted Ria as best he could, whispering softly into her ear between bouts of coughing, and stroking her back and her hair.

I stood to the side, shivering in the cold of the early morning dawn. All but the brightest of stars had faded away and the moon was but a faint shadow of its former self. An orange sun painted the eastern sky in bright pastel hues. Far off in the distance, a lone bird winged toward an unknown destination.

* * *

After we had completed our descent back down the chimney hole, everyone began to speak at once.

"What happened up there?" Gray Elk questioned us anxiously. "All of the sudden, we saw someone fall into the chimney! And then a spear fell down! It landed in the flames, but I pulled it out before it could catch fire."

Gray Elk still held Puh's spear.

"That was me, and it was my spear. Many thanks for rescuing it for me," Puh said.

"I should have known it was you," Gray Elk gave Puh his spear. "You smell like a smoked haunch of venison. But I fear your spear suffered a bit of damage. The tip has broken off the head and the shaft is fractured length-wise down the grain. See here?" Gray Elk pointed to the place. "We have any number of spears for you to choose from. Perhaps it is one way I can repay you all for making such a long journey to bring your dogs to me."

"I think that is a very fine idea," I agreed.

"Yes," Puh nodded. "And I have an idea, myself. It has occurred to me that we may be able to simply melt the snow at the cave entrance, rather than shovel it out of the way. It is an enormous amount of snow; it would have to heaped inside the passageways at least until we are able to create a path to the outdoors. Melted snow would have considerably less volume. While it will make things rather damp, it may be the fastest and easiest way to clear the entryway."

Gray Elk and Buttercup grinned widely. They approved as well.

We stopped to rest a short while and eat a breakfast of dried foods before we commenced work at the cavern's entrance.

We tested the depth of the snow at the top of the entryway's opening and found that it was relatively shallow there. So I crawled up the sloping wall of snow to the ceiling and using my spear and an axe, I stabbed and chopped away at the dense snow until I had reached the outside. I worked to widen and deepen the hole until it was big enough to allow the fire's smoke to escape, as Puh cleared away the chunks of snow that collected below me. We then started our fire and gradually built it up until we could lean chunks of wood against the snow under the hole and let them burn.

As Puh said, it was a wet project, but we kept adding more and more wood until finally we had a sizable blaze going and the opening at the top of the entryway had expanded until it exposed the entire ceiling of the entrance. By sunset, there was a very adequate pathway to the outdoors, even if we had to use some of Gray Elk's hard-won firewood to make a dry path that spanned the large puddle of water left by the melting snow.

Chapter Six

Rain falls in heavy drops as we trudge down a thin trail. Suddenly a woman comes into view. Her face is hidden by her long, sodden dark hair. Her head moves slightly as she perceives our presence. "Run!" she says.

It was the same scene that had played out in the earlier Dream. I recalled Great Gran's words about reporting any additional details to her should the Dream revisit, but nothing new was divulged.

I was wrapped in my cloak, lying on the matting by the hearth. My disassembled boots and most of my clothing were spread out around the fire, as were Puh's. The previous day's work had saturated almost everything we wore, so I had kept the fire going all night, periodically rising to add more wood to dry our things before we were due to leave in the morning.

A few of the pups had slept with me, but most of them were now dispersed around Gray Elk's cave, more than likely keeping company with his grandchildren. The children were quite taken with the young dogs and lavished attention on them, often playing with them and feeding them tidbits.

I sat up and peered sleepily at the slowly dying flames. Gray Elk stocked quite a bit of wood at the far end of the great chamber, so I slipped the cloak from my shoulders and went to retrieve an armload of fuel for the fire. I had just returned to the hearth when Buttercup emerged from the room she shared with Gray Elk.

"Oh, Tris!" she said with surprise.

"Did I startle you? I am sorry," I said to her.

"Well, I knew you were here, but I just did not expect to see you in this state of undress," Buttercup said, shyly averting her eyes.

I was wearing a loincloth, so I was not completely naked, but I realized that my fair, freckled skin probably presented a ghastly sight for those used to viewing the tawny complexions of The People.

"I am sorry. I will see if my clothes are dry," I apologized hastily.

"Oh, there is no need to apologize," Buttercup laughed a little. "I did not mean to sound at all critical, it is just that it has been many years since I have seen a young man's physique, and certainly never one as impressive as yours." Buttercup approached a few steps and her brows furrowed as she inspected me at close range. "Your body tells the story of many brushes with violence."

"It is not as bad as it looks," I assured her. "Many of those scars are leftover from when I fell in the White River last year. The rocks scraped off a good deal of flesh, as I was knocked about quite a bit. But the marks are fading. I believe they will disappear over time."

"I hope so," Buttercup nodded.

"What do you hope?" Gray Elk asked, yawning and scratching at his scalp as he exited their bed chamber.

"I was just noticing that Tris carries quite a few scars," Buttercup told him. "He said fell into the White River and was battered on his way downstream, but hopefully the scars will be gone someday."

I felt somewhat self-conscious as Gray Elk closely observed me, too.

"Indeed!" he exclaimed, "you are a lucky young man to have survived that perilous plunge. It was a miracle you could break from the current and extricate yourself."

"I had a lot of help," I admitted. "I know this sounds incredible, but a cow mammoth pulled me from the waters." I shook my head at the memory. "I can scarcely believe it myself."

My clothing was now dry. I beat and bent the items a little to soften them up so I could don them once again, first tying on the leggings and then pulling my tunic over my head. Next, I situated my boots' new sole inserts inside each boot and followed it with the boot liners before shoving my feet in them. Last, I lashed the boots to my lower legs. Now, other than rolling up my cloak and gathering up my pack and spear, I was ready to leave. No doubt Puh, Ria, and I would eat our morning meal before we left, but I was eager to get going.

Ria came out wearing a bright smile and wished us a pleasant morning as she breezily retrieved Puh's clothing from where it was hung by the hearth. We returned her greeting, and after she disappeared back into her room, Buttercup's gaze lingered after her.

"She is such a happy little thing," Buttercup noted.

I smiled as I remembered Ria's fierce determination while she faced the snow leopard.

"Yes," I agreed, "most of the time she is."

Puh, Ria, and baby Mror soon joined us, Puh now dressed in his dried clothing. We ate a breakfast of dried meats. It was a lighthearted meal as the children played with the pups, the little ones squealing with delight and the puppies frolicking with abandon. Even Gray Elk's older dogs seemed to enjoy the noisy fun. They had not yet resumed their usual stations at the entrance to the cavern, as it was still far too wet there. I thought that Gray Elk seemed pensive, despite all the frivolity. One of his daughters seemed to notice as well.

"What is it, Da?" she asked him. "Why are you so serious?"

"I was just thinking," Gray Elk responded. "We are very fortunate that Tor, Ria, and Tris happened to stop by when they did." Gray Elk paused a moment before going on, "I mean, it would always be pleasant to have their company, and . . . I am glad they brought these young dogs to us, but how fortuitous that they arrived before the avalanche! Just think what it might have been like to be caught up in that wave of snow! Plus, it is good that we had their assistance in clearing away the snow, both from the chimney and our entryway."

The young woman's eyes opened wide with comprehension.

"Oh, Da! Besides that, what if our mates had come back to find the mountainside awash with snow! How would they have found their way home?" she exclaimed.

"That is true, as well," Gray Elk nodded. "We are indebted to you all," he continued, looking at us.

"You have always been very kind to us; we are very pleased we could help," Puh said, gesturing toward Ria and me, indicating that he spoke for us.

Baby Mror had been watching us all intently and he piped up with a series of babbles that made it sound as though he was trying to agree with his father, and he clapped his hands.

"Now it is time to wave farewell," Ria said to Mror, waving her hand by way of demonstration for his benefit. "Like you did before. Wave like this."

Little Mror grinned and waved to our hosts.

* * *

Our return trip to the Fen of Falls was somewhat treacherous in the beginning as we navigated the field of snow left behind by the avalanche. In some places it was densely packed, and in others it concealed a spot where some obstruction had created an air pocket under the smooth white surface, and we would suddenly find ourselves waist-deep in snow. Puh and I took to walking ahead of Ria, probing the snow cautiously with the butts of our spears. We were relieved to finally leave the remnants of the avalanche behind us and walk on the still-moist but comparatively solid ground.

It was a two-day journey back to Willow Woman's summer abode. As always, the roar of the falls foretold our imminent arrival. Even baby Mror's face perked up at the sound.

Black Wolf wore a bittersweet expression when he saw us. He welcomed us and then said, "I suppose this means you will want to leave for home tomorrow." He then sniffed the air. "You all reek of smoke! What have you been doing? You did not encounter another wildfire, did you?"

"No," Puh said, shaking his head. "We cleared some snow from Gray Elk's chimney."

Black Wolf still looked bewildered.

"Tor, that is not your spear," Black Wolf pointed out.

"That is correct," Puh agreed. "My spear developed a crack, so Gray Elk was kind enough to give me this one."

"It is smaller and lighter than Tor's was, but it is finely made," Ria chimed in.

"Why do I have the feeling that you are leaving much unsaid?" Black Wolf questioned.

"I do not wish to withhold anything from you, old friend, but I was thinking that we will have plenty of time to catch up while we are on the trail," Puh told him. "For now, you may prefer to spend your remaining time with Willow."

"That is true," Black Wolf nodded. "Just the same, I believe Willow would like to see you all before we leave. I will go and tell her that you all have returned so she can make plans for this evening's meal. I am sure she will wish to make it particularly festive. Why do you not go to the rooms you formerly occupied and get resettled . . . perhaps rest from your travels."

I returned to my room and set down my pack and spear. The space seemed lonely and empty without the puppies. I missed them, but it helped to know that not only were they in good company, but that they might help to alleviate the distressing situation in which Gray Elk and his family had found themselves. Gray Elk was a good man; I liked him and his kin immensely and I earnestly wished that the young dogs might help to reverse their fortunes.

I must have been very tired, because the next thing I knew Puh was at my side, gently shaking me to a state of wakefulness.

"Dinner is ready," he announced.

"Oh . . . I fell asleep. I did not realize that I had been sleeping," I said groggily.

"No Dreaming?" Puh asked lightly.

I knew he was teasing.

"If I was, they ran away before I was conscious enough to store them in my brain."

Puh thumped my shoulder heavily and he grinned.

"They were just regular dreams then," he surmised.

"Yes," I said, and then I shrugged. "But considering that my Dreams of late have not made much sense, it has not made much difference."

"How so?" Puh asked.

"I have been Dreaming of a woman . . . a woman I do not know. She appears to be an Old One, but she has brown hair. Gran says that it may be an ancient memory," I explained.

"*Ancient memory*," Puh repeated. "I have not heard that term in many, many years. Maybe since I was a boy. Does Gran think the ancient memories visit you as well?"

"She seems to think it is possible." I rubbed the last vestiges of sleep from my face. "Gran also says that some kinds of ancient memories visit everyone . . . that they are usually attributed to instinct."

"Well, Gran would know. Let us join the others."

I was famished and did not need any further encouragement. I hastily rose to my feet and accompanied Puh to the clearing at the front of Willow Woman's dwelling, where everyone was gathered.

I was amused to see tiny Ria sitting next to Willow Woman, who looked even more massive than usual in comparison. Each woman held her baby on her lap and the little boys seemed to be enjoying each other's company as much as their mothers were. Although Mror was three moons older than Oak, Oak was slightly larger. Both Ria and Willow Woman were first-time mothers, despite being old enough to instead be first-time grandmothers. They were an unlikely-looking pair: Ria so small and pale, and Willow Woman so large and dark. Ria's skin was thoroughly speckled with freckles, while Willow Woman's skin was heavily tattooed. But none of this mattered. They sat companionably together as though they might have been sisters.

The chat was momentarily interrupted as food was served. As Black Wolf had indicated, a sumptuous meal indeed awaited us. White Cloud had prepared a variety of roast meats: boar, venison, and geese, and an array of tubers and early greens. After a few days of sparse eating, while we had made an attempt not to consume too much of Gray Elk's limited stores, we hungrily set upon the many victuals with unbound enthusiasm.

"Are you relieved to be free of the dogs?" Black Wolf asked me as we ate.

"Yes and no," I replied. "I know they had to go, but I do miss them."

"Was Gray Elk happy to receive them?" Black Wolf went on.

"Oh, yes. He was down to four dogs. He seemed very pleased," I answered.

"Four dogs?" Black Wolf sounded surprised.

I immediately regretted mentioning the number of dogs. I knew that Puh was hoping to hold off on this conversation until after we had left, so as not to dampen Black Wolf's last day with Willow Woman. But then Willow Woman herself came to my rescue.

"So tell me, Tris," she started, speaking loudly to be heard over the nearby rushing water "Black Wolf says that you have visions. What sort of visions do you have?"

"I have Dreams," I said, faltering for a moment. "But I suppose you might call them visions. They show me brief scenes. Often, I do not know what they represent until later."

"Do you ever see my son in a Dream?" Willow Woman inquired.

Now I knew why she was questioning me in this vein. This was not the first time that someone had hoped to garner information about the future from my Dreams.

"I am sorry, but no; not that I know of. As I said, very often my Dreams do not make any sense to me." As I saw her disappointed look, I added, "but I do sometimes Dream of children. Perhaps he is one of those children."

Willow Woman smiled. She was wise enough to know that I was seeking to comfort her. Little Oak carried the seeds of her hope that he would one day become a great leader of his people. Just now, however, he was a very vulnerable baby. But like an acorn, he had the potential to one day sprout into a mighty tree.

* * *

The next morning Black Wolf reluctantly set off with us to make our way home. Puh then told him the complete story of what we had found when we arrived at Gray Elk's, the loss of the grandchild, the suspected loss of Gray Elk's sons, and the avalanche that had buried his home. Black Wolf looked grieved over the mention of the lost child and men. He shook his head and was silent a moment.

"I remember the child, poor little thing. What a shame; Gray Elk and his family must be heartbroken. I have not seen Sky Fire and Running Buck in many years . . . I know that they depended heavily on those men to bring in meat and haul firewood up the mountainside."

"I am sorry that we bear this awful news," Puh told Black Wolf.

Ria and I also expressed our condolences. Black Wolf just nodded grimly.

"So that is why you carry one of Gray Elk's spears," Black Wolf suddenly resumed speaking. "It must feel funny to carry one so light. I believe it is even lighter than mine, but then mine is quite a bit longer than Gray Elk's."

Spears were made to be longer than their owner, so that if he tripped while carrying it, he was not accidentally impaled on his own weapon. Therefore, Black Wolf's spear was very long compared with most.

We Old Ones carry particularly thick, dense-grained spears so that they will stand up to the rigors of lancing the body of a large animal, and then subduing the wounded creature until it passes from life.   Even so, our spears sometimes cracked or snapped in two under the strain.

"You must have been missing your bow and arrows when you had to fend off that leopard," Black Wolf said to Ria.

"Yes," she agreed. "If I had had them, he would be dead. Tris's spear was a bit too big for me . . . and so heavy! But it kept the snow leopard at bay. And Tris pulled my Tor out of the chimney . . . that is all that matters."

"He is good at that!" Black Wolf laughed. Seeing Ria's quizzical look, he explained, "Tris once pulled me out of a hole, too. Back when Tor and his brother Mror went missing and Tris and I went out to look for them . . . Tor probably told you about how he ended up in the bear trap with his deceased brother and the dead bear. Well, after we saved Tor — and I was acting the fool with some rope — I ended up in the same trap. But Tris stopped my fall when he grabbed my arm. If he had not pulled me out, I would probably still be there, yet."

"We would have gotten you out somehow," I said, even though I knew that we had just barely escaped with our lives.

The fragile soil surrounding the trap had very nearly broken down and swept us all into the deep pit.

I pushed the terrible thought from my mind.   Life was full of peril and it did no good to worry about it. All you could do was to face life's challenges as best you could.

***

The ground continued to be damp and spongy beneath our feet while we crossed the open plains. I was just thinking that it would be nice to dry my boots by a fire tonight and finally be able to warm my wet feet when I noted movement in the distance and saw great hulking mammoths, their broad strides carrying them quickly over the ground. No doubt, they were in search of a fresh source of fodder. They observed our presence, too, and trumpeted the news to all within hearing range. This was a herd of cows and young mammoths of various ages. We would stay well away. Herd members were devoted to one another, and the infants and juveniles were tended with special care; it would not do to rile these animals.

All the same, it seemed that one of the mammoths was particularly interested in us. She stood stock-still and stared in our direction, trunk raised as though she were trying to draw in our scent. Suddenly, it struck me that there was something familiar about this creature. Even from this far away, the distinct curve of her left tusk, which had grown unevenly and crossed her right tusk, was the same as that of the cow who had rescued me from the frothing waters of the White River last year. Would she recognize me from her remembrance of the bloody half-drowned man she had pulled from the raging waters?

"That cow is watching us," Black Wolf announced. "Well, she can stay over there! I have no notion of doing any mammoth hunting. I had quite enough of it the last time."

Ria grinned up at Black Wolf, reaching out to pat his hand.

"I am very grateful for your presence at that hunt. You and the others made it possible for Tor to fulfill my silly brothers' ridiculous demand of a mammoth so that we could be paired." Ria paused. "I am sorry about what happened to you, though. That bull could not have chosen a worse moment to empty his bowels. . . ."

"Do not remind me!" Black Wolf hastily cut her off. "I remember it all too well!"

"No, there will be no more mammoth hunting," Puh started. "My oldest brother was killed by a mammoth, so I felt as though, in addition to being the requirement exacted of me to win Ria, that bull paid for his death. But now, especially after one of them has saved my son, I feel as though I owe them a life." Puh then noticed that the cow mammoth and I were still gazing at each other. "Tris, does she look familiar to you?"

"Yes, she does," I replied. "I believe that she has the same uneven tusks as the one who fished me out of the river."

"She is a big animal," Ria stated. "She looks as though she is the matriarch of her herd."

"Listen to her call out!" Black Wolf laughed. "I think she is talking to you, Tris. She is asking if you have been swimming lately!"

I smiled and shook my head at his good-natured ribbing.

"No swimming for me if I can help it!" I assured him.

We continued to walk through the yellowed grasses that were still somewhat flattened from the past winter's snow and strong winds. Some of the grass had been worn down to mud by overgrazing and too many animals trampling the area. A few of the muddy spots were now being used as wallowing holes and the many tracks around these trenches attested to their popularity.

The mammoths also recommenced their trek, and seemed to be moving roughly parallel to our course. The matriarch still cried out from time to time, but not in a threatening or alarmed manner as we would usually expect. The other mammoths kept a keen watch on us as well, but the lead cow almost seemed happy to see us.

"Is it just my way of thinking, or does it seem as though the big cow is pleased that we are here?" I asked.

Puh pondered my question for a moment.

"She does seem to be avidly following our progress. She appears calm, but interested," he stated.

"Yes," Black Wolf agreed. "I do not sense any agitation . . . very unusual. While the bigger mammoths have positioned themselves around the younger ones, they do not seem upset at our presence."

"We may need to step up our pace," Puh suggested. "It would be good to reach the river before the mammoths do. If they arrive first, not only could they prevent us from reaching our only nearby source of potable water, but even if they do not intercept us and drive us off, we might have to go a long way upstream to find unsullied water."

We all nodded. This was true. I had seen how much sediment a lone mammoth could stir up, never mind an entire herd. We hurried onward.

Still some distance away, the herd seemed to keep up with us, but we were relieved to see that it halted some distance from the river. The beasts appeared to be milling around a certain spot. Something had definitely captured their interest. In the meantime, we refilled our water bags and drank from the icy-cold waters, and then indulged in a quick meal of dried meats and roasted nuts.

The mammoths were now trumpeting vociferously and producing rumbling utterances. I turned to watch them again.

"Something has happened," I said.

My companions also stopped what they were doing and gazed across the expanse of open grassland. The mammoths were now quite agitated and circled around something, calling out to one another as though they were having a very anxious conversation. I was not sure if I really wanted to know what was at the center of that mob of behemoths. It might be a cave lion or some such predator. But, given that I owed my life to one of those mammoths, I felt a strong level of concern for them.

I walked to a small rise in the land in hopes of gaining a better vantage point. Puh and the others followed me. There, we took stock of the situation.

"Your lady friend appears to be beside herself," Puh observed.

She was alternating between bellowing with angst and cooing tenderly.

"What strange behavior!" I nodded.

"She is too far from the river to be rescuing another swimmer," Black Wolf mused.

"She is acting like a worried mother," Ria said, snuggling little Mror tighter.

Something about Ria's words rung true. The matriarch's lively running about and vocalizations were not those of an aggressor. She was more than worried; she was scared. I began to walk toward the mammoths, and again, the others followed me. I sensed that they were hesitant to accompany me, but they were also unwilling to let me proceed by myself.

We continued across the top of the rise and were perhaps fifty or sixty paces away before the mammoths noticed us. For a short while, we stood and stared at one another. The only sounds were those of the wind, the rustling of the grasses, and the mournful cries of a creature hidden within their midst. Then the mammoths seemed to be speaking to one another.

They all collectively stepped back, except the matriarch, who hovered close by. She looked right at me and called out with a few short blasts.

I locked eyes with her as well as we continued to slowly approach. She called out again and stepped toward a large, muddy wallow — and then I saw it. A mammoth calf, not more than a half-moon old, was mired in the muck. The sides of the wallow were too deep for the infant to climb, and the depression was too small for a mammoth to get in behind the baby and push it out. The matriarch's tusks were thoroughly encrusted with mud and grasses. She must have tried to shovel out the calf, but evidently she had not met with success. It was possible that her huge tusks actually prevented her from coming close enough to reach it.

We were dangerously close to the herd. But the animals, although still obviously distressed, allowed us to come nearer and in fact backed away still farther. My gaze had seldom left that of the matriarch. She now swayed back and forth with anxiety, calling out as before.

"The baby must be saved," I stated. "The rest of you stay here. I think I can push it out by myself."

"I will help you," Puh volunteered.

I turned to answer Puh and saw that he was calm, but Ria was wild-eyed. Her mouth worked as though she wanted to say something, but she could not put the words together.

"I can do this, Puh. This is my debt to pay," I insisted.

Besides, I felt that the mammoths would be less threatened by one lone man, especially one their matriarch seemed to know.

"All right," Puh nodded reluctantly, "but I will be ready to assist if needed."

"Me, as well," Black Wolf promised.

I smiled at them in gratitude. "I hope it does not come to that."

In reality, there would be little they could do if the mammoths suddenly turned on me. The only way I could see that they could possibly help was if the calf were too heavy for me to rescue by myself.

This was going to be a messy job. I took off my pack, boots, and cloak and gave my spear to Puh to hold for me. I then removed all my clothes except my loincloth and turned to the squawking infant. The chilly breeze raised bumps on my skin, and the wet ground squished up between my toes. As I came to the rim of the wallow, I paused to again look at the matriarch.

"I am here to help your baby," I told her, speaking softly. "I will be gentle. I have babies, too. I know how it is to worry for your child."

I was unnerved at the nearness of the enormous creatures. I could smell their musty, earthy odor, and see that they were shedding big patches of their heavy winter coats. Never would I ever have believed that I would come be standing this close to so many mammoths. They could end my life without a thought. However, although they all watched me carefully, they made no move to come any nearer. Even the matriarch stood by, now silent except for her heavy breathing.

Looking down into the wallow, I could see the muddied calf. It cried piteously, begging for a rescue. This youngster probably weighed more than I did, so I had to exercise considerable caution when I lowered myself into the muddy hole, lest I be injured myself.

I slid down the side of the wallow, causing the baby to cry out in panic and throw itself futilely at the walls of the trench.

"It is all right, little one," I said. The baby's mother also cooed to her child, and although it seemed to settle down for a moment, when I again moved, the infant resumed its terrified thrashing and crying. "Easy now, little one," I whispered, slipping as I tried to position myself in the muck. "I am here to help you."

The infant did not seem to appreciate this rescue mission. It bawled loudly for its mother and did its best to get away from me. I then realized that I would have to move fast before the baby's frantic cries whipped the adults into a state of panic. I decided to use the baby's fear to my advantage; I moved to step closer to it, causing it to lunge away from me, so I quickly lowered by body so I was under its behind and abruptly raised my torso as best I could, with the wet, furry calf's boney rump now on my shoulder, as its legs scrambled for purchase on the steep slope. My own feet were barely able to keep from sliding out from under us, so I dug in with my heels and kept pushing the infant up the slope. When the poor creature finally became exhausted and stopped struggling, I too paused just long enough to catch my breath.

"One more time, little one," I said, bracing my legs as best I could. I made an effort once again to straighten up and push this balky baby toward the rim of the wallow.

The action alarmed the calf once more, but this time, its forelegs reached the upper edge of the hole and I continued to shove the baby until at last it was standing on the muddy ground. At this point, I could see that it was a little bull. The poor thing was trembling with fright and exertion, but it took a few wavering steps toward its mother, who ran over and greeted it joyously. She caressed her calf with her trunk, speaking to it tenderly. Then, she suddenly moved closer to me; I leaned against the side of the chest-deep wallow, watching the heartfelt scene. The matriarch reached out with her truck and touched my face ever so gently. Her eyes bored into mine. I knew those brown eyes so well. I often saw them in my dreams.

"Beautiful lady," I spoke to her, barely above a whisper. "We meet again. You see? There was a reason you saved me — so I could save your baby. All the same, I am eternally beholden to you. Without you, I never would have returned to my family, and that means more to me than anything else in this life. Many thanks to you, again, beautiful lady; many thanks to you."

I slowly reached out until I could touch the matriarch's trunk and stroked it. The fur was still damp and dirty from caressing her baby. At this proximity, her breathing was clearly audible, but she was completely calm. Only then did I notice that my companions had approached us and stood at the far end of the wallow.

"I will help you out," Black Wolf offered as knelt down and extended his hand toward me.

"Many thanks," I said to him.

I then felt faint vibrations shaking the earth. I turned to look at the mammoths, but they were now quickly walking away, no doubt headed to some new locale where they could graze and recover from the day's trauma.

Black Wolf looked up at them, too.

"I believe that mammoth cow is enamored with you," he said with a grin, grasping my hand and tugging me up from the wallow.

I could now appreciate the calf's difficulty. The sides of the wallow were so slippery it was no wonder it could not get out. However, with the aid of Black Wolf's strong right arm, I was soon standing on the well-trampled muddy grass again.

"I do not know if she is enamored with me or not, but I am quite fond of her, myself. And I am very glad I was on hand when I could be of service to her. Seeing her again was almost like meeting up with an old friend," I mused.

"Let us go back to the river," Puh said. "There, you can wash off all that mud and mammoth fur. Looking at you now, one can hardly tell if you are man or beast."

Black Wolf sniffed the air in my direction.

"One cannot tell by the smell, either," he quipped.

We all chuckled for a moment and then retraced our steps to the river, but not before I turned to peer over my shoulder at the retreating herd. Their hulking forms steadily lumbered across the plains under a rising sun.

* * *

It was not until I began my ablutions that I realized how begrimed I had become. Even my hair was thoroughly saturated with mud. I had to undo the many coiled cords that Morning Star had so carefully arranged and dunk my head beneath the surface of the frigid waters. It was only after a good scrubbing that I felt I was ready to don my clothing once more. When I sat down to put on my boots I noted that my bare feet were bleeding in a few places where I had stepped on the sharp stubbles of last year's grass and other pointy, prickly brush that cut up the soles of my feet.

"Oh Tris, look at your feet!" Ria also took note of their condition. "After a long winter of wearing boots and trudging through so much soggy terrain, your poor feet are softened like a hide that has been soaked for cleaning! When you take your boots off tonight I will dress your wounds with a salve to help them heal more quickly."

"Many thanks, Ria. And Morning Star will also be grateful that you are watching out for the well-being of my feet. She mentioned that she was worried I would not take care of them while I was away."

Ria paused before answering, adjusting the sling that baby Mror was carried in. He was asleep, with his head comfortably resting on his mother's back.

"I am sure that Morning Star worries about everything upwards of your feet, as well," she said.

"I hope that is true," I said with a smile.

Chapter Seven

When we strode back onto the family compound some days later, we found our collective families gathered as they prepared the evening meal. Morning Star leapt up from where she knelt by the hearth and ran toward me. I ran the last few steps to meet her and as she threw her arms around my neck, I lifted her off her feet in a one-armed hug, holding my spear to the side, and swung her around joyfully.

"Oh, I am so glad you are home!" Morning Star said as she covered my face with kisses. I then set her down and while she still had her arms around me, she looked me up and down. "And you are all in one piece!" Morning Star continued, grinning.

"It is so good to be back! Our trip was more or less uneventful," I told her with a smile and planted a kiss on her cheek. "The pups are safely ensconced with Gray Elk, and he was very happy to have them. Does Raena seem to miss them?"

"No — well, maybe a little. But I find myself missing the silly creatures!" Morning Star responded.

"And Fox constantly asks where they are. But I am glad that Gray Elk was happy to receive them,"

"How about me? Did you miss me?" I inquired lightly.

Morning Star looked around at all the people who were near enough to overhear our conversation and she suddenly seemed self-conscious.

"Of course I missed you," she whispered.

I pulled Morning Star closer and rested my forehead against hers.

"I missed you, too," I said, giving her a long kiss.

I then felt a familiar touch on my leg.

"Puh-Puh!" Fox held his arms aloft in a wordless request to be picked up. I cheerfully obliged and kissed him several times, too.

"Where is your sister?" I inquired.

"Nee with Tee," Fox announced.

My younger sister Twie soon arrived with Pony in her arms. I was somewhat taken aback to note that even though I had only been gone a half-moon or so, Pony had grown noticeably while I was away. Pony reached for me, too, so Morning Star took my spear from my other hand and Twie slipped the baby into my grasp. I gazed at Morning Star while snuggling our two children and saw her beaming back at me. At that moment, I did not think that life could possibly be any better.

I was quickly brought back to reality when Pony gave my beard a strong tug. Morning Star came to my rescue as she untangled the baby's fingers from my whiskers and took her from me.

"Nee bad!" Fox proclaimed.

"No, she is just a baby. She does not know any better," I said to Fox. "Besides, I remember when you used to pull my beard."

"Fox no bad. No pull Puh-Puh's bear," Fox insisted.

"Not pull your Puh-Puh's *bear*," Morning Star teased. "What a funny boy you are. Say *beard*, not bear!"

"Bear," Fox repeated. "*Bear.*"

"Dinner will soon be ready," Morning Star reported. "I am looking forward to hearing the stories about your journey. The weather was good, was it not? We have had no rain."

"Yes, some of the days were cloudy when we first left, but other than that, the skies were clear," I said. "There was still a little snow at Gray Elk's."

"Come, take off your pack," Morning Star began to pull the straps off my shoulders. "You must be so tired of having it on your back."

It was a pleasant homecoming indeed. I had hoped it would not be necessary to leave my family again until the fall hunt when the deer began their rutting season. But then, one day while Black Wolf, Puh, Bror, and I were laboring to chop downed tree trunks into manageable sections, we paused to rest a moment. Black Wolf scanned the nearby trees.

"So many of the remaining trees are either so huge that it would take an exceedingly long time to hew them or so spindly that they are not worth our while," he said.

"That is true," Puh nodded.

This was not the first time we had discussed our firewood situation.

"The deer have still not returned in any number," Black Wolf persisted.

"No, they have not," Puh agreed.

Puh looked at Black Wolf expectantly. It was evident that he was leading up to something.

"We might relocate, but where would we go?" Bror questioned, wiping the sweat and tiny bits of wood from his brow.

"While I was staying with Willow, I posed to her that very question. She suggested that we explore the lands to the north. They are relatively unpopulated and full of game," Black Wolf replied. "When my family decided to distance themselves from the Village, they went north. I think we might do well to go there, too."

The Village was a settlement of The People comprised of numerous clans. It was located about a day's trek from our compound. The Village was a crowded, dirty place that was steadily losing population because of the same challenges we now faced: dwindling resources.

"But we cannot just take our families into unknown territory," Bror pointed out. "Ru will have her baby in a little more than three moons . . . she cannot go any such distance for a while."

"Yes," Puh nodded again. "We could make forays throughout the summer, traveling fast and light to look for potential places to resettle. But it would mean missing another summer at the coast."

Black Wolf hung his head at this thought. He had never seen the ocean. He and his family were supposed to go to the coast with us last summer, except we were not able to go because the Wolf-men were staying with us. Black Wolf had often spoken with enthusiasm about seeing the great expanse of sea for the first time and he was obviously disappointed to put it off for another year. Morning Star would be dismayed as well.

"I guess it is the only time it makes sense to explore these areas," Black Wolf reluctantly agreed.

"You have often told us about all the food that is available at the coast," Bror started. "Would it not make sense to move there? That would be only a day's trek from my Muh and my brothers."

"Yes, there is plenty of food there, but every year when we go back we see evidence of the great storms that have ravaged the coast in our absence. They are bad enough that we must bury the materials we use to rebuild our homes every summer to prevent them from being washed or blown away," Puh solemnly explained. "If not for that, I would be inclined to agree with you."

"I see," Bror sighed resignedly.

I knew Bror missed his family badly. He was thrilled to be paired with Ru and expecting his first child, but he had not seen his mother or brothers since he and Ru were joined early last winter. This was the first time he had ever been away from his family for so long.

"What does Willow Woman say about the lands to the north?" I queried. "Is it mountainous or flat? Is it wooded? And what about water?"

"She says that from what she hears, it is wooded in places, largely flat and open . . . not mountainous," Black Wolf's smile returned. "Much game: mammoths, reindeer, wisents, aurochs, horses . . . ."

"Big animals," Bror noted.

"Elk and deer as well. The reindeer come through during their migrations. There are also rivers full of fish," Black Wolf added.

It went unspoken that lots of game also meant lots of predators — predators that did not distinguish between two- and four-legged prey. We had managed to keep most of them away from the family compound by generations of inhabitants marking the borders with urine. We would have no such invisible barrier at a new location.

"We should discuss this with the others over the evening meal," Puh suggested.

I understood why this was prudent, but I dreaded it just the same. We had only returned from a lengthy trip just a few days before. Morning Star had remarked many times how glad she was that I was home, and I could foresee that she would be very displeased to learn that I would soon be leaving to hit the trail for another long journey.

"When would you want to go on the first foray?" I asked.

"We must bring in more meat before we leave our families again," Puh pointed out.

"Yes," Black Wolf concurred, "maybe by the full moon."

We were halfway through the moon cycle now. I was relieved to know he did not want to depart immediately. Unlike the rest of us, Black Wolf was always glad to have an excuse to be away from home.

"Unless we can bring in another animal or two before then," Black Wolf went on.

For the first time in my life, I actually hoped we would not have a successful hunt for as long as was reasonably possible.

* * *

I was weary by the time we were all seated around the fire for our nightly sup. Fox ate while comfortably situated on my lap, and he was rather droopy as well. Morning Star, holding Pony, was next to me, and I noticed that she looked at me often. She had sometimes told me that I wore my thoughts on my face, and she must have seen that I was preoccupied. I was not only troubled with the impending storm that was sure to be unleashed when she found out about our upcoming trek, but also by the distressing notion of abandoning the only home I had ever known. The place where untold generations of my clan had lived . . . and been interred. I choked up on the thought of leaving my mother's and brother's gravesites to be neglected and lost to the ages. Nonetheless, we had to survive, and to do that we had to find ample meat and wood.

When everyone had finished eating, Black Wolf suddenly cleared his throat.

"Tor, Tris, Bror, and I have been talking today," he began.

Morning Star gave me a sidelong glance. I tried to smile at her encouragingly.

"We believe we must make plans for the future," Black Wolf continued.

"What sort of plans?" Morning Star asked. "Do you worry about getting in enough stores for the winter?"

"We still have some dried stores from last year, and so as long as we can add enough meat, fruits, vegetables, and grain to supplement those stores, we should be all right for this winter," Black Wolf said. "But it is the following winters that worry me. And it is not just harvesting meat. We have lost many trees in this area over the past few years. First a great storm knocked down a good many of them, and then there was the fire, which burned many trees we might have otherwise used for firewood."

"What are you saying?" Little Fawn cried. "Do you mean that we will have to move to some other place? We only just joined Tor's family here last year. I do not want to move again so soon!"

"I do not want to leave, either," Puh said, turning to Little Fawn, "I do not think any of us would want to go. The thing is that we may not have a choice."

I ventured a glance at Morning Star. She was alert and listening to this exchange intently. She was clearly distraught. I reached over and clasped her free hand.

"I like our little home," she said in a low voice.

"I do as well," I admitted to her. "I hate to think of leaving this place."

Morning Star smiled a little and she squeezed my hand, "Yes, this is your home. But wherever we go will also be our home. All that matters is that we are together and we have enough to live on."

"We think we should explore the lands to the north this summer," Black Wolf resumed. "We will work to bring in some fresh meat before we commence our journey so that you will have plenty to eat while we are gone."

"You will go away again?" Morning Star whispered harshly. "You just got back!"

"Let us speak of this later," I said quietly.

Morning Star looked into my face and she must have seen my grief there. Her expression softened.

"Yes, we will speak of this later," she agreed, squeezing my hand once again.

The others in our families were all somber at this discussion. Not only did this mean potentially giving up our homes and relocating to a strange new place where we would have to start anew, but they also knew it meant forgoing our annual trip to the coast. When the long cold winters seemed to drag on forever, it was the thought of spending a moon or two of carefree existence on those golden shores that gave us the heart to get through until spring: those warm days and balmy nights by a bright blue sea, lulled into a state of peacefulness by the sounds of the persistent breezes and foaming waves washing the sands. The bountiful sea and adjacent lands were teeming with foodstuffs for the reaping. It was extremely disappointing to know that long-awaited pleasure would be put off yet again.

Later, after Morning Star and I had put the children to bed, we began to talk.

"I am sorry, Tris," Morning Star apologized. "I should not have snapped at you. I know it must be very hard to even think of leaving your boyhood home behind."

"Yes, it is very hard," I nodded. "It may be just a futile hope, but perhaps we can return in a few years, once the wildlife and the forest have had time to recover from the fire."

"A few years?" Morning Star repeated. "The wildlife may come back that soon, but how quickly will the trees grow?"

"You are so clever," I smiled at her regretfully. "But you are right. I may have been foolishly optimistic at that."

"That is one of the many reasons I love you," Morning Star said, snuggling up against me.

The truth was, I would have given anything to be wrong in agreeing with her. What I wanted more than anything was to live right here with Morning Star, my children, and our families, for the rest of our lives. I had always cherished the thought that my children would go on to raise their children, and they would raise their offspring in the same locations where their ancestors had lived since time immemorial.

I found myself taking in the little details of the home so familiar to me, details I had not noticed before but now seemed so important: the care with which some long-ago relative had crafted the fireplace in the main house; the sturdy antlers driven into the densely packed earthen and stone walls at precise intervals from which to hang things; the slender section of tree trunk that was firmly affixed floor and ceiling, from whose lopped-off branches hung water bags and other heavy items. How many years back were those things crafted and installed?

Gran found me making this inspection after I had stopped by to speak with Puh but, and not finding him there, lingered in my old home.

"Are you reliving your past life?" Gran asked with a smile.

"Perhaps a little," I replied. "But mostly I am just looking. I came to find Puh, only after I arrived I saw that no one was home . . . at least until you walked in."

"We have taken this place for granted, but there is much to see here, is there not?" Gran stood next to me and ran her hand along the smooth wood from which the water bags were suspended. "Do you know who made this?"

"No," I shook my head.

"I was told that my great-grandfather made it. And he only replaced the one that was there before." Great Gran paused to look up at me, her eyes shining, "My father made the shelf over here. He carved it out of the dirt in the wall and then laid those stones along its surface so that anything set down on that shelf would not rest on the soil."

There were numerous shelves fashioned the same way.

"Did your father make all the shelves?" I questioned.

Gran shook her head.

"No," she stated. "I do not know who made the others." Gran gazed down at the floor, covered with layers of matting and hides. "It is sobering to think of how many feet have walked this floor. How many of our ancestors have lived, laughed, and loved in these rooms. Have died in these rooms. And soon, all that will come to an end."

"You must be very sad," I remarked with sympathy.

"It is sad," Gran said with a weak smile. "But I trust Tor to make the right decision. If he thinks the family needs to go somewhere else to make a new home, I am sure he is right."

"Do you know where Puh is? I wish to speak with him about tomorrow's hunt. I saw deer tracks by the upper creek this morning. I have not seen any there since last summer," I told Gran.

"Your Puh and Ria have taken your younger siblings on a jaunt to gather greens for this evening's sup. They should be back before long," Gran said. After a slight hesitation she went on, "What of your Dreams as of late? Do you see the brown-haired woman still?"

"Just one other time. Like the earlier vision, it is raining. She says, *run*. Then it is over. I have also been Dreaming of mammoths, but I believe that is because we ran into the cow who saved me from the White River last year." I grinned at the recollection. "I think she remembered me."

"You saved her infant," Great Gran grinned back.

"I hardly need to tell you anything," I teased Gran. "Did you see all that went on while we were away?"

"I saw you in two Dreams. I saw you pushing a muddy mammoth calf, and I heard the blasting trumpets from the older mammoths as they cried out for the baby," Gran said. "They must have been very relieved that you helped that little one out of the wallow."

"You said two Dreams. What else did you see?"

"The second Dream showed me you and Tor. I saw your father fall down a dark hole. It almost stopped my heart." Gran closed her eyes as though to block out the image. "But then you pulled him out." Gran patted my arm. "I am so grateful for your quick action and strong arms."

"It was Gray Elk's chimney hole. We were trying to clear the snow from around it when a snow leopard appeared. It must have been watching us from nearby rock formations that actually kept most of the snow from coming down on Gray Elk's home," I speculated. "Then when it saw that we were preoccupied, it snuck up on us. An avalanche had just taken place, so we were not expecting to find anything else alive on the mountainside. It just goes to show that you cannot be too sure of anything. But when Puh stepped back to shore up his stance with his spear, the snow gave way under his foot and he disappeared into the chimney. Ria kept watch on the snow leopard while I helped Puh climb out."

"An avalanche?" Great Gran repeated. "That must be why I saw so much snow in the Dream."

We then heard the voices of approaching children. Black Wolf's dogs were snoozing, as always, outside Black Wolf's home and they rose to their feet to greet the returning residents with a few happy barks and wags of their tails. Puh's new dog, Ochs, had accompanied them on the excursion, and I thought he seemed especially pleased to rejoin his canine friends. I momentarily wondered if Ochs missed his littermates, who had left the family compound almost a moon ago now. If he did, there was no sign of it.

I waited for Puh to set down his bundle and help Ria remove little Mror's sling from her back so he could be set down on a mat to entertain himself while his parents sorted through their gatherings. The others were also separating their prizes by type, putting fragile greens to one side, roots to another. When Puh reached the bottom of his sack, I grinned to see that it was full of rocks, some of them rather large. I hefted one of the stones.

"Flint . . . very nice," I said to Puh. "And a piece of agate, too."

"Yes, I was very lucky today," Puh nodded. "When Ria saw what I was collecting, she took most of my vegetables from me and carried them in her basket. Even so, I am afraid that some of the remaining tubers were crushed during transport."

"Oh well. At least we have vegetables in abundance at this time of year," I responded.

"Indeed!" Ria said cheerfully, kneeling protectively by Mror as he played with an empty sack, flapping it around energetically.

Just then, my brother Ty approached with several bows in his hands.

"Ria," Ty called out. "May I show you these bows? I would like to see what you think of them."

Ria rose to her feet and accepted the bow that Ty placed in her hands. She adopted the familiar pose, with the bow thrust out in her left hand and fingers of her right hand on the bowstring. She drew back on the bowstring, although she had not armed it with an arrow. There was an ominous cracking sound, as the middle of the bow gave way.

"Oh, Ty! I am so sorry!" Ria looked crestfallen as she examined the fractured bow.

Ty managed to hide his disappointment.

"The wood is too brittle," he said, also briefly examining the bow. "But here . . . try this one now. It is made of the same wood, but I made it thicker in the middle."

Ria appeared a little trepidatious as she grasped the bow.

"Perhaps I should be more gentle?" she questioned.

"No," Ty shook his head. "Draw back exactly the same as you always do. If the bow cannot stand up to the rigors of normal use, it is no good to us."

Ria nodded with understanding and again, drew back on the bowstring. This time, the bowstring let go, causing the bow to suddenly jump like a living thing, but Ria held onto it. She picked up the loose end of the string and held it up to her eyes.

"The cord did not break, but the loop has come undone," she announced. "I can fix it and try again."

Ria sat down cross-legged on the matting next to Mror, with the bow across her lap. Mror crawled closer to watch his mother as she mended the loop.

"Tor, pick up the baby, would you?" Ria asked Puh. "I want to restring the bow, and I do not want the baby too near just in case it comes loose again."

Puh did as bidden and lifted little Mror into his arms.

Ria stood and restrung the bow with one swift, deft motion and then poised the bow to try again. The bowstring made a satisfying twang.

Ty smiled broadly and offered Ria his last bow.

"Now this one," he said as he took the other bow back. "This one is made of a different wood. As you can see, it is a quite bit longer than the others. I hope that it might be better-suited to someone taller, like Tris."

Ria drew back on the bowstring, grunting slightly with effort.

"It has a hard draw," she pronounced. "I think it is a good bow, but I must say, my arm would be very weary if I had to use it all day. I can shoot my little bow tirelessly. But then, it is very small and no good for felling bigger game animals."

"What size animal do you think could be killed with the larger bow?" I inquired.

I knew that her bow was only appropriate for small deer and other modest game. But if we could use a bow and arrow to kill animals like elk or wisents, or even to defend ourselves from bears and lions, this would be a huge boon.

"I am not sure," Ria shrugged. "We would have to take it out and see how powerful it is."

"You mean actually shoot an arrow with it?" I was eager to try. I had never attempted to use a bow and arrow before, and Ria had never volunteered to let me use hers. She guarded her weapon jealously, so fearful was she that someone might accidentally break it.

"Yes," Ria started, "but we will have to make longer arrows before we can try to shoot with that bow. You see, my arrows would be far too short."

Ria selected one of the arrows from her quiver and placed its notch on the bowstring. As she pulled back, it was quickly apparent that her arrow would not be able to rest against the bow if she were to draw back all the way.

"You see?" she said again. "Unless we can draw back fully, we cannot tell how powerful this bow might be."

"We can bring the new bow with us on our next hunt for a trial run," Puh suggested. "I can make some longer arrows before we go."

"So can I," Ty said, nodding eagerly.

I was so intrigued at this that I had almost forgotten that I meant to tell Puh about the deer tracks, but Puh's remark reminded me.

"Puh, I meant to tell you that I saw deer tracks at the upper creek this morning," I announced.

"The upper creek? That is close!" Puh exclaimed.

"Yes. I was thinking that we may not have to go so far afield to find game if this one comes around again," I said.

"Or we can let it settle in and hope some of its friends will come around, too," Puh said after a pause. "Maybe we can hope that the animals will return faster than we had thought."

"I was thinking that same thing last night," I admitted. "And then Morning Star reminded me that we still have to have firewood."

"That is so," Puh agreed.

"It would be nice if we could stay," Ty broke in. "When you leave me here to protect the family while you are out hunting, I have the comfort of knowing that predators have been avoiding our home for many years and that we are relatively safe. It would take a long time to achieve the same effect in a new place."

"I was thinking on that, as well," Puh said.

"So was I," I told them.

"That has worried me," Ty went on. "I do not think I can hold off a large predator by myself."

"You might with this," Ria said, holding up the large bow.

We exchanged glances.

"I will make more bows," Ty stated determinedly.

* * *

We determined that we would try out the new bows the next day. We also decided that we would not attempt to track the deer that had visited the upper creek; in fact, we trekked in another direction in hopes of finding other game. It was likely that we would not be relocating for another year or more, so it would not do to either kill or scare off what few animals that chose to repopulate the area. As Puh had said, it would be good if they could be coaxed into resuming their old haunts.

Black Wolf, Puh, Ria, Bror, and I set off early the next morning into the misty landscape. The trees were just beginning to leaf out now, and the dew dripped wetly from the foliage overhead. We did not speak, just walked briskly down the trail and closely observed our surroundings. Even Black Wolf was unusually quiet. Most often, he liked to sing while we hiked, but he seemed oddly introspective. The peaceful hike lulled Little Mror to sleep, and he napped securely in his sling at his mother's back. With luck, we would come across game before he awakened.

Ty had given me the big bow, and Puh had made eight arrows to fit the weapon. We wanted to save the precious arrows for when they could be used with deadly force, so I had not yet attempted to make one fly. Ria had shown me how to draw back with the arrow and how to allow for the movement of the animal when I took my aim. I could only hope that all would go well. Ria made it look so easy. She could draw back and aim all in one effortless motion and send several arrows aloft within the span of a few moments.

After we had covered some distance we slowed our pace. Now was the time to be stealthy. We knew that a small glade was ahead, and the new late-spring and early-summer grasses and tender foliage would be attractive to deer. Their droppings littered the ground here and there. This would be a good place to await potential prey.

It was now midday and the sun was warm. The still air was filled with the sweet songs of birds and the hum of insects. As we came to the edge of the tree line, we scouted for a place to lie in wait. Puh pointed to a tree. Ria found it preferable to shoot from a higher vantage point, so often he would boost her up onto a tree branch, where she would have a clear line of sight. Ria, with Puh's assistance, situated herself on the thick limb, the baby on her back still sleeping soundly.

I placed myself by another tree, just a few steps away. Bror stood nearby, his spear in hand. Black Wolf stayed close to Puh and Ria.

And we waited. And waited.

I was hungry and thirsty. The insects buzzed around us, sometimes flying into my eyes and up my nose. I tried not to move, as stillness was imperative.

At last we heard the sounds of sizable animals moving through the brush. The steps were slow and hesitant, as though the creatures were unsure of their surroundings. They were upwind, but they may have been naturally cautious when approaching an open area where they would be exposed to anything that might be looking for a meal.

A roe deer tentatively thrust its head into the clearing, not far from where we stood. Dark eyes blinking and nose and ears twitching, it stepped out into the tall grass. It was a doe, and she was soon accompanied by several other does with young fawns and yearlings. We would have to act soon. It would not be long before they sensed our presence and scattered pell-mell.

Ria's arrow had been poised for some time, and I saw her pull back on the bowstring. I had also armed my bow and I followed suit. In the past, we had had to conceal ourselves behind trees or bushes and lance our prey with our spears. Since Ria had come to live with us, armed with her small bow, she could often wound the animals seriously enough that we could then finish them off with our spears, thus saving us close encounters with these animals until they were already badly injured.

When I heard the twang of Ria's bowstring, I also let my arrow go. The bowstring unexpectedly slapped the inside of my left forearm. I stifled a grunt of pain. The deer bolted before I could get a second arrow in place, however, Ria managed to shoot two more before the deer were gone.

Little Mror was awakened by the flurry of movement from his mother, and he chattered happily as we walked into the field to examine the area where the deer had been shot. A blood trail led us to a doe near the edge of the meadow; she was already dead. Another blood trail led us to a yearling doe. She was still alive, but we quickly dispatched her and brought her over to the other deer, so we could gut them both at once.

I located my arrow amidst the grasses where it had fallen. It may not have found its target, but at least it was still undamaged.

"I will need much practice before I can hit anything," I observed. "I must have done something wrong. After I let go of the bowstring it snapped against my arm."

I held out my injured limb, which now displayed a large red welt.

"Oh, that does hurt! I can show you how to hold the bow so it is less likely to happen. We are in an open spot here; why not try to hit that dead tree over there?" Ria suggested. "It appears pretty rotten. I think you could shoot the arrows into it without harming them."

"That is a good idea," Puh agreed. "We will take care of the deer. Ria, why do you not take Tris over there and help him with his technique?"

"Yes," Ria nodded.

Together, she and I approached the dead tree. Its bark was gone and most of the branches had broken off of it. The remaining wood was quite soft.

"Left hand like this . . . do not hold on too tightly. Twist your elbow slightly so that your arm will be farther away from the bowstring," Ria instructed, pushing my arm into position.

"The arrow wants to fall away before I can shoot it," I said, struggling to keep the missile in place as I attempted to maintain the correct form.

"Not so tight. Relax your hand," Ria advised, prying the fingers of my left hand away from the bow until they were loosened. "Twist your elbow." She again tugged my bow arm until she was satisfied with its placement. "Now draw back with one smooth motion . . . close shots like this you must aim low, but remember, when the arrow has farther to go you must to allow for the arrow to drop in its flight."

It felt awkward, unlike my spear, which functioned almost like an extension of my body. However, I realized it was important I learn to become proficient with this tool. Ria had me start with short-range shots, gradually moving me back to shooting from greater distances.

The arrows were easily pulled from the rotted wood, so I was able to reuse them over and over. Ria and I practiced at the far side of the meadow, almost opposite to where the deer had been butchered. By the time Ria and I decided that we had enough for the day, the others had finished with the deer and tied the does' ankles to hewn saplings so they could be transported home. Although I still had not mastered the tool, I was clearly improving. Nevertheless, it would not do to linger in this clearing with two dead animals and heaps of entrails nearby.

I had two arrows left in my quiver and I was about to suggest that I shoot those off before we quit the meadow when a large brown bear suddenly charged out of the trees and headed straight for us. Poor little Mror began to scream in terror at the sight of the bear. Bror dropped his knife and reached for his spear, as did Puh and Black Wolf. Ria also readied her little arrows, but they would be pitifully in adequate against a beast of this size. My spear was leaning against a tree, perhaps eight or ten paces away. Even if I ran for my spear, the bear would be in our midst by the time I could lay my hands on it.

Bears were bullies when it came to taking over the kills of others, particularly the bigger boar bears. They often let other creatures take down an animal and then they would run off whatever had made the kill and enjoy a free meal. Sometimes, we would just back off and let the bear have our hard-won prey, but we needed these deer. It was not worth our lives, but there were enough of us that we hoped to discourage the bear, or kill it if need be.

Unfortunately, little Mror's wild cries seemed to incite the bear. It roared and focused on Ria and the baby. Ria's arrows flew one after another until she had emptied her quiver, each one hitting the bear in the face, chest and shoulders, but still the bear came at us. I drew back on an arrow and let it fly, but the bear was moving too quickly and it missed its mark. Puh, Bror, and Black Wolf intercepted the bear and blocked my next and final shot. The bear knocked the men aside as though they were mere afterthoughts, even though each one had stabbed the animal viciously with his spear. Now that no one stood between us I drew back with my last arrow. I waited until the bear was nearly upon us and let fly.

The arrow hit the bear in the chest, and it lodged deeply. The boar faltered his last few steps and finally fell to the ground, almost at our feet.

I had been so fixed on accomplishing my task that I had momentarily blocked out everything else and only now became aware that not only was Mror still crying, but Ria was sobbing hysterically. I turned to look at her and put my arms around her to comfort her and the baby. She was still holding her bow poised in front of her.

"It is over now," I told her. "It is over."

Puh, Black Wolf, and Bror picked themselves up and limped toward to us. I backed away so that Puh could now console Ria and the baby. Mror was removed from his sling so he could be held and cuddled. Black Wolf and Bror both clapped congratulatory hands on my shoulders. They and Puh were bloodied, but they did not seem to be badly injured, except for a stream of blood running down Bror's right arm.

I took a moment to look at the bear bristling with arrows as I walked past him to gather the rest of my arrows from the dead tree. If I could learn to shoot consistently well, I now knew that this bow was indeed a fearsome weapon.

Chapter Eight

Mror hiccupped as his weeping subsided. He clung to Puh as though he would never let go. Poor Ria was thoroughly rattled. After Puh's gentle words soothed her, she came up to me and hugged me tightly.

"Oh, Tris! Many thanks for slaying that bear! All I could think was that my arrows were having no effect and I could not protect my baby." Ria appeared to be struggling mightily to suppress another round of sobbing, "I feared that the bear would kill us and that you men would be injured or killed trying to protect us."

"I am just glad that my last arrow was enough to take him down." I was a bit shaken too.

Black Wolf knelt by Bror, who was now sitting on the ground and sporting a savage slash across his meaty right shoulder. Black Wolf had dumped the food from a bag into his pack and sliced the bag's seams open, thus laying it open so it could be used to quell the blood flow by binding it tightly over the wound. We had already used most of our rope to tie the deer to the saplings, so we had to sacrifice my food bag, too, and slice it into strips that could be used as ties. We each had lengths of cured gut, but we feared that the thin gut would cut into Bror's shoulder too tightly, whereas the broader strips of hide would keep the makeshift bandage in place and put even pressure on it as well.

We were well into the afternoon by now, and we still had a long trek ahead of us before we would arrive at home. Although we hated to leave the bear's meat and hide behind, we had to leave as soon as possible. Bror assured us that he was ready to hit the trail, but I worried for him.

The roe deer were both small. Black Wolf and I carried the bigger one between us, and Puh and Bror took the yearling, carrying it so that the pole rested on Bror's good shoulder. We hiked swiftly, warily watching the forest around us for more predators that might wish to steal our deer.

We reached the family compound just before sunset. Poor Bror was pale and looked grimly pained. Ru hastened to his side as soon as she saw him.

"Oh, Bror! What has happened?" she cried out. "Come with me!"

"My shoulder is injured," Bror said simply.

Bror followed Ru to the fire pit, where the fire's glow would allow her to continue ministering to him in the rapidly fading daylight.

The rest of us worked to butcher the two deer as quickly as possible. I noticed that Black Wolf shifted his weight from one foot to another as he helped to butcher the deer. We had been trekking more than usual lately, and although Black Wolf did not complain, I knew his feet caused him much discomfort.

Some of the meat was roasted immediately and hungrily consumed as we worked; the rest was cut into slices and draped over smoking racks to preserve it for future meals. We were exhausted by the time we sat down around the fire. The coals still glowed at one end of the fire pit where the food had been cooked, and the aroma of our repast still hung in the air. It was an uncharacteristically quiet meal.

"Now that we have brought in fresh meat, we should depart for the first of our explorations tomorrow," Puh broke the silence. "Bror, I think you should stay here and recuperate. You bled out quite a bit. You not only need to heal; you will need to build up your blood again."

"Yes," Bror nodded, grinning sheepishly. "I will not argue with that."

Ru sat very close to Bror, holding onto his good arm and leaning against him.

"I am so glad you will stay home where I can take care of you," she said. "I would be crazy with worry if you left in this state."

"I will stay behind as well," Ria announced.

Puh looked at her in surprise, but I thought he was probably pleased with her proclamation. He had suspected that this day would come, and I knew he was concerned that the baby could be endangered if he continued to accompany us on hunts. Today's misadventure had amply demonstrated why we left children safely at home when we pursued prey. Not only were they defenseless against predators, they tended to produce high-pitched sounds that often excited predators to attack.

"I will miss you both, but I think it is a good decision," Puh said, squeezing her hand.

"I am glad Ria is staying, as well," Ty piped up, "I will be making more bows and lots more arrows, and she can advise me as I work."

"Your big bow and Tris's good aim saved us," Ria told Ty. "I do not know how many of us would still be here without that."

The family had already heard the story, but Ty nodded, his face beaming with pride.

"Someday, spears will be a thing of the past," Black Wolf predicted.

* * *

They were men of the Old Ones, but their hair was dark. They held large bones in their hands as they sat around a fire, beating upon something that produced deep, resonating tones. When they opened their mouths they sang — not with words, but with a kind of harmonized noise.

It was such a strange Dream. Like the woman from my earlier Dreams, these people had brown hair. I hoped to see Great Gran before we left so I could tell her about it and get her perspective, but the sun was still at the horizon when we set out and it was likely she had not yet arisen. The previous day's bear had also visited me in my sleep, rushing at us again and again as I fumbled with the bow and arrow. I tried and tried to seat the arrow's notch on the bowstring, but no matter what I did, I could not do it. The bear kept coming and coming as I struggled with the arrow. I was profoundly grateful that the real-life situation had had a happier finale.

Just as I had when we embarked on the journey to Gray Elk's, I staggered along half-asleep after a night of little rest with Morning Star. Now that summer was in full swing, we were dressed only in our loincloths and boots, carrying our rolled cloaks bundled over our left shoulders. If we were more familiar with the territory we would be visiting, we might have even left our boots at home, but since we could not be sure that the ground would be forgiving to our feet, we decided to err on the side of caution.

I was sorry that we had to leave Bror behind. He was extremely strong and very resourceful, and besides, it would have been pleasant to have someone of my own age for company. That said, Puh, Black Wolf, and I had been on many travels together, and we were quite accustomed to working and hunting with one another.

However, on this trip, we did not know exactly where we were going. We simply began to walk north, taking note of landmarks along the way once we left familiar territory. We did not know for certain how long we would be gone, so we hunted small game whenever it presented itself and stopped to drink and refill our water bags whenever we came across a stream. But other than that, we just hiked briskly. This time, Black Wolf did sing. He had a vast repertoire of songs, but he favored various versions of *The Mighty Hunter* tune.

> *The mighty hunter is bold and brave*
> *The mighty hunter does not fear the grave*
> *The mighty hunter finds his prey*
> *Even if it hides away. . . .*

Black Wolf's theory was that his songs, sung at a lung-bursting volume, kept predators at bay. So far as we could tell, this was largely true. I wondered if he also sang to help him keep his mind off his aching feet.

Each night we stopped before sunset to build a fire and erect our lean-to. It was early summer, and the weather was pleasant. It was too soon to be plagued by mosquitoes, but the small biting flies more than made up for their absence.

"These insects are a trial!" Black Wolf said in frustration as he slapped at yet another fly.

"This place does not yet have much to recommend it," Puh agreed.

"Do I have as many welts as you two have?" Black Wolf asked, taking a moment to look at his limbs.

Puh paused just long enough to take a gander at Black Wolf and then at me.

"I cannot tell," he shrugged.

"How can you not tell?" Black Wolf persisted.

"Well, most of your skin is hidden under a layer of fur," Puh quietly pointed out. "So it is difficult to see whether or not the insects have left their mark on your flesh."

"I see," Black Wolf began. "Well I can assure you that they have indeed . . . *ack!*" Black Wolf swiped at another bug ". . . have indeed managed to locate my flesh!"

We had been traveling for eight days, during which we had seen signs of spring migration routes. It seemed as though reindeer passed through some of the areas, and bigger animals like wisents, aurochs, and woolly mammoths as well. The farther we moved from the family compound, the more animals we saw. This was good, because this was about as far as we wanted to travel from home. But now, we just needed to locate a place with easy access to potable water.

We were pleased to find a river, but the landscape around that running body of water was largely open. If we could find a forested area, one sizable enough to provide us with ample shelter and firewood, that would be perfect.

On the ninth morning, Puh and I worked to disassemble our shared lean-to while Black Wolf built a small fire. It was a cool morning. The sun hid behind the clouds and we could smell the coming rain.

"I guess the fair weather could not last forever," Black Wolf mused, looking skyward. "I think I just felt a raindrop."

I, too, felt a raindrop splat as it landed on my face; however, the rain did not begin in earnest until later, although the rate was still a rather slow drizzle. We trudged along on what appeared to be a trail, the first we had seen in many days. It took us to a section of woodland that seemed promising. The trail continued to a stand of scrubby saplings and brush. Although we had left the river behind some time ago, the ground was a bit soggy, even on the pathway.

"This does not look good," Black Wolf observed. "It is too wet. Perhaps we should go back to those woods."

"I agree," Puh nodded, "The mosquitoes will be brutal here, later in the season. But I would like to see where the trail leads. There is a rise in the land over there and we may have a good view of the surrounding area from the hilltop."

"It is apt to be drier at the top too," Black Wolf said with a grin. "It is bad enough that the damp falls from the sky, but here it percolates up from underfoot, as well!"

* * *

We had not gone much farther when we were surprised to see a woman sitting alone on the sodden ground. Her dark hair was wet, and although her face was hidden, I could see that her skin was dusky. At first I assumed she was a woman of The People, but then when she turned toward us I saw that her hands were bound, and her upturned face showed that she was a woman of the Old Ones.

"Run!" she said through clenched teeth. She pulled at her bindings in an attempt to face us more directly, but they were secured to a nearby tree so she could only see us by looking over her shoulder. "Go away! Run away as fast as you can!"

We were startled at her words. We had expected that she might ask to be freed from her predicament.

Then four men stepped out from the brush. They were Old Ones, and they too were dark; perhaps they were her family and had come to release her. They were so well-disguised that it took me a moment to realize that these were in fact men. They wore mud to help mask their features, and their hair is filled with twigs, moss, and grasses. Their clothing was obscured with dried foliage as well. The men carried spears, but they held their spears casually, in a non-threatening manner. I was bewildered by these people. Then, three of the men each brought a hollow reed to his lips and blew into the end. I felt a fly bite my neck. Puh and Black Wolf also moved as though to brush away an insect.

Suddenly, I felt woozy.

* * *

I awakened in a strange place. My head throbbed and my mind moved slowly. I could not focus my eyes or my thoughts. An array of odors assaulted my senses. The dirt floor so near my face was thoroughly infused with the fetid scent of decomposing flesh.

A woman's voice whispered to me, "I told you to run! Why did you not run?"

My mouth was dry. I tried to formulate words, but I could only croak random sounds.

"Hush!" the woman hissed at me. "Do not draw attention to yourself!"

I pushed my tongue around my mouth in an attempt to lubricate it with saliva and tried to speak once more.

"Where are we?" I asked quietly, my voice still husky. "I feel so strange."

"You are in a cave," the woman responded in a low voice. "You feel strange because the men have stung you and your friends with a magic serum which has temporarily disabled you."

"Are the others still with me?" I questioned, feeling a sudden dread.

"Yes. The tall one and the shorter one. They are here. They have not moved yet."

"Are they nearby?" As I spoke, I felt a gentle touch at my calf.

"Yes, the shorter one is just at your back," the woman answered. "The tall furry one with the long black beard is on the other side of him."

The shorter one. She must be speaking of Puh, and Puh was letting me know that he was there, and awake. I wondered if Black Wolf was conscious, as well.

"Where are our captors?" I was now coherent enough to realize that I was lying on my right side and bound at my hands and feet, with my arms tied behind my back.

I was very uncomfortable. My hands were numb and the arm I was lying on tingled alarmingly. Additionally, my bladder was quite full, and unfortunately, it did not seem likely that I would have an opportunity to empty it any time soon.

As my vision slowly returned the woman came into view. I was stunned to see that she was beautiful. She had been lying alongside me, but she cautiously sat up and craned her neck to see over the piles of unidentified clutter. Just then I had a moment to observe her. The woman was very thin, but yet she still owned an admirable figure. She was near my age, perhaps a bit younger, and she had wavy deep brown hair, large dark eyes, full lips, and smooth, tawny skin.

"I cannot see them. They are the father and his three grown sons, and a boy. Disgusting men. The boy is a simpleton. He may be the child of one of the sons. I do not know what happened to their women. Perhaps they ate them."

"*Ate them?*" I repeated incredulously.

"Keep your voice down! I do not know for certain whether or not they have left the cave!" the woman whispered harshly. "Yes, *ate* them! The only reason you have not been trussed up and bled out yet is because they had happened upon a wounded roe deer a few days ago and since then they have been eating off the carcass. They do not cook their food, so they prefer fresh meat. They are keeping you alive until they are ready to butcher you."

My mind reeled at this news, and I felt Puh shift a little, but he remained silent.

"But why would they butcher men?" I asked. "I do not understand."

"Did you get a good look at them?" she responded.

I stopped to think. I remembered only being surprised that the men were so well-camouflaged. Their bodies and clothing were almost completely obscured by mud, twigs, leaves, and grasses.

"No, I did not. I only saw them for an instant."

"They are not in good shape. They are barely able to hunt," she said.

"Not in good shape? What do you mean?"

"The father is old. He walks with a stick to aid him. One of the sons has lost his right arm. Another is missing a portion of his left foot. Only the lastborn is whole, but he cannot bring down much game by himself. So, although they do take in animals when they can, they have found it is easier to hunt men. Besides, it seems that their stinging darts do not have enough magic to work on bigger animals, but they can make men sleep for a short while."

This was disturbing news. I wondered about this young woman. Who was she and how was she related to the men?

"Are you a captive, too, or are you paired with one of the men?" I asked.

"I am not paired with any of them, although each of them, except the boy, has made what could euphemistically be called romantic overtures toward me. I think the only reason I have not been forced into a . . . a relationship . . . with one of the men is that they cannot come to an agreement on which one of them will have me, and fortunately, they are too jealous to share me. They have fought over it several times. Ugh! They are vile creatures!" She spoke adamantly and with apparent revulsion. "They came upon my family and me and stung us with their little darts, just as they did you. I was newly paired; I had only just met my mate for the first time. One by one, they killed and ate my family . . . my mate. I was spared only because they decided that I would be useful to lure victims into range." The woman spoke calmly, almost in a monotone, but I noticed that she trembled as she told her tale. If she had been newly paired, she must be very young. Perhaps the same age as my sister Ru, who was fifteen winters old.

I was momentarily struck dumb.

"That is . . . that is incomprehensible!" I shook my head in disbelief. After a pause I went on, "I am Tris. My father is the man behind me; he is Tor. And next to him is our friend, Black Wolf. What is your name?"

"Aessa," she said. For the first time since we had met she smiled, but just slightly. "I can help you escape. Just take me with you . . . I will be your woman."

"Uh . . . um. . . ." I stammered.

I was more than willing to take her with us, but I had not expected the second part of her offer.

"I will find a way to free you from your bindings! Just take me with you! I will give myself to you!" Aessa spoke more animatedly this time as the idea grew in her mind. "You have strange eyes and fiery hair, but you are a fine-looking man . . . ."

"But I am already paired," I hastily whispered to her. "My mate waits at home with our children." I then saw Aessa's crestfallen appearance and I realized that she did not understand. I knew that most pairings were not bonded with love and that monogamy was rare, so she must have thought that I was rejecting her, personally. "You are a very attractive woman," I assured her. "But Morning Star is my life. I love her as I could never love another. When I became paired with Morning Star, I vowed to always do my best by her. I would protect her from all harm and danger. Not only from starvation, or people, or animals that would do her injury, but even, or should I say, most especially, from any hurt that I might cause her." Aessa still looked confused, so I went on. "As one who claims to love and protect Morning Star, it would be the height of insult and hypocrisy for me to inflict such an unspeakable pain on my mate."

As I saw a look of comprehension cross Aessa's face, I thought I heard a small sound from the shadows of the cave. Aessa heard it, too.

"I see," Aessa nodded. "I think I hear one of your companions awakening. But if I free you, will you take me with you?"

"I will take you, but we must also take my Puh and our friend Black Wolf," I insisted.

"All right," Aessa agreed. She again tried to change her position so she could see where our captors might be. She was bound as well, but her hands were tied before her instead of behind her back. I was curious as to why they should take less care with her to ensure that she did not release herself, but perhaps they feared her less than they did three grown men. "Here they come! Act as though you are still unconscious!" Aessa ordered.

I instantly closed my eyes and went limp. My hands and the arm pinned beneath my body so pained me that it took every bit of my self-control not to squirm with discomfort. But I was soon distracted from these annoyances.

"*Be careful!*" My head was down, so I was unable to see the owner of this loud voice, but it sounded as though it came from an older man, presumably the father. "You almost broke my favorite clanger, you beetle-brained, puss-nosed lout!"

"You left it in a stupid place," another voice answered. "You left it right where it could be tripped over. So you must not care about your stupid clanger very much, you mangy old butt-sniffer!"

"Argh," growled the first, "you stepped on your own basher last night, so who is stupid, now, eh, poophead?"

This was the most bizarre conversation I had ever heard in my life. I struggled to maintain a bland expression on my face, in case any of the returning family happened to look my way; otherwise they would surely note my shocked and confused countenance and realize that I was now lucid. My mind was awhirl with a myriad of thoughts. What was a clanger? What was a basher? And what son dared to call his father such disrespectful names?

Apparently, the father did not care for the terms, either, and a resounding thunk met our ears, followed by a howl of pain.

"There, see?" the father said triumphantly. "I may have stepped on my own basher, but it still works! That was a musical tone if ever I heard one!"

"Poop-head! Poop-head! Stupid old poop-head!" the other voice chanted, as his brothers giggled.

"Ha! You have a buzzard beard! I have seen better beards on a cow wisent!" yet another piped up, but I could not tell to whom he was referring.

Evidently the insult struck home to someone, because a scuffle ensued. I heard a cacophony of sound as things were knocked over, blows were landed, and bodies hit the ground. Insults were flung as handily as objects.

I felt Aessa cringe and she edged closer to me. A moment later, another being joined us. I turned my head just enough to see that it was a small boy. Despite Aessa's wrists being tied, she put her arms around the child and pulled him to her, holding him tightly as he clung to her.

Finally, the violence was over and the men panted as they recovered their breath.

"My good hand is bloodied!" one of the brothers complained.

"You stay here and bandage your poor little hand," his father replied. "The rest of us will retrieve the last of that deer meat and prepare it for our evening meal. Then, if you are feeling well enough, you can join us for dinner. In the meantime, clean up this mess! And if our captives start to waken, dart them again . . . we will work on them tomorrow. The young one may be all right, but the two older ones . . . *bah*! They will need some tenderizing or they will be tough as old bucks that have seen too many ruts!"

"The younger one will have big heavy bones! We will get good bashers out of him!" one of the siblings exclaimed.

"The older ones might be tough and stringy, but they might make good clangers," another said cheerfully. "The tall one looks as though he owns a fairly resonant skull. It is so high and rounded at the top."

It sounded as though they were using their victims' bones to perform music!

"I have thought on that very thing," the father agreed. "I am eager to give him a try. I would be tempted to give his head a few raps while he is alive, but . . . *bah* . . . he is much too big. If he were to awaken he might break loose from his bindings and throw me across the cave."

"He would not! That is good rope! I spent days making that rope!" an indignant voice protested. "Can you not even tell a good new rope from a rotted poor rope, old man?"

"I can tell that you are a matt-headed slack-jawed twit who does not have the sense that resides in a toad! Let us go, now! And *you*! Why are you not cleaning yet?"

Shuffling steps indicated to me that some of this unusual family had vacated the premises, but the remaining man muttered unkind sentiments under his breath about his parent and also his brothers, who at this moment were more favored than he. Rather than cleaning up, he sullenly kicked at the debris that was scattered about the cave, still uttering an unceasing torrent of unflattering remarks regarding his kin.

"Stupid! Stupid poop-heads! Mammoth fart-smelling, ferret-faced, stupid, stupid, poop-heads! I will not clean up after them!" There was a pause in his tirade. "Aessa!"

Aessa started. Although I was supposed to be feigning unconsciousness, I opened my eyes and saw that her own were bulging. She turned to face the man, squaring her shoulders.

"Yes, Rowit?" she replied with a tremor in her voice.

"You will clean. Make everything neat."

Neat? That was an onerous request indeed! I closed my eyes again as Rowit approached us. I heard Rowit squat next to me and I guessed that he was untying Aessa. I have inhaled many scents during my lifetime, but Rowit's personal aroma was almost enough to make me gag. I held my breath for as long as I could, and I was relieved when he moved away and I could once again breathe the still putrid but relatively fresh air of the cave.

Now that Aessa was moving about the cave, the boy stepped over my prone form and hid behind me. I was somewhat dismayed at this, because I hoped to use the boy for cover so I could occasionally peer past him to see how Aessa was faring. But within a few moments, I realized that the boy was not just hiding behind my bulk. I felt the light touch of his nimble fingers as he worked at the knotted ropes that bound my hands and feet.

A few moments later, my hands were free. I dared not move too much and thus attract Rowit's notice, but I was desperate to flex my numb arm to hurry the restoration of feeling. The boy then crawled to my feet. I kept a keen eye on Rowit as the child again labored to loosen the coarse rope.

As luck would have it, Rowit's attention was focused on Aessa, ogling her as he ordered her about. He was gruff but he spoke to her considerably more amicably than he had to his father and his brothers. I used this time to cautiously stretch my arms and legs and wriggle my fingers energetically. Pain shot through my right arm as sensation returned. I massaged my hands vigorously and I ventured a glance at Puh and Black Wolf, who both stared at me, imploring me to move quickly. The boy was now at Puh, eyes narrowed in concentration as he tugged at the bindings.

Suddenly, a roar of rage met my ears.

"Stupid boy!" Rowit bellowed.

Rowit brushed Aessa aside as he rushed past her, knocking her off her feet and sending her sprawling onto a heap of assorted bones, both animal and human.

I rose to my feet to intercept his charge, bracing myself as best I could, considering that I was still recovering both wits and bodily function.

This was the first chance I had to assess my assailant. He was not as tall as I, but he was a burly man. He was powerfully built, especially in his right arm, which was his only remaining upper extremity. He was quite unkempt, with long, dark, stringy, untamed hair and a scraggly beard. His ill-fitting clothing was thoroughly stained and begrimed.

"You are a strange-looking beast!" Rowit proclaimed, laughing as he came at me. His torso was partially lowered as he prepared to tackle me, leading with his right shoulder.

His vocal laughter threw me off; I had never known another Old One to laugh this way. I just barely had the presence of mind to evade his swinging arm. Rowit frowned that his intended strike had missed its mark and continued to advance toward me as I retreated. He picked up a large femur to use as a club and I, too, picked up the closest thing at hand, which was a reindeer skull still sporting one antler.

Again, the arm swung mightily and the brandished bone whistled as it passed my head.

Holding the reindeer skull before me, I still backed away, struggling to keep my balance as I trod on the uneven piles of detritus that littered almost every surface of the cavern. I fervently hoped that Puh and Black Wolf would soon be free to join me in fending off this crazed person.

When my feet finally found solid footing, I waited for Rowit to come at me once again, and as he raised the femur to strike, I swung the reindeer skull with one hand into the stomach of my antagonist with a blow that sent him reeling backward. The skull must have been very old, as it immediately shattered, leaving me holding just a bit of bone, which I flung away. Then, without hesitation, I launched myself at my opponent, grappling him around his middle.

Rowit's midsection was a solid target — in fact, he reminded me of the wounded bear we had come across last spring, in both build and smell. At this proximity Rowit's stench made my eyes water, but there was no avoiding it. Our feet crunched over brittle bones and slid over the fresher, moister ones. I continued to drive Rowit back until I slammed him into the stone wall, where his head made contact with an ominous thunk, sounding much like an axe hitting a tree trunk. Rowit slumped to the ground as soon as I released him. There was no telling how long he would be down, so there was not a moment to lose.

I turned to see that Puh was rising to his feet. Puh and I quickly helped the boy to finish untying Black Wolf, and then we met Aessa at the center of the cavern, where she waited with a collection of items, including her small bundle of personal belongings and our packs, knives, and spears. Within moments, Aessa and the boy led the way as we dashed clumsily — since Puh, Black Wolf, and I still suffered the aftereffects of being bound — through the bowels of the long cave toward the entryway. There, we looked about us anxiously. We had no idea where the other men had gone, and we particularly wanted to avoid them if we could.

"Which way do we go?" Puh asked Aessa.

Aessa, too, gazed around us uncertainly.

"The young deer was hung up over there," she pointed down a path leading away from the cave. "But I am not sure where they are now."

"If they are downwind, we will surely know it," Black Wolf piped up.

At that moment, Rowit appeared at the entryway to the cave. He still seemed dazed, and he leaned heavily against the side of the entrance.

"They are escaping!" he cried out. "All of them! They are escaping!"

Chapter Nine

We did not deliberate any further on which direction we should take. We set off running blindly through the brush. I was at the lead, pulling the boy by the hand behind me. The child could not keep up with me, so I swept him off his feet and ran with him slung over my shoulder.

All at once, my feet became tangled in something and I fell face-first to the ground. I glanced up to see the boy on all fours beside me. Aessa, Puh, and Black Wolf came to a stop as well. We were shocked to behold what had tripped me up. We were surrounded by the discarded bones of many people. Aessa clamped her hands over her mouth as though to keep from screaming. Even at a glance I could see the bones bore signs of butchering and smashing to get at the marrow.

I hurriedly got back on my feet and we quickly resumed our hasty departure from this terrible place.

Shouts followed us as we ran. The boy seemed to be trying to get my attention. Finally, he was outright pulling on my arm with both hands and attempting to drag me in another direction. Aessa had described him as a simpleton, but I thought I saw the glimmer of intelligence in his eyes. Puh noted this as well.

"Stop a moment," Puh said. "What is it?" he asked the boy. "Do you want us to go somewhere?"

"I have never heard him speak," Aessa told us. "I do not think he can talk."

The child opened his mouth, but all that came out were *ahhh-wahhh-ahhh* sounds and he continued to tug at my hand.

"Let us follow him," Black Wolf suggested. "He helped us escape, so I think it is unlikely that he would wish to see us caught again."

"Yes," Puh agreed.

Puh bent down so he was face to face with the child and nodded vigorously to him. The boy grinned and let loose a happy squeak. We began to trot through the brush after him, soon coming to a river.

The sounds of pursuance had drifted away, so we halted our mad dash to catch our breath for a moment.

"I cannot go any farther without relieving my bladder," Black Wolf suddenly announced. "The urgency was bad enough before, but now that my ears are filled with the gurgle of running water, I must make a stop."

We were all of the same mind, or at least Black Wolf, Puh, and I were. We paused long enough for everyone to urinate. Before proceeding onward, Puh recommended that we break out some food that could be chewed as we continued our trek. Puh, Black Wolf, and I opened our packs, and each let out a small gasp of astonishment.

As I examined the contents of my pack, I realized that almost nothing in it was actually mine. I recognized one of my food bags, but some of the items I knew to be Puh's, and a few other things belonged to Black Wolf.

"Tris, these are yours," Puh said as he passed my hatchet and water bag to me.

"Puh, I think these are yours, and Black Wolf, I have some of your things, too," I nodded as I took the proffered items from Puh.

We all traded goods until each had his own belongings restored to him.

"I am afraid that was my doing," Aessa spoke up. "The men had dumped out your packs. I think they intended to sort through your things later. The clothing they wear, the tools they use, almost all of it comes from their victims. So, when Tris and Rowit fought, I just tossed all your belongings back into the packs — in the hope that Tris would succeed in overwhelming Rowit — so that then we could leave as quickly as possible."

"That was very clever," Black Wolf said, smiling at Aessa. "Here, take this." He must have seen the hesitant look on Aessa's face. "It is dried elk meat," Black Wolf assured her. "Give this piece to the boy. Let us move on as quickly as possible."

"Yes, and it might be a good idea to walk in the river," Puh added as he stepped into the water's edge.

"They will have a much harder time tracking us if we are wading."

This made sense. The water was quite chilly, but the thought of being stung by another one of those darts and returned to the cave was enough to harden our resolve to endure the cold. The boy still held my hand and led the way, as though he had some destination in mind, but the depth of the water soon overwhelmed him, and I carried him once again.

"Puh, do you have any idea where we are?" I inquired.

Puh looked up at the sun, which was low in the sky.

"We are moving roughly south," he replied, "but beyond that, I have no idea."

I winced as I stumbled over a submerged rock.

"The boy seems to know where we are going," I observed. "Aessa, how much do you know about him?"

Aessa shook her head as she sloshed through the water, hugging herself for warmth.

"I know hardly anything about him at all," she started, ". . . even though I have been with those men for several moons. As I said, I have never heard him say anything coherent. I believe he is the child of the oldest son. I do not even know if he has a name. They have just ignored him. He did not get much to eat, poor little thing. I tried to sneak some food to the boy whenever I could. I foraged for tubers, roots, and greens for my meals . . . sometimes I could find mushrooms, too. I would not eat with the men . . .," she said, shuddering at the thought. It went unspoken that she would not share in their food for obvious reasons.

"So he belongs to the family," I said. "He is not another captive?"

"Captive or relative, they do not seem care about him," Aessa answered. "The only attention they show him is when they are angry or annoyed with him, so he stays out of their way or hides behind me."

"Where were you going when you were captured?" Black Wolf inquired.

"We were returning home," Aessa answered. "We had just traveled to my mate's clan, where he and I were paired, and we were four days into our trek home when we were attacked."

"A very short pairing," I noted. "I am sorry for it. You must miss your mate and your family terribly."

"Of course I grieve my family . . . my poor younger siblings!" Aessa agreed. "But my mate — we had spent only a few days together. He seemed nice enough, but unfortunately I never had the chance to get to know him. He seemed kind of sweet — I will never forget what those horrible men did — I will loathe them for as long as I live."

"One can hardly blame you for that," Puh said gently. "But anything you can tell us about them might help us evade them. Do you know anything about their hunting skills?"

Again, Aessa shook her head.

"I only know that they must have come from a line of good hunters — considering all those large animal bones both in and outside the cave . . . horses and reindeer, mostly. But most of those bones look as though they have been there for many years. During the last moons, I have only known them to hunt as you have seen. They camouflage themselves and lie in wait, and then sting their prey with those little darts. Once my mate and family were . . . gone . . . they were then forced to hunt again," Aessa said, again beginning to tremble. But this was more than shivering with cold; she was shaking with fear. "That is when they tied me to a tree in hopes of using me to lure potential victims to come to my aid."

"You have been through a harrowing experience," Puh said, touching Aessa's shoulder. "We will do our best to get as far away from them as we can, as quickly as we can."

Suddenly, the sound of a distant voice came to my ears, heard even over the rush of the river. We froze in our tracks. When the boy realized that we had stopped, he turned and looked around quizzically. He patted my shoulder and grunted a bit, pointing ahead of us in an effort to keep us moving forward.

"There!" Puh indicated a ridge high over the river.

Sure enough, the men had somehow found us.

Aessa gasped at the sight of them, and the boy made a cry of despair.

"We tarried too long on that bank," Black Wolf lamented.

"I think it is time to get back on land!" Puh said, working his way back to the shore.

Once we reached the bank we could move faster, and we immediately headed for the wooded area, where we would be hidden from view by the trees and brush. Just as before, the boy still seemed to have a destination in mind. He continued to grunt and point back to the river.

The wooded area was becoming swampier, slowing our progress as the wet, mucky earth sucked at our feet with each step. We soon found the reason for this waterlogged section of forest. An old beaver dam blocked a substantial portion of the river. Although the dam allowed some of the water to flow through, it bridged the span handily.

"Maybe we should cross the river here," Black Wolf suggested.

Puh's gaze canvassed the area, but he again noted the boy's persistent tapping on my shoulder, which now had become a steady pounding, and motioning toward the river. I set him down on the ground and rubbed my shoulder where it had been hammered on for several moments.

"What is it?" Puh asked the boy.

The child stared blankly at Puh for a moment, and pointed at the river once more. Puh hesitantly pointed at the river, too.

"Show us where you want us to go," Puh said.

The boy still looked at Puh blankly, but then he suddenly seemed to have an epiphany and he grinned.

He waded into the water up to his neck, where he reached the side of the dam. Then he ducked underwater and disappeared.

"Where did he go?" Aessa questioned, deeply concerned. "No one could hold his breath for so long!"

"He's inside the dam!" Black Wolf answered. "I wonder — is it big enough to fit all of us?"

"We will know in a moment," Puh replied, retracing the boy's steps into the water. "We can take off our packs and shove them before us up into the dam. I do not think there will be room to bring our spears inside, but we can tuck them into the dam's foundation under the water and retrieve them after we come out."

Then the boy's head popped up just long enough for him to wave to us to follow him. One by one, we stepped into the river. Puh saw that Aessa was frightened. Old Ones have heavy bodies, and we are not good swimmers.

"I will help you," Puh said to her. "Take a deep breath and grasp my hand."

Aessa nodded. They both took deep breaths and dove under the water.

Black Wolf and I exchanged glances. We dared not wait too long, since our captors might catch up with us at any time.

"You go now," Black Wolf instructed me. "I will be right behind you."

I filled my lungs with air several times as I sloshed my way into the river until I reached the spot where the others had disappeared. Then I crouched down and put my head underwater. There, I could just barely see the dark opening of the dam. It was not very big, but I reckoned I could squeeze through.

The tree trunks and branches that made up the tunnel scratched my arms, legs, and shoulders as I crawled in, shoving my wet pack ahead of me. There was no room to crawl in the normal way; I had to wriggle my way through. I moved as quickly as I could, knowing that Black Wolf was left exposed on the riverbank until he too could join us.

I had no sooner found my companions than I felt Black Wolf coming up the tunnel behind me.

"This is going to be cozy," he muttered, positioning his great length as comfortably as he could. "I hope the beavers do not choose to come back while we are camped out in their home."

Our crawl into the dam had left us quite wet and adorned with fine cuts and scrapes that wept small amounts of blood. Although a little light came through in spots, for the most part it was rather dark. There was just enough light to see that the space was about four paces long and three paces wide. The ceiling was too low to allow us even to sit up.

"I think this dam has been abandoned," Puh said quietly. "I did not see any fresh beaver tracks in the area, or newly gnawed trees. All the wood used to make this dam was harvested years ago."

Luckily, the mud floor of the dam provided a relatively smooth, dry surface for us to lie on. We had only a short time to assess our cramped and musty hiding place when we heard a faint voice in the distance.

"Their footprints lead down to the river!"

We tensed and hardly dared to breathe as the approaching voices grew louder. The boy noted our drawn knives and alert state and cowered by Aessa, his eyes shut. As before, she held him tightly.

There was a break in the men's conversation as they neared us, but we could hear them pushing through the brush as they searched for clues to our whereabouts.

"One thing is sure, they have reentered the river, no doubt hoping to hide their trail," the father finally said. "We could have had them long ago if you could keep up, you slow-footed imbecile! I can move more quickly than you, even though I rely on a walking stick!"

"I cannot help that part of my foot was frozen off last winter! I stayed out with a wet boot for so long after I broke through the ice only because you did not want to delay our return home by stopping to build a fire and a shelter, which would have saved my foot, you cranky old man!" the owner of the damaged extremity retaliated. "At least I remembered to bring my spear! The rest of you are barely armed!"

"They stole my Binty," another stated. "He may be a useless bit of flesh, but he is mine and I want him back!"

"Never mind him; that bag of bones has been a waste of food for the past ten winters! I want Aessa returned to us!" Rowit insisted.

I supposed the Binty they referred to was the boy in our midst, and I was shocked to learn that he was ten winters old. I would have guessed he was much younger, perhaps five or six winters old at most.

"She would never want you, buzzard beard! I will have her!"

"*Bah*, as though she would give herself to you! Besides, you have already had one mate. I am still waiting for mine! You would just beat her to death as you did your first one, or you would kill her with your foul breath! Such a stench as issues from your mouth is bad enough to make water run uphill!"

A few thumping blows and an assortment of insults were exchanged before the men were brought back to the mission at hand by their impatient father.

"Stop it, you two! Why can you not behave with the decorum of your youngest brother; see how he stands calmly like an aurochs chewing his cud? You two have not the sense of a slug! Do you not see that we have more important things to concern us? If those people succeed in escaping, then our hunting habits and our whereabouts will be known to others and they will surely broadcast the news far and wide. At best, people will avoid our territory, and no one will ever come through here again. We will have to journey to distant lands to find our prey. At worst, they will come back with a larger group of men and hunt us down and kill us!"

There was a silence as these thoughts were presumably digested by the former combatants.

The men then climbed up on top of the dam to gain a better view of the surrounding area. As they walked on the dam's structure the individual branches creaked under their weight and debris loosened from the dam's surface filtered down to us, coating us with a bits of dried mud, bark, and various plant matter.

Although gaps in the dam let in some light, I was unable to see our former captors clearly; I could make out only the shadows they cast as they trod over us. Finally, they decided that we must have evaded them upriver, and they moved on to continue their search.

When the sounds of their departure faded and were lost amidst the subtle noises of the river and the evening's serenade provided by nearby frogs, birds, and insects, we all sighed with relief.

"What do we do now?" Aessa asked.

"I suggest we have a little something to eat and drink," Black Wolf said as he began to dig through his soggy pack.

"Yes," Puh nodded, "and then we can get some sleep. I think we are fairly well-protected in here, and although there is not much room, we will be safe and warm for the night. We can leave at first light and start working our way home."

I expected that our evening meal might be somewhat damp, given that our packs had been submerged in the river, but the leather ties on the food bags had actually sealed out the water surprisingly well. The boy ate voraciously, but the rest of us nibbled at the dried meats and sipped just enough water to help slide the food down our throats.

In the waning light we noted that the beaver dam had numerous underwater exits and entryways. Apparently, the beavers had taken pains to ensure that they would not be trapped in their dam if a predator found an opening to their home. I wished I still had my cloak for warmth, but it was left behind at the cave. However, I was too weary for the chill to keep me awake. I fell asleep to the soothing sounds of the river lapping against the dam.

* * *

I awoke to dim light coming through the few tiny gaps in the dam's sides. For a moment I was confused about where I was. I was vaguely aware that someone was lying at my back, and yet another person was curled at my front. The arm of one of my companions was draped over my side. Black Wolf snored softly, and the birds had just begun to twitter. As the light grew stronger, I could see that the boy Binty was nestled between Aessa and me, and it was Aessa's arm that rested on my side.

Puh was not amongst us, but I could hear someone walking outside the dam, so I assumed he must have arisen before the rest of us and exited the structure on his own. I decided to do the same. I gently pushed Aessa's arm aside and left the same way I had come in, shoving my pack down the tunnel ahead of me. The river's water was colder this time. My air-filled pack popped to the river's surface, and I had to hold onto it as it bobbed on the water's surface. Grasping onto a shoulder strap, I ducked back down to retrieve my spear from where I had left it tucked in the dam's foundation, and then sloshed to the riverbank to join Puh.

"Pleasant day to you, Tris," Puh said, grinning at the sight of me.

Puh stood by a small fire in the chill morning air to dry and warm himself. I leaned my spear against a tree and stood by the fire as well, shivering as water ran off my hair and loincloth and puddled at my feet.

"Pleasant day to you, too, Puh," I replied, wiping water from my face and wringing out my hair. The heat from the fire felt good. "Have long you been up?"

"Long enough to get my bearings," Puh stated. "I do not think the men brought us very far from the place where we were captured. I climbed that tall tree over there and from one of the uppermost branches I was able to see the course of this river for quite some distance. I think that if we follow it roughly south, it will lead us toward home."

Home. How long had it been since I had been home? I missed Morning Star and the children terribly, but it seemed as though it might be a frustratingly long time before I would see them again.

Our companions soon joined us. Little Binty ravenously attacked the food handed to him. I had never seen any living thing, man nor beast, eat so quickly, stuffing the food in his mouth and hardly bothering to chew before cramming in more. It was alarming to watch. Words were useless. He completely ignored us. Puh attempted to gently persuade Binty to eat more slowly by kneeling next to him and holding back his hand so he was unable to thrust additional food into his mouth until he had chewed his first mouthful. Puh demonstrated by biting off reasonable amounts and chewing each bit thoroughly. Binty watched with interest, but while he did moderate his mad pace, he was still consuming his breakfast like a famished bear fresh from hibernation. Binty eventually relaxed a little and leaned against Puh as he ate.

"He trusts you," Aessa said. "Poor thing has lived like a wild animal. I do not think he trusts many people."

"Maybe he senses that I am a father who is used to caring for children," Puh suggested.

"Perhaps," Black Wolf began, "but it does not seem that his own father showed him much kindness."

"No, he did not," Aessa agreed. "Are you planning to go after those men?" Aessa watched our faces carefully as she waited for a response, her own countenance clearly anxious.

"I believe we should," Black Wolf said, trading glances with us. "Those four maggot-brained miscreants will just go on to murder unsuspecting people until they are stopped."

"Ha! *Maggot-brain!*" Aessa echoed. "That is what one brother called the other recently."

"Well, it fits," Black Wolf nodded solemnly. "If we are going to start tracking them, we should leave soon. It is convenient that they may start to move even more slowly once the one with the injured foot begins to falter on that sore limb, but it is remarkably inconvenient that they are also looking for us."

We set to packing up what little we had removed from our packs, and topped off our water bags upstream from the beaver dam before hitting the trail again. Binty did not have enough stamina to keep up with us, so I placed him on my shoulders once more and he rode there comfortably. Although he was twice my sister Saree's age, he was no heavier than she, and he was easily carried over long distances. It was only later when we stopped for a midday break and I set him down and removed my pack that I realized that he was resting his behind on it and crushing the contents at the top. The parcel of dried foods fared reasonably well, but the honey seedcakes were smashed to tiny bits. No matter; those tiny bits still tasted fine. I shared them with Binty, and he finished off the packet. No more worries about crushed seedcakes.

We did not have a plan thus far, other than to track our supposed pursuers and hope to catch them before they could catch us. Their sign was easily followed, given that one of the brothers was missing part of his foot and limped, his awkward gait becoming more pronounced as time went by. Also, the father's steps were accompanied by periodic divots where his staff dented the ground. We guessed that we might overtake them in a day, at most.

It was not long before we left the wooded area near where the man-eating clan lived and were once again out on the open grasslands. The river still ran alongside us, cheerfully burbling in the morning light. The sun had not yet reached its zenith when we discovered the place where the men had bedded down for the night. They had found a patch of brush near the river where they had created a nest amongst the bushes and thick bunches of weeds. A small fire pit still contained warm ash. As we moved on, we lost their tracks. A herd of animals — horses, we suspected — had gone through, and in doing so, their many hoof prints and piles of dung had obliterated all traces of the men's passing.

We soon saw the horses up ahead where they grazed placidly. Since there was still no sign of the men, we decided to hike to the highest point, where we could scan the landscape in hopes that we might see them in the distance. A knoll stood out against the horizon, but we would have to leave the trail to reach it. The horses in the herd often lifted their heads to watch our approach, eyes alert, noses snorting and twitching, and ears swiveling nervously. Considering that we had spent the night in a beaver dam, we may have carried a confusing array of scents to their sensitive nostrils. Confusing or not, they decided to gallop away in a thundering mass as we neared them, leaving us a clear path to the top of the hill.

We were somewhat startled to see what lay on the other side. At the bottom of the steep precipice, which was littered with scrubby patches of brush and a few rocks, was a vast array of animals. Most notably, mammoths ambled across the plains a short distance away; they, too, seemed agitated by our presence. Farther on, we could see reindeer. They were so numerous that they appeared to be one seething throng of moving antlers, heads, and legs. I set Binty down and rubbed my shoulders now that they were free of his weight. He was starting to feel heavy after a long morning of trekking.

Suddenly, a rush of movement caught my eye. At first, I thought it was a small bear, but when it straightened up and produced a club, I realized it was a man. Rowit. The raised club smashed into the side of Black Wolf's head; he reeled and then fell in a heap.

Aessa's mouth opened as though to scream but she made no sound. Binty cried out in alarm at the sight of his relatives. I charged Rowit with my spear, but I was intercepted by his younger brother, who also wielded a spear. Our weapons clashed and both snapped under the strain. Spears were not made to withstand this kind of use. Holding a length of broken spear in my hand, I quickly glanced to see how the others in my party were faring. Puh was fending off Rowit's father and his other brother, and Rowit was now tackling Aessa; it seemed that he was attempting to bind her again, but she fought him fiercely. Binty was now nowhere in sight. I had only a moment to take all this in before the youngest sibling was coming at me again, swinging what remained of his fractured spear like a cudgel. I held the ends of my broken spear shaft with both hands and met his blow, stopping it. I then pushed back with all my might, pressing him forward until he had to retreat several steps, whereupon he tripped over Black Wolf's prone form.

Black Wolf did not move, and he was bleeding from his ear. My heart ached to see him like this; I could only hope that he was not mortally wounded, as I had no time to help him. While the younger brother scrambled to untangle his legs from Black Wolf's long limbs, Rowit now came at me. Rowit still held his club, and I was yet armed only with my broken spear. I cast about to see if there was anything I could use to defend myself. Black Wolf had collapsed partially across his spear, but perhaps I could eventually pull it out from under him, if I could do so without exposing myself to potential injury from my attackers.

I worked my way toward Puh. We stood a better chance if we could fight back to back. Puh's eyes met mine for just an instant as I sidled up to him. We were taken by surprise and we were outnumbered. Although it apeared they were armed with only hastily manufactured weapons, it was all we could do to keep them from lancing or hitting us.

As I looked into the savage faces of Rowit and the youngest brother, all at once the latter faltered and he dropped to the ground. Behind him stood Aessa, brandishing a bloodied knife, tatters of rope still dangling from her wrists.

Rowit spun around to her in a rage, and he immediately took in what had happened. Aessa sprinted away, still holding the terrible dripping weapon. I feared that Rowit would take the knife from her and plunge it into her chest, so I followed, soon catching up with Rowit, and I threw myself at his back.

We both crashed down on the ground, and again my nose was assailed with the gut-wrenching odor that emanated from Rowit's person. We landed at the cusp of the downhill slope, and Rowit and I rolled to the bottom, the contents of my pack flying in all directions as I went. There, I attempted to stagger to my feet as I collected my tumbled wits.

Rowit had somehow managed to hold onto his club throughout his fall, and he advanced on me, smiling.

"You will die here!" he announced menacingly.

Suddenly, we were shrouded by a large shadow. I turned to see a huge cow mammoth, the herd matriarch, and my spirits soared to see my old friend. She bellowed with rage as she ran the last few steps, mowing Rowit down with one sweeping movement of her formidable tusks.

Rowit was no longer so self-assured. He had been soundly knocked about. He fought to regain his footing when she wheeled and struck him once more. Now that he was down again, she determinedly raised a massive forefoot and brought it down on him. I had to look away.

However, Puh and the others were still at the top of the knoll, so I paused with the cow mammoth just long enough to stroke her trunk and say, "Many thanks once again, kind lady!" before I grabbed Rowit's club and dashed up the hill.

There, I was relieved to see Black Wolf upright and grinning, although he was leaning heavily on his spear. Puh stood with Aessa and Binty, his chest heaving after the excitement of the fracas and the expenditure of so much effort. The father and last remaining brother were both dead.

"I am telling you, Tris," Black Wolf said as we watched the mammoth return to her herd, trumpeting triumphantly, "that cow has a crush on you."

I was still catching my breath after my frantic sprint up the hill.

"I am just thankful not to be the one she crushed!" I said.

Chapter Ten

Puh was battered by his encounter with our combatants, and Black Wolf's head had obviously suffered from its buffeting. I was a bit worse for the wear, myself. Puh gazed at me with concern.

"Are you all right?" Puh asked as he looked me up and down.

"I rolled down the hill with Rowit. I may be a little bumped and scraped and cut, but I am well enough to travel," I answered. "And you, Puh? Black Wolf, you are bleeding."

"I am fine," Puh assured me. He added, speaking to Black Wolf, "You should sit and let us take a look at your head."

"It hurts," Black Wolf admitted, sinking to a sitting position on the ground.

Black Wolf gingerly touched his still-bloodied ear and winced. Puh bent to gauge the severity of the blow, pushing Black Wolf's braids aside so he could better see the injury.

"Your scalp has been split wide open over your ear," Puh stated. "We will need to bind your head. Plus, the swelling has already begun."

"I can feel it. It is causing the skin the pull under my braids," Black Wolf said.

"I am afraid we will have to unbraid your hair, my friend; at least on this one side," Puh told Black Wolf.

"You may as well undo both sides," Black Wolf began. "Leaving the braids on one side would just look silly!"

Aessa listened to the exchange without comment, but at this, she traded glances with me. I was used to the appearance of Black Wolf's spider hat hairstyle, but to most, it looked rather silly under any circumstances.

"Binty, that brave boy," Aessa started, "he took Black Wolf's knife from his belt and freed me after Rowit tied me up again. I will clean your knife before I give it back to you, Black Wolf."

Black Wolf smiled, although he still grimaced now and then as Puh removed his plaits. His braids left little kinks in his shoulder-length hair, which now jutted out in all directions and gave poor Black Wolf a maniacal appearance.

"I see that you also put my knife to good use," Black Wolf gestured toward the weapon that was still in her hands. "You and Binty both deserve praise."

* * *

We had no desire to linger at this place, nor did we care to bury the bodies, as we usually did with our own dead. The presence of the permafrost made digging an onerous task, and we had no shovels or other tools with which to excavate earth, in any case. And none of us wanted to go near Rowit's horribly smashed body. As soon as we had bandaged Black Wolf's head and picked up our various belongings that had been well-dispersed all around the top of the knoll and hillside during the fight, we rolled the father and two brothers down the hill to join Rowit.

As we recommenced our journey homeward, I felt a distinct sense of relief that our former captors had been killed. I scanned every sapling we passed. I was toting the hafted end of my broken spear, but I needed a new one. When I spotted an appropriately sized tree, I hastened to look at it more closely. My companions followed me off the trail.

"Do you plan to make a spear?" Puh questioned.

"Yes, this one will do," I replied.

I removed my pack and dug out a hatchet. Then I swiftly began to strike at the little tree's limbs until they were almost all cleaned off. Now I could attack the base of the sapling, and I began to hew the tree. I did not want to spend much time on the production of this weapon. We had to resume our trek as quickly as possible. After I had felled the little tree, I struck off the remaining upper limbs and quickly sharpened the end to a point. I could refine the spear later, smoothing its wooden surface and heating the tip in a fire to strengthen the wood. Later, I would add a spearhead. In a matter of moments, we were back on the trail.

* * *

We had walked some distance when, to my surprise, Aessa began to silently weep into her hands.

"What is the matter?" I inquired.

Binty, too, looked up at her with a worried expression. We halted our trek. Aessa could not walk with her hands over her eyes and she would not take away her hands, even when I tried to gently pull them from her face. Aessa leaned against my chest and I looked around at the others helplessly. I was somewhat disconcerted by her nearness. Seeking to console Aessa I patted her back awkwardly.

"What is the matter, Aessa?" I asked again.

Black Wolf stood there with his head inclined to one side, one of his huge hands over the bandage. He was obviously in considerable pain. Binty clung to Aessa with both arms wrapped around her middle, looking as though he wanted to cry, too. Puh shook his head at the pitiful scene.

"She has coped with the unimaginable for such a long time. Let her cry. She has lost her family and the future she had counted on." Puh said. "Aessa, would you like to rest a while?"

"Many thanks, but no," Aessa finally spoke. "I just want to get as far away from here as possible." Aessa wiped her eyes and she surrendered a small smile. "Binty and I owe you all so much. Both for rescuing us from those despicable men, and taking us away with you. I regret that you had to experience this awful misadventure, too, but I am so grateful . . . so grateful."

Tears began to course down her cheeks. "I only wish my family and my mate had not perished . . ."

I thought that she might begin to weep in earnest again. Certainly, no one could blame her if she did, after all she had endured. But she swallowed her grief and wiped her eyes once more as she started to walk.

At that moment I was angry for Aessa, and for Binty too. They had seen terrible things at a very young age, things that no one should ever have to see. We walked until the sun was low in the sky. We then found a little wooded place where we could set up a shelter. We still had our lean-to, but it was too small for the five of us, so Puh and I built one of our circular huts, made from saplings bent over a small clearing until they met in the center, and there we lashed their tops together. Next, we cut boughs off fir trees and placed them against the saplings until they covered the structure. It would not be water-tight, but it would provide us with ample shelter for the night. Aessa and Binty foraged for firewood and then built a fire while Puh and I did our work.

Black Wolf wanted to help, but he looked so uncomfortable that Puh bade him to sit, which he did, still cradling his head. Black Wolf would not join in eating our evening meal. He claimed he was not hungry, and in fact, at one point he bolted to his feet and lunged for the nearby brush, where we heard him vomit.

"This is not good," Puh whispered to me, "I have never known Black Wolf to turn down food, and I have never seen him vomit before."

"What can we do?" I questioned.

"If Gran were here, she would know what to do," Puh said. After a pause he added, "I am very worried for Black Wolf."

"We need a healer," I nodded. "Willow Woman has a very good healer. The Fen of Falls is closer to here than home."

"Yes," Puh agreed. "If Black Wolf can keep up the pace, we could be there in three days, instead of the seven or eight days it would take to get home."

"Keep up the pace?" Black Wolf said as he resumed his seat next to us, "Keep up the pace to where?"

Black Wolf's eyes were closed with misery. It was true that he did not look at all well.

"The Fen of Falls," I told him. "You need a healer."

"Willow," Black Wolf smiled slightly. "I need Willow."

"You need Gray Owl, too," I insisted, referring to Willow Woman's healer. "Can you make it there?"

"I can make it to Willow. And my little Oak," Black Wolf replied.

Aessa was confused.

"Who? What?" she asked.

"It is a long story . . .," I started, but Aessa cut me off.

"Why must we travel for three days to find a willow . . . and an oak?" Aessa persisted, "Surely, we will see plenty of those before three days have passed. If we can find a willow, we can harvest some of its inner bark and that may help to alleviate his pain."

"She is right," Puh suddenly brightened. "That may make him comfortable enough to travel more easily."

"But an oak tree," Aessa went on, "those are more plentiful. My mother used to crush their leaves and place them over wounds to help reduce the swelling . . . why are you laughing?"

I had begun to chuckle.

"It is just that Willow is a person . . . Willow Woman," I answered. "And Oak is Black Wolf's son with Willow Woman."

"Oh," Aessa said, but I could see that she was trying to work it out in her mind. It could have been that she had never known anyone belonging to one of The People from the East's tribes and she did not know that they did not have real names, as our people did, but instead were named for things.

"Willow Woman's father was named Standing Oak," Black Wolf said, apparently having observed Aessa's troubled countenance as well. "So we named our son in honor of his father and grandfather: Black Oak."

"That is a very nice name," Aessa told Black Wolf. "It is a very strong name."

"Yes," Black Wolf agreed. "And I like your idea of foraging for willow bark and oak leaves. I am sore, indeed. The only good thing about the pain in my head is that it takes my mind off the pain in my feet. You are a wise young woman!"

When Aessa smiled at Black Wolf's words I again noted how beautiful she was. Not the same as my Morning Star, with her raven hair and gracile figure, but lovely, just the same.

* * *

It was a restless night. Black Wolf could not get comfortable lying down, so he was forced to try to sleep while sitting up in our hut. He snored vociferously. He also shifted position frequently, and when he did manage to doze, he often groaned in pain.

The next morning, when Puh removed Black Wolf's bandage to check the wound, I could see from my vantage point behind Puh that the side of Black Wolf's head was now quite swollen and grotesquely discolored.

Sadly, there were no willow or oak trees in this area. We would have to keep walking to find potential relief for Black Wolf, who trudged and sometimes staggered doggedly along with us.

Another day passed before we finally found woodlands that contained oak trees, where Aessa faithfully harvested a good supply of oak leaves. She crushed them up in her hands and then flattened them out again, so they could be laid over Black Wolf's injured head before it was bandaged again. Black Wolf smiled gratefully and told Aessa he was sure it would make him feel better, but I could see no change in his outward condition. Aessa placed a fresh application of the leaves on his head again that night, but poor Black Wolf again spent another night in severe pain.

The next day I was pleased to see that we were nearing a small stream, where we could hope to find some willows. Around midday, we finally found a stand of willows and Puh hurried to strip the inner bark from some of the branches. These were not trees, but the sort of willows that grew soft catkins each spring. Aessa also began to remove some of the bark.

"See?" Aessa showed me a section. "This is what we are after. We must collect as much as we can so Black Wolf will have enough for the journey."

"Yes, that is right," Puh joined in. "I have not seen any willow since we left that river to the north."

Aessa took a handful of the inner bark to Black Wolf and gave it to him.

"Chew this," she instructed. "I know my oak leaves did not help you much, but this may be more effective."

"I know you are doing your best," Black Wolf assured her. "I am grateful."

Black Wolf popped the bark into his mouth and began to chew.

"You should try to eat some food, as well," Puh said. "You have not eaten in a few days now. You need your strength."

"Even the thought of food makes me ill," Black Wolf complained. "But I will try . . . just let me chew this . . . *ugh* . . . bark for a while, first."

The bark did seem to give Black Wolf a little relief, and although he still vomited almost everything he tried to eat, he did finally manage to keep a little food and water down.

We were all exhausted after another restless night, but at least we knew that we would reach the Fen of Falls soon. We had found the White River, but rather than hike along its rocky banks, we traveled a bit farther inland so Black Wolf's aching head would not be subjected to the full blast of the torrent's incessant roar.

At last, we reached Willow Woman's abode. Black Wolf was near collapse by the time we arrived. While the willow bark had relieved some of the pain, the side of his head was now swollen enormously, and it was horrifically bruised. I had never seen anything like it.

Willow Woman was aghast at his appearance. In fact, I could see that she was fighting back tears, but she mastered her emotions and called for Slow Bear to bring Gray Owl to her, right away.

As it happened, Gray Owl was out with some of the men, foraging for his medicinal supplies while they harvested foodstuffs, however, Slow Bear knew where they had gone. He and some others left at a trot to bring them back as quickly as possible.

While we waited for Gray Owl to return, Willow Woman asked that Black Wolf be carried to her bed.

"I can walk," Black Wolf insisted indignantly.

"Do not be ridiculous," Willow Woman was undaunted. "You can hardly stand!" Willow Woman turned to me, "Tris, please carry Black Wolf for me. I will show you where to bring him."

I looked at Black Wolf and shrugged to him. Black Wolf glowered and frowned, uttering a few indistinguishable words under his breath. He sullenly gave Puh his spear and then took off his pack and handed that to Puh as well.

"All right," Black Wolf said resignedly. "I am glad my daughter chose a mate so large, one big enough to tote me around," he grumbled as I hefted him into my arms and followed Willow Woman to her quarters. Puh tagged along, carrying Black Wolf's belongings, and Aessa and Binty trailed after him.

Willow Woman anxiously watched Black Wolf's head and feet as I carried him, warning me if I came close enough to strike one end or the other of Black Wolf on some obstacle. At last, I set Black Wolf upon her spacious sleeping platform. He groaned as I lay him down.

"I cannot lie down," he complained. "My head hurts too much."

Puh and I helped Black Wolf to sit up while Willow Woman gathered armloads of blankets and pelts, which she placed at his back.

"Try to lean back now," she suggested. "I will remove your boots."

Willow Woman sat on the end of the bed and began to unlace Black Wolf's footwear.

"Oh! Oh! How long has it been since you have taken off these things?" Willow Woman cried out, nose wrinkled. "I will have them burned . . . new boots will be made for you."

I was surprised to see Willow Woman open one of the movable panels at the end of her quarters, exposing a view of the outdoors. She then heaved Black Wolf's huge boots through the opening and promptly closed it again. Bustling around with an air of efficiency, Willow Woman collected more blankets and spread them over Black Wolf's lap.

Black Wolf's eyes had been closed and he was silent, but then he spoke, "Stop a moment."

"What? What is it?" asked Willow Woman.

"You have not kissed me yet," Black Wolf said to her.

"I guess there is hope for you if you still want a kiss," Willow Woman said, smiling a bit as she bent to gently kiss his lips. But Black Wolf embraced her and put a hand to the back of her head to hold her there a moment before he let her go.

Just then, Gray Owl and Slow Bear made their breathless entrance. Apparently, Gray Owl could tell at a glance that something was desperately wrong.

"Black Wolf!" Gray Owl exclaimed, shaking his head as he approached his patient. "I am so sorry to see you looking this way! Let me get the bandage off you."

As Gray Owl carefully pulled away the wrapping, numerous crushed oak leaves fluttered to the floor, which Slow Bear quickly collected. Gray Owl gasped and quickly turned to Willow Woman.

"I want everyone out of the room, except one person to assist me," he said to Willow Woman.

"I will help you," Willow Woman volunteered, as did Slow Bear, and Puh and I as well.

Gray Owl was a small man, and he was dwarfed by Willow Woman's great bulk, but he gazed up at her resolutely and solemnly for a moment.

"No, I cannot have you here. You are too close to the patient." Then, seeing that she was about to protest, he held up a hand and went on, "I know you are very strong. But in matters of the heart, sometimes even the strongest falter."

"Do as he says, Willow," Black Wolf instructed quietly, eyes again closed.

Daring to oppose Willow Woman was unheard of, and the room went silent.

"Yes, my dear Black Wolf, " Willow Woman began. "I will leave . . . ."

"But kiss me first," he went on, interrupting her.

Willow Woman nodded and leaned in to kiss him once more. As she backed away, I noted that she had tears in her eyes as she hastily left the room.

"I will stay to help," Slow Bear said again.

"No," Gray Owl told him. "I need you to draw lots of clean water for me and to bring me as many large basins as you can find. Tor, will you stay and assist me?"

"Yes, of course," Puh agreed, placing Black Wolf's spear and his own spear against a wall, and setting their packs on the floor where they would be out of the way. Before leaving the room I stepped up to Black Wolf.

"Be well," I said, touching his arm. "I will be close by if you need me."

"I know," Black Wolf spoke quietly. "But I am sure all will be fine. Is Gray Owl not the best healer? He will see that my head is set to rights."

"Yes, he will." I grasped Black Wolf's hand and gave it a squeeze. I then straightened up and paused just long enough to meet Puh's eyes. Puh's face wore a mixture of relief that Black Wolf would finally receive the help he so desperately needed and grief that his lifelong friend was so badly injured. I put a hand on Puh's shoulder.

"Let me know if you need me," I whispered.

"Yes," Puh nodded.

"Come with me," I said to Aessa and Binty, escorting them out.

I found Willow Woman just outside the room, still in tears and arms crossed in front of her chest. White Cloud was attempting to ply her with offerings of food and drink, but she would have nothing. Willow Woman suddenly noticed us.

"Perhaps our guests would like to go with you to get something to eat," she suggested to White Cloud.

"Many thanks, but I will remain here," I responded. "I promised to stay close by in case they need me."

Willow Woman smiled at me gratefully.

"Take . . . what are their names?" she questioned.

"This is Aessa and this is Binty," I made the introductions. "Aessa, Binty, this is Willow Woman, she is Head Elder of The People from the East. And this is White Cloud; he handles most of the household's food preparations."

Aessa had seemed a little taken aback at Willow Woman's appearance when we first arrived, but now that she had become accustomed she was able to give Willow Woman a polite smile and a nod. Binty, however, stared at Willow Woman with open-mouthed fascination. Considering his deceased relatives' eating habits, I wondered if he was contemplating how many meals a person like Willow Woman might provide.

But it was a different kind of meal entirely that was in store for him. White Cloud motioned for Aessa and Binty to follow him, and he led them away.

Slow Bear soon passed through the room, bringing water bags and large vessels into the next chamber, and then he left Puh and Gray Owl alone again. We could hear hushed conversation, water sloshing, and occasional grunts and groans from Black Wolf, but no one came out to retrieve me. Willow Woman grew tired of standing and pacing.

"Tris, sit with me," she invited.

I joined her on a broad platform that was covered with a layer of pelts.

"I want to talk to you," Willow Woman continued. "I owe you an apology."

"You do?" My mind had been far away, thinking of many things: Black Wolf and his future recovery, my family, who awaited me at home, and the repulsive family that we had left dead at the base of the hillside. Willow Woman's words caught me off-guard.

"Yes, I do," she persisted. "I am so sorry I referred to you as a Big Red Buck when we first met."

This was an unexpected conversation indeed. It had happened several years ago.

"You have not called me that in some time," I pointed out.

"I know. But still, it has preyed upon my mind," she admitted. "That was before Black Wolf and I were together, and my mate had been dead for a few years. I had just lost my beloved father and I was not myself. And besides all that, I was frantic to have an heir to pass on the Head Eldership. I am not a young woman. I will be forty winters old in a few years. I was afraid that if I did not have a child, my family and our tradition of Head Eldership would die out with me. I was foolish enough to commission a number of men to make likenesses of me that could be passed around so that they might bring about some interest in helping me to have that child, and oh, that was the worst decision of my life! They not only made many likeness of me, but they made them badly! None portray my height . . .

my lovely skin! My beauty! They just show me as short and fat with these pathetically skinny little arms, no face, and *no clothing*! I cannot even tell you some of the awful things they carved into those figurines! Much to my shame, they even began to barter the likenesses for other goods!"

Her embarrassment was a heavy presence in the room.

"Perhaps you can have them found and destroyed," I said, attempting to comfort her.

"But I have digressed," Willow Woman resumed. "When I first saw you, I was very much taken with your fine form. Of course, once I saw Black Wolf, I knew who he was instantly because I had heard that he was a very tall man — taller than anyone else — and he was so very handsome! I knew I could never consider another. But when I saw you, I had never seen an Old One before, never seen such red hair and light eyes before, and I am afraid that I behaved very badly. And then as I came to know you over the past few years, I found that you were not only well-made, but also quietly intelligent, caring, and a devoted friend to my darling Black Wolf." She paused and took my hand. "Please accept my sincerest apologies."

I had always known Willow Woman to be a loud, brazen, and powerful leader. I had never seen her to be gentle and introspective as she was now.

"Of course," I said. "It has never occurred to me that you had anything to apologize for."

"You are a very sweet young man," Willow Woman said to me, giving my hand a pat before she let it go. "I do hope that Gray Owl is fixing my Black Wolf. He simply must make him well again." Willow Woman stifled fresh tears. "Black Wolf is the great love of my life . . . I cannot live without him."

"I understand," I told Willow Woman, putting an arm around her shoulders and drawing her closer. While consoling Aessa had given me a distinctly unsettled feeling, somehow I had no such misgivings about comforting Willow Woman. "I feel the same way about my mate, Morning Star."

"Black Wolf's daughter . . . ."

"Yes. Morning Star is my light — as necessary as the air I breathe; she and our children are the most important things in my life."

"I suppose it is unlikely that I will ever get to meet your family, but I would very much like to." Willow Woman sighed. "But all things considered, I guess that would not be wise . . . ."

"I guess that is so," I agreed. "However, if it were possible, I would very much like for you to meet my family as well. My son Fox and your Oak are less than a year apart in age. I hope that at least they will know each other."

Willow Woman nodded absently. She appeared preoccupied.

"I so wish my Black Wolf did not have to expose himself to dangerous tasks like hunting. My mate was killed on a hunt, and I am very much afraid that Black Wolf will suffer the same fate," she said.

I then realized that we had not yet explained how Black Wolf had come to be injured.

"Black Wolf was not wounded during a hunt," I told her. "He was clubbed on the side of the head by a man."

"What?" Willow Woman turned to me wide-eyed. "Why would anyone want to hurt my dear Black Wolf?"

I took a moment to compose my thoughts.

"Black Wolf, Puh, and I were exploring the lands to the northwest of here when we came upon Aessa, who was tied to a tree," I started to explain. "She told us to run, but before we could react, four men stepped out of the brush and blew into hollow sticks, causing a poisoned stinger to come out and hit each one of us. I became very dizzy and fell asleep. When I awoke, we were all in a cave that was filled with heaps of bones, some that had been there for many years. Our captors were not paying attention to us at that time and Aessa whispered to me that the men were eaters of human flesh and they intended to butcher and consume us. Aessa and Binty untied our bindings so that we were able to escape . . . ."

"But you cannot be serious!" Willow Woman broke in. "Do you mean to say that they actually eat people?"

"Yes, we saw evidence of it everywhere, and Aessa told us that the men had killed and eaten her family and her mate," I said grimly. "We got away from them and then realized that merely escaping was not enough: we had to track them down before they could inflict their gruesome practice on other unsuspecting travelers. But they snuck up on us when we lost their trail after it was trampled over by a herd of horses, and the first thing they did was hit Black Wolf on the head."

"Of course! Catch your victims unawares and take out the biggest threat!" Willow Woman spoke angrily. "But you and Tor obviously managed to handle the four men."

"Well, we had some help." I admitted, "Aessa borrowed Black Wolf's knife and stabbed one of the men. Another one of the men rolled down a hill and blundered into a mammoth that —well — made sure he did not get up again."

Willow Woman's mouth dropped open for a moment and she looked at me incredulously.

"Now I can truly appreciate why you and your father look a bit battered," she said. "I will ask Gray Owl to attend to you two when he is finished with Black Wolf. But tell me, who is the child Binty? Is he Aessa's son?"

"No, he is the child of one of the men we killed. As best we can tell, he is about ten winters old and he has been severely neglected." I replied.

"Ten winters? I would have guessed him to be no more than four or five," Willow Woman shook her head. "I will ask Gray Owl to look at him as well."

"You are very kind to ask Gray Owl to tend to me, but really, I am well," I assured Willow Woman. "I just need to wash and, once Gray Owl has completed his ministrations on Black Wolf and made him comfortable, a meal and a good night's rest will set me to rights."

Slow Bear then hurried through again and we got a glimpse of the scene in the next room in the brief instant as the movable panel exposed the goings-on. Black Wolf was still sitting up, but he was leaning forward against Puh's shoulder as Gray Owl worked on him. It appeared that Black Wolf's hair had been shorn short so that the damage to his head was now more visible. The split over his ear now yawned wide. It was a sickening sight.

When the panel swung shut again, I turned to gaze at Willow Woman and saw that her dark skin had blanched as she still stared at the closed doorway.

"Tris," she started, "I have not yet thanked you. Thank you for bringing my Black Wolf to me."

* * *

Sometime later, Puh, Gray Owl, and Slow Bear came out as Willow Woman and I sat companionably on the platform. I was weary and nearly nodding off, but their sudden presence jolted me to a state of alertness.

"How is my dear Black Wolf?" Willow Woman was instantly on her feet. "Is it all right if I go in, now?"

"Yes," Gray Owl answered. I thought he looked tired, too. Gray Owl and Slow Bear's arms were piled with assorted impedimenta while Puh held open the movable panel for them to pass through.

Willow Woman hastened to Black Wolf's side, but not before quietly thanking the men who had tended to her beloved.

Puh and I stood in the doorway, where I could see that Black Wolf was now semi-reclining against the heap of blankets piled at his back. His eyes were closed and he looked drawn and pained, but he opened his eyes as Willow Woman took one of his giant hands in hers.

"How are you, my dear?" she asked him gently.

Black Wolf smiled and his long fingers curved around her hand.

"I am hurting right now, but I will soon be well again," he responded in a low voice. "Gray Owl had to cut my hair," Black Wolf then lamented.

"No matter," Willow Woman brushed his concern about his hair aside. "It will grow back. I will bring Oak in to see you when you are feeling up to it."

"My little Oak. I would like that. But for now, I would like to sleep." Black Wolf's head was drooping. Willow Woman then lay down at his side and rested her head on his chest as he encircled her with one arm.

"Sleep, my love. I will keep you company," she said, "I will lie here and listen to your beating heart."

Puh nudged me, and we both stepped back so that he could swing the door closed.

* * *

"I want to wash my hands," Puh announced as we began to walk away from Willow Woman's chamber, Puh carrying his pack on one shoulder and spear in one hand.

"Me, too," I agreed. "And the rest of me, as well. Did Gray Owl give you any notion as to how Black Wolf will fare?"

"Well, he believes that Black Wolf will have a long recovery. He does not want Black Wolf to attempt a trek home for some while," Puh said grimly.

"I guess that means we will have to go home without him once again." I did not like to think of this possibility. Whenever Black Wolf stayed away for extended periods of time, it only deepened the rift between Black Wolf and Little Fawn and caused more anxiety for their offspring.

"Yes," Puh nodded. "Slow Bear has already offered to accompany us home with a few other volunteers. They did not wish us to travel without an escort, since you and I are cut up enough to attract attention from large predators. And they would likely consider Binty and Aessa to be tasty morsels, as well."

"I wish we did not have to leave Black Wolf behind, but I am eager to return home," I admitted.

"As am I," Puh started. "I have never been away from Ria for so long, but I do feel somewhat better, knowing that Bror is there while we are away. I know that Ty does his best, but it is a heavy responsibility he bears."

"You would know," I smiled at Puh.

After Puh's father and oldest brother were killed, he and my uncle, at fourteen and sixteen winters old, respectively, were left to procure all the necessities of life for their family. And when his older brother was paired and moved to the territory of his mate's family, Puh, still not yet fifteen winters of age, had borne the burden alone.

When we were outdoors once again, I was amused to see White Cloud standing by Aessa and Binty, hands on his hips and shaking his head. Aessa and Binty were lying on the mats near the hearth, sound asleep, hands still clutching the food they had been eating.

White Cloud grinned when he saw us.

"I will let them sleep," he whispered. "That little fellow can eat! He put away more food than a fully grown man!"

Puh and I smiled and nodded to White Cloud, but continued our walk to the frothing waters of the White River. By now, we had visited the Fen of Falls enough to know the best place to access water for bathing. A short distance up the riverside path there was a spot where the rocky bank jutted out, providing a place where we could sit on the boulders and dangle our feet into the fast-moving waters, or step on one of the stones and squat down as we splashed water on ourselves. It was still a somewhat daunting process, as the nearby falls thundered and shook the landscape, but there the flow was actually much calmer than it was even a short distance away.

The Dreamer IV ~ THE CAVE OF BONES

Puh and I set down our gear and finally washed off the blood and dirt that we had been wearing since we left the knoll.

Chapter Eleven

As always, the evening meal was a pleasant affair. Black Wolf and Willow Woman did not join us, but most of the remaining household occupants were there, including Gray Owl. I was ravenous and eating almost as voraciously as Binty when I noticed that Gray Owl was staring at him. Gray Owl suddenly turned toward me and took note of my gaze.

"He is an unusual child," Gray Owl stated with a smile. "He is quite small, but if he keeps eating like this he may experience a substantial growth spurt."

"He does not speak," I told Gray Owl. "He oftentimes seems to exist in his own dream world."

"Yes, I have observed that very thing," Gray Owl agreed. "I believe he does not hear sounds. As I said, most unusual. His *dream world*, as you so aptly put it, may be how he has coped with life."

"*Does not hear sounds?*" I repeated. "I do not understand how a being cannot hear."

I thought on all the sounds heard on a day-to-day basis that I took for granted: Morning Star's voice, songs of the birds, the wind in the trees. What would it be like to live in silence?

"It is very rare, but some people do not hear. Sometimes they are born that way, sometimes they become deaf at some point during their lives," Gray Owl mused. "It would not surprise me to know that little Binty had been bashed just over the ear, as Black Wolf was, and had the hearing knocked out of his head."

"Will Black Wolf go deaf, too?" I asked, alarmed.

"No, I think not," Gray Owl assured me. "Although he does complain of hearing noises in his ear. Black Wolf was lucky that his assailant was significantly shorter than he. The man had to stretch up to hit him with the club, and the blow was nowhere near as bad as it might have been if he had been struck by someone closer to his own height."

"That is lucky," I agreed. "The man who hit him was very strong. He had only one arm, and that one arm was indeed mighty."

"*One arm*?" Gray Owl's eyes widened. "In that case I would hazard a guess that if Black Wolf had been of average height, he would likely be dead."

A little later that evening, Oak was brought out to socialize with us before his bedtime. Willow Woman and Black Wolf still had not appeared, but I was happy to see Oak and, in fact, to hold him for the first time. He was a solid baby; I guessed that he was perhaps eight or nine moons old. His hair was as black as a moonless night, and his skin was tawny. Although I was a stranger, he was content to sit in my arms, staring at me as though I were some odd creature. I could well imagine that my pale skin, fiery hair, and green eyes contrasted sharply with those he was accustomed to viewing. He held up his forefinger and poked my cheek several times, as though to test my skin and be sure it felt the same as everyone else's. He came rather close to also poking my eye and I involuntarily blinked.

"Black Oak!" Slow Bear cried out. "Have a care!"

Poor Oak jumped at hearing his name called out and I snuggled him comfortingly.

"He did not harm me," I told Slow Bear. "I am used to little ones."

"It is good that you are!" Slow Bear responded. "He has been known to pull beards, too."

"I am used to that, as well. My mate has often had to rescue my whiskers from the clutches of our children," I said with a laugh.

"How I envy your time in life," Slow Bear said, shaking his head. "I have already enjoyed those years of living with my mate and raising a family," Slow Bear sighed. "My mate has been gone a long time now, and our boys are grown with families of their own."

"Where are your sons now?" I had never seen any sign of Slow Bear's family, other than an occasional mention.

"Last I knew they were settled in another region, many days' journey to the southeast. I see them only when they come to the annual Gathering of the People." Slow Bear now grinned as Oak began to chant

Da-Da-Da-Da. "Every year I am on edge until my boys show themselves and I know they are all right. I wish that they could have relocated to somewhere nearer, but as you know, it takes a lot of resources to run a household, and they needed to find open lands where water, game, and wood were plentiful."

"Yes," I said thoughtfully. "We were looking for such a place ourselves when our misadventure began and Black Wolf was clobbered on the head."

"Where was that?" Slow Bear inquired.

"Three days' hike to the north of here," I answered. "There were a lot of game animals, but also a lot of swampland. The forests were rather spotty."

Oak was now hammering on my chest with his little fists, jabbering and sometimes continuing to chant *Da-Da-Da-Da.* I shifted him in my arms to encourage him to do something other than pound my chest and he responded by grunting and scrunching up his face until it turned red. As a parent, I knew what this meant. So did Slow Bear. He called one of the household staff to come and take the baby away.

"The child has a very healthy digestive system," Slow Bear stated after Oak was removed from the dinnertime assemblage.

"It appears that is so," I nodded.

Puh had been mutely taking in our conversation, but now he broke his silence.

"The Gatherings provide a great opportunity to exchange information," he mused. "I know you must be quite busy at that time, Slow Bear, but are you able to speak with the other attendees?"

"Yes, of course! I actually seek out as much news as I can. When we are at the Gathering Willow Woman is quite wrapped up in her duties as Head Elder, so she counts on me to relay to her as much information as I can garner."

"Think on this, if you would," Puh began. "Based on what you hear, where would you advise a clan such as ours to relocate?"

Slow Bear's brow furrowed in thought as he considered Puh's question.

"If I were looking for a place to go, I might try the Lake Region," he finally said. "No People from the East have settled up there, so it is still largely unclaimed, so far as I know."

"My uncles live there," I chimed in happily. I had not spent but a number of days with my mother's older brothers, but I had enjoyed that time immensely and I would be very pleased to live near them.

"Yes, Ria's brothers live there, too," Puh added without enthusiasm.

Ria's brothers were a couple of conniving simpletons, and Puh was understandably not seeking to foster a closer relationship with those men.

"Well, it is a sizable area. Surely there would be room enough for your families, as well," Slow Bear pointed out.

"And surely it would be better than that insect-infested swamp we recently trekked to," Puh admitted.

"Many thanks, Slow Bear. I will talk it over with our families. And, of course, with Black Wolf when he is a little better."

* * *

Puh and I were both weary from our long day and the preceding long nights of poor Black Wolf's frequently shifting position and groaning and snoring, so we excused ourselves early to at long last get a good night's sleep. Aessa and Binty had already been led to a room right after the evening meal and I was sure that they were probably sound asleep by now.

"What do you think of Slow Bear's idea?" I asked Puh as he and I lay down on the floor matting in our chamber.

"Do you mean his idea about going to the Lake Region?" Puh answered.

"Yes."

"I think there will be plenty of meat . . . and wood, too. But the winters will be a little longer than what we are accustomed to," Puh paused. "It may also mean that we are too far from the coast to venture there every summer as we have always done until recently."

"Oh," I said glumly. "I had not thought about how far it would be from the coast. That would be a long way to travel with our mates and little ones."

I recalled our last summer at the shore, two years ago. Morning Star and I were just paired, and it was an oh-so-pleasant time of warm days by the ocean and warm nights making love to my new mate. Puh and I still worked hard while we were there as we trapped fish and hunted seals, but somehow, that is not what I most remembered. I was sad to think that we might never return.

* * *

Puh and I were awake as soon as the sun rose the next morning. We were eager to depart for home, so we packed our few belongings, including the carefully created cloaks made from wisent hides that were given to us by Slow Bear. Puh and I then collected our spears before heading out to join the others for breakfast. Aessa and Binty were already there, happily stuffing their faces before we set off. Slow Bear, again accompanied by Roe Buck and Crow Feather, were also ready to leave as soon as we had eaten.

Black Wolf and Willow Woman honored us by coming out to see us off. Black Wolf was still using his spear as a staff to help support himself, but he was smiling, and his color looked a little stronger. All the same, Black Wolf appeared very thin, and he still held his bandaged head to one side, as though it were very heavy. For the first time since I had known Black Wolf, he actually looked old.

As we said our good-byes, Black Wolf gently chided Puh and me. "Do not look at me so pityingly, as though I am going to die. I will be fine, and I will be home sooner than you think."

"I know that, old friend," Puh assured him. "I just hate to see you suffering."

"Me, as well," I added. "I wish you a speedy recovery and hope to see you before long."

"You will," Willow Woman chimed in. "But do not look for him too soon. I do not want to give him up until I must."

Black Wolf and Willow Woman embraced first Puh, then me. Next, they hugged Binty and Aessa, too. Lastly, Black Wolf removed my hastily made spear from my hand, and gave me his.

"Take my spear, Tris," he said. "I will not need it while I am here, and I know I can make another one before I leave for home."

"Many thanks, Black Wolf," I nodded gratefully. "I do feel more secure to be headed home with a proper spear in my hands."

Black Wolf's spear was somewhat longer than mine, but it was beautifully made. He smiled to see my pleasure at his gift.

We did not tarry long. The sun was rising, and we had to be on our way. Despite the uncertainties on our horizon, I was lighthearted. I was going home.

* * *

Aessa was understandably curious about where we were bringing her. She asked many questions about the people who lived at our family compound and where she and Binty might live once we arrived. Puh thought that she might like to live with him and Ria, Great Gran, and all the children in the main house.

"Yes, I would like that. Many thanks," Aessa agreed. "But you mentioned that there are dogs; are they friendly?"

"Yes," Puh replied. "They dislike only people or animals who would attempt to do us harm. But other than that, they love to cuddle and be petted."

"I have never had a dog, but I guess I will see what they are like soon enough," Aessa said, still seeming a little trepidatious at the notion.

I wondered what Binty would make of his new home. Since he was not able to verbalize most of his thoughts, I expected that he would be quite confused. Just the same, he trotted alongside us happily, sometimes merrily skipping his steps and making little birdlike sounds. Considering the vile home he had come from, he was indeed a resilient child. Harkening back to Aessa, I then recalled that she and my sister Ru would be about the same age.

"I have a sister around your age," I told Aessa, "and my mate Morning Star also has a sister who must be nearly your age as well, so you will have an opportunity to make new friends."

"Oh, that would be wonderful! It might be just like having sisters!"Aessa said, brightening at the idea. "I have never had a sister before!"

The others smiled at this exchange. Poor Aessa and Binty certainly deserved a chance at happiness after all they had been through.

* * *

That night, in our combined lean-tos, Aessa lay with her back to me.

"Tris," she whispered, "tell me about your sister Ru."

I was awake, lying on my back so I could see the vast nighttime sky from the entryway to the lean-to, but I was hesitant to answer, afraid our talk would keep the others from sleeping.

"She is a little taller than you. She is very good at keeping a home," I whispered back. I was not sure what kind of information Aessa was seeking.

"What does she look like?" Aessa persisted. "I want to see her in my mind."

"She has dark red hair, and dark green eyes," I began unsurely. "She has freckled skin like Puh and me."

"How does she wear her hair?"

This was getting to be a bit much.

"She twists her hair into coils and wears them up, affixed to the back of her head."

"Affixed . . . how does she do that?" Aessa wore her long hair loose or gathered simply at the base of her neck.

I pondered on the notion that perhaps her clan did not dress their hair as our people did. But then our traditional stories told us that our hair provided us with a second sense, so to heighten that acuity it was seldom cut. Plus, our hair was dense and curling, so it required taming or else it was very difficult to manage.

"I do not know." I cast about for an answer that would satisfy her. "She uses wooden rods . . . her hair just sort of stays there."

"I have seen that," Roe Buck piped up. "The rods are pushed through the masses of hair and that keeps it from falling down."

"Yes," Slow Bear agreed, "sometimes the hair is wound with a strip of leather . . . ."

Aessa rolled over to face me and she giggled silently as she listened to the men discussing how women did their hair.

"See what you have started?" I teased her.

"No matter," she replied. "I am just giddy at the thought of being safe and going somewhere safe."

"I am glad for that," I told her.

"Tris," Aessa said.

"Yes?"

"I always feel safe with you."

"I am glad for that as well."

Soon, the conversation died down and I heard the soft snores and gentle breathing from my sleep mates, telling me that all were slumbering. I continued to look up at the firmament overhead. The moon had set early, leaving just a sprinkling of stars across the sky. Somewhere in the far distance, wolves howled. Aessa snuggled up to me. I found this to be disconcerting, so I subtly rearranged my new cloak so its bulk was between us. Oh, when would sleep come?

* * *

We were near home when I heard my dog's familiar woofs. Raena was standing in the middle of the trail, barking and wagging her tail so madly that her whole body swayed back and forth. She rushed up to me and placed her paws on my chest, straining up to lick my face. I had only time for a quick glance at Aessa as she cringed behind Puh in horror. Raena was a bit more wolf-like in appearance than many dogs, so I could understand her apprehension.

After giving Raena a few quick pats and kissing her nose, I pushed her down.

"Come on, girl! Let us go home!" I said to Raena, starting to run.

Raena woofed and loped easily alongside me the rest of the way to the family compound. It was late in the day, so most of the compound's occupants were finishing up their day's tasks or preparing the evening meal. Morning Star was just turning from the fire pit to see what had set the dogs to barking when I swept her off her feet and swung her around, my lips on hers.

Morning Star held me tightly and returned my kisses joyfully.

"Oh, Tris! I am so happy you are home!" Morning Star exclaimed.

"And I am so glad to be here!" It seemed as though we said the same words every time I came home, yet it was undisputable that we were both elated to be together again.

Puh was also having an enthusiastic reunion with Ria.

It was only after several moments of enraptured kissing that I remembered that we had guests. Slow Bear and his companions were being seated by the fire as Aessa and Binty stood by, clinging to one another.

Great Gran approached them, peering at Aessa and Binty keenly.

"Come and sit," Great Gran invited. "You must be very hungry and thirsty. I will get something for you to eat and drink."

Gran quickly retrieved gourd cups and dispersed them amongst our visitors. Then, moments later, as some of the food was ready to eat, that, too, was handed out. I was eating heartily when Gran sidled up to me.

"Who are those two children?" Gran questioned.

"They were living in very hard circumstances." I did not want to tell the gruesome story while we were beginning to eat our nightly sup. "So Puh and Black Wolf and I took them away."

"Where is Da?" Morning Star suddenly asked in alarm, looking wildly about. "I do not see Da! Where is he?"

"We had to leave your Da with a healer," I told Morning Star gently.

"Da is injured?" Morning Star gasped.

Black Wolf's mate Little Fawn had just exited her home as Morning Star said this. At first, Little Fawn's eyes flew open wide, but then she frowned.

"He has a head wound, but we believe he will recover. However, he is not yet well enough to travel," Puh told Morning Star.

"When will Da be able to come home?" Morning Star queried anxiously.

"It may be a little while," Slow Bear responded. "We will return home after we have rested a day or so and then when Black Wolf is ready, we will bring him back."

Morning Star turned to look at me, as though trying to decide if she were being told the truth or if we were acting in concert to protect her father from the ire of his family.

"Your father promised us that he would return as soon as he is able. He has a bad gash on the side of his head. The healer had to cut off most of his hair," I explained.

"Cut his hair?" Little Fawn said dryly. "Black Wolf must be beside himself."

"Um . . . back to the children," Gran tried again. "Are they going to live here?"

"Yes," Puh answered. "If that is their wish. They appear to have nowhere else to go."

"The young woman is not exactly a child," my brother Ty pointed out. "In fact; I would say that she is quite well full-grown."

"Indeed," Crow Feather agreed, looking at Aessa from across the compound.

Morning Star did not appear pleased.

"*Really*, Tris!" she began indignantly. "First you and your father bring home Ria and now you bring home this woman. You really must stop bringing home strange women!"

"But look how happy Puh and Ria are," I feebly retorted.

"I guess," Morning Star relented with a wry smile.

"Besides, we could not just leave Binty and Aessa where they were. I will tell you more about it later. It is not a very nice story . . . we should eat first," I said, reaching for the slab of roasted meat offered to me by Morning Star's younger sister. "Many thanks, Petal."

"Eat up, Tris," Petal grinned pleasantly. "Bror and Ty brought in a small deer. We have lots of fresh meat just now."

"Many thanks, Petal," I said again.

As was usually the case, mealtimes were noisy as everyone talked. Aessa and Binty stayed close to Puh. The compound's children were very curious about Binty, and they vied to sit with him and offer him the choicest morsels from their shell bowls.

After the meal was finished, it might have been a time for stories before everyone retired for the day, but it was necessary to relate what had happened while we were away. Puh matter-of-factly told the tale, using the fewest words possible, but highlighting Aessa and Binty's bravery during the ordeal. After he was through, everyone sat in stunned silence.

"You have left out your own feats," Aessa spoke up. "Without you, Tris, and Black Wolf, Binty and I would still be at the mercy of those awful men. And anyone else who ventured near that area. I will be grateful to you for the rest of my life, and although Binty cannot say so, I am sure he feels the same way."

Morning Star and I did not stay long; our little ones were nodding off and we were most eager to go home and finally have some time to ourselves. While we readied to leave, Morning Star was deeply involved in a conversation with her mother. I could only catch a few words here and there, but both were very serious. Gran took the opportunity to speak with me.

"So, this must be the dark-haired woman of your Dreams," Gran said, motioning toward Aessa with a nod of her head.

"It appears so," I agreed.

"Then it was not an ancient memory." Gran stated. "And the men had dark hair, too?"

"Yes," I replied.

"Funny. I have never known Old Ones to have brown hair, but I guess if The People from the East can have black hair, it must be possible for clans from different places to be a little different as well." Gran shrugged, but then went on, "I do hope Black Wolf will survive his injuries. It does sound as though he is in a bad way."

"Yes," I said again. "I hope so, as well. He did not look well when we left him. I can only be comforted that the Head Elder's healer is no doubt the best in these lands. If anyone can save Black Wolf, he can." Then something occurred to me. "Have you not seen Black Wolf's future in your Dreams, Gran?"

Gran shook her head soberly.

"No, I have not," she replied.

I felt a stab of fear go through my heart. We wished each other a pleasant evening, and then Morning Star rejoined me. With Raena trotting by our side, we walked up the hill to our little home. There, the flickering flames of a low fire were all that lighted the place.

Pony was already asleep. In the semidarkness Morning Star laid Pony in her cozy nest-like bed, while I did the same with Fox. Fox's eyes were barely open as I lay him down, too, and covered him with a blanket, kissing his forehead. Then Morning Star and I changed places and she kissed Fox while I kissed Pony.

Morning Star began to fluff the dried grass and moss padding under our bedding while I fussed with the fire. In-ground homes like ours tended to be cool and a bit damp, so even during summer we kept small fires alight to take off the chill and brighten the main chamber. Once these chores were attended to, we fell into bed fairly quickly and it was only much later when we lay in one another's arms in the now darkened room that I began to drift contentedly and peacefully off to sleep.

"Tris," Morning Star said.

"Yes?" I tried to summon my wits to return sufficiently to speak.

"Mama and I were talking," she went on.

"Oh?"

"Yes, and when Slow Bear and the others return to the Head Elders, Mama would like you and me to go with them."

I was now wide awake.

"What?" I was both incredulous and dismayed. I had just returned home, and I really did not want to go anywhere. "Why should we do that?"

"Mama is concerned about Da. And frankly, so am I," Morning Star said firmly. "I want to see Da's condition and let him know that I worry for him. Mama would go herself, but she does not want to either impose my four younger siblings on anyone else or bring them on the trek. And, besides, I do not think that Mama feels up to a long journey. She has not traveled farther than the Village since I was a child."

My mind ran amok with images of all the things that might result from such a trip, and most of them were not at all desirable.

"My sweet," I began, "I would do anything to make you happy, but it is a three-day trek and it is not like our trips to the shore. We have to press hard to make it in three days. If we go, we must bring the children. And while you can carry Pony, Fox is much too restless to be toted for long periods, and he walks too slowly to set the pace for the others." I then recalled my last hunting excursion with Ria, and how the bear had charged her and Mror. "And besides, there is also the very real danger that the children will attract large predators to our procession."

Morning Star was undaunted.

"Why can we not bring Da's dogs and a sled or two on which Fox could ride and also, they could carry extra supplies?" she asked. "The dogs would not only pull the sleds, but they would do much to protect us — and they would deter predators, too."

"Actually, that is not a bad idea," I mused aloud, but then I immediately regretted my words. What would Black Wolf say if I were to arrive with Morning Star?

"You see?" Morning Star pounced on this. "It is not so impossible! One might think that you do not want to leave so you can stay close to that woman you brought home."

I was momentarily confused.

"Why would I want to be close to her . . . she is all the way down the hill at Puh's" — and then I had an epiphany. "You do not think . . . you do not think that I am interested in her?"

"She is quite taken with you," Morning Star said hotly. "She stares after you with those big doe eyes of hers."

"She said something to me once and I told her in no uncertain terms that I am paired and that I will never love anyone but you." My fervor must have impressed Morning Star, because I felt her relax against me.

"I am sorry, Tris," she whispered, kissing me. "I should not have said that. It is just that she is so pretty. I feared the worse when I saw her and knew that she had been traveling with you for all that time."

"But you are the one I love. And you are the mother of my children," I murmured to her. "You have nothing to fear from other women; no one could be more dear to me or more beautiful than you are."

It seemed that our sleep would be delayed yet again, but I was not displeased. I had waited to be back with my cherished Morning Star for so long; I felt as though I could make love to her forever.

* * *

We were not long arisen when Morning Star picked up our discussion about venturing to see her father once again. Under the barrage of her many reasons we should go, I at last relented.

"All right!" I held up my hands in surrender. "I will speak with Slow Bear. If he is in agreement and if your mother will allow us to take some of Black Wolf's dogs and sleds, we will go."

I thought she might regret her determination to make this trip; it would not be an easy one for her. But that was her decision. Black Wolf, on the other hand, might never forgive me.

Chapter Twelve

The trek to the Fen of Falls took us four days instead of the usual three, but it turned out to be quite enjoyable. The presence of the dogs, some of which roamed free and canvassed the area around the trail and up ahead of us, and some of which pulled travois sleds, made the journey much less taxing and much more worry-free. Morning Star and the children and I shared a lean-to, while Slow Bear and the others shared another. The dogs spent the night at the front of the lean-tos, where they could keep watch on their charges. At home, our pets were cheerful and affectionate; out here, they were deadly serious about their duties.

Up till now, I had always envied Puh and Ria their ability to be together when we made long trips. I found that sharing this experience with Morning Star and our children was far more pleasant than I expected — surprisingly so. Morning Star gasped at the beautiful violence of the roiling White River, and again, when we arrived at the Fen of Falls, at the grandeur of those cascading waters. But perhaps most of all, she was impressed by the sight of Willow Woman's summer home. This was by far the largest structure she had ever seen. In fact, the only building I had ever seen to be bigger was the enormous hall where The People's annual Gathering took place.

Our journey reached its end near midday, and we found White Cloud at the hearth before the great dwelling, where he was already starting to build up the fire so it would burn down to coals by the time he was ready to cook over it. White Cloud stared at us with curiosity evident on his face. The dogs were all panting from their exertion and the warm temperatures. Fox was napping, sprawled across one of the sleds, so I removed the dog from the sled's harness so Fox could slumber in peace and released the other dog from his burden, as well. The dogs immediately went to the river to slake their considerable thirst.

"I will just go inside and announce you to Willow Woman," Slow Bear said.

"Many thanks," I nodded to him. "Come and meet White Cloud," I said to Morning Star.

Morning Star held a dozing Pony in her arms as she accompanied me to greet White Cloud. I was glad that Pony was asleep so that her first impression would be an agreeable one, rather than one of a squalling infant. But Pony's temperament, like the weather, could change at any moment.

White Cloud rose to his feet and he also began to walk toward us.

"Pleasant day to you!" White Cloud welcomed us. "Tris, it is a surprise to see you again so soon! And you have brought a beautiful woman with you! We have not seen such beauty since Aessa left us!"

"Many thanks," I said, inwardly cringing at White Cloud's hapless remark, but smiled to him just the same. "This is my mate, Morning Star, and our daughter, Pony. Our son, Fox, is on the sled just there." I pointed toward Fox, a few steps away, who seemed to be sleepily rousing from his snooze. "I will get Fox," I said, hastening to lift him up so he would not be frightened at awakening in a strange place. Fox rubbed his eyes as I returned to Morning Star and White Cloud, who were chatting amicably as White Cloud admired Pony.

"Can you say *good day*, Fox?" I asked him, but Fox responded by dropping his head heavily on my shoulder. "I do not believe that he is fully awake just yet."

I suddenly saw Morning Star's eyes widen in alarm and turned to see what had caught her gaze. Willow Woman was exiting her home and she was waddling toward us with great dignity.

"This is Willow Woman, the Head Elder," I whispered to her.

Morning Star nodded dumbly, clutching Pony to her a little tighter. Fox now seemed to come to life, and he grinned at the sight of Willow Woman.

"Lady!" Fox called out, pointing. "See lady!"

I was thankful that Fox did not choose to comment on any of Willow Woman's physical attributes. Toddlers, despite owning a limited vocabulary, can be brutally honest at times, and it would not do for him to announce to the world such obvious characteristics as were peculiar to Willow Woman, such as her great size or the fact that she was tattooed almost from head to toe. But the day was young.

"Tris!" Willow Woman said as she hugged me, a bit awkwardly, as Fox was still in my arms and he wriggled at being caught in between us. "I am so glad to see you again. Thank you for bringing your family to my home. You know I have often said how much I would like to meet them!"

"It is I who must thank you for allowing us to impose on your hospitality," I returned, ever grateful to Slow Bear for going in before us and preparing Willow Woman for this meeting.

"And this must be Morning Star! So pretty!" Willow Woman bent to embrace Morning Star, too, "Black Wolf has told me so much about you! You are his pride and joy!"

This much was true. Morning Star had always been her father's favorite.

"Thank you," Morning Star said shyly, but beginning to regain her composure. "I am very eager to see my Da. I am very worried about him."

"Of course, come with me." Willow Woman waved us to follow her. "He will be so pleased to see you. But be forewarned, you may find him much changed."

Morning Star visibly swallowed, and her step faltered for a moment, but she still managed to gaze about her in awe as we passed through the rooms to Willow Woman's chamber at the far end of the structure. There we found Black Wolf sitting up in bed, his head misshapen on one side, the bruising still painfully obvious, and shorn hair sticking out awkwardly.

Black Wolf grinned at the sight of us. Morning Star quickly passed Pony to me, who somehow remained asleep as I held both children at once.

"Da!" Morning Star cried as she flew to Black Wolf and wrapped her arms around him. "Oh, Da! You look horrible!" Morning Star blurted out and she began to sob.

Black Wolf hugged her tightly and stroked her hair as she wept.

"*Horrible?*" he echoed. "How disappointing. Everyone keeps telling me how much better I am looking. I must have been truly hideous before."

"Oh, Da, I am sorry," Morning Star sat back and wiped her tears from her eyes. "I was just so shocked to see you. You do not really look horrible. But you do look . . . *injured.*"

Black Wolf laughed. I was relieved to hear that his voice sounded strong again. He also seemed to be a little less thin than he had been when I was last here.

"Well, I fear I was indeed injured," he agreed. "Thankfully, I was brought here where I could be tended by the wisest and most skilled healer known."

Willow Woman sat on the other side of the bed platform, next to Black Wolf.

"Gray Owl has worked much magic," Willow Woman said. "We are all so very grateful to him."

"I would like to meet him," Morning Star responded. "That is, if it would not be too much trouble."

"Of course," Willow Woman said with a nod. "I will bring him to you later."

"Thank you," Morning Star said, smiling though she continued to dry her eyes. Every time she looked at her father, her tears began to flow again. "And thank you for taking such good care of my Da."

Fox was now squiggling to get down.

"Down, Puh-Puh!" Fox insisted, "Fox *down*!"

"Let him down," Black Wolf said. "Come and see me, my little Fox! We have a playmate for you here! You can meet him when he arises from his afternoon nap."

Fox trotted over to Black Wolf and eagerly clambered up the side of the platform, where Black Wolf set him on his lap. Morning Star seemed comforted to see her father speaking and behaving normally, even if he did not look the same.

Black Wolf asked Fox many questions about our journey here, and Fox charmed his grandfather and Willow Woman with his replies.

"See bird!" Fox exclaimed. We had not seen many animals, because the dogs discouraged their presence, "And rabbit, and . . . um . . . bird . . . and fox! *Fox* name like me!"

"Like you?" Black Wolf repeated. "Did he look like you?"

"*Noooo*," Fox said, shaking his head emphatically. "No big nose!"

"Did you see the big water outside?" Black Wolf questioned.

"Loud!" Fox covered his ears.

Willow Woman suddenly stood up.

"I will go and see to your lodgings," she said to Morning Star and me. "Of course, you are welcome to stay here for as long as you desire."

"Many thanks," I replied.

Willow Woman paused momentarily at my side to peer into Pony's sleeping face. She gave me a warm smile and gently squeezed my hand.

"Thank you very much," Morning Star added.

Willow Woman gave us a parting smile as she left us. It then occurred to me it was likely that she had already instructed Slow Bear to take care of our accommodations. She was giving us time to speak with Black Wolf without her presence.

"I am sorry to appear unexpectedly like this," Morning Star told her father.

"I am sorry that you are not here under happier circumstances," Black Wolf admitted.

"I heard that you were hurt, but still . . . I did not envision . . . would it be all right if I looked under your bandage?" Morning Star asked.

"Gray Owl will change it this evening, perhaps then. When the children are not here," Black Wolf said, looking pointedly at Fox. "And if you have the stomach for it. I myself am glad I cannot see it."

Morning Star hugged her father again and began to weep anew.

"What? What is this?" Black Wolf said to her gently, patting her back. "Such tears from my stoic daughter! I am not dead yet! It was just a rap on the head; I should have expected it after hearing them discussing the probable musical qualities of my skull."

Morning Star gave her father a puzzled look, but then she took note of his left arm.

"Da! What have you done to your arm?" she cried out.

Black Wolf's normally furry forearm was shaved to the skin and decorated with the same lines and zigzag markings that covered most of Willow Woman's body.

"Is it not exquisite?" Black Wolf said as he looked at the limb admiringly, despite that the fresh tattoo still looked rather red and swollen.

"Will it wash off?" Morning Star asked hopefully.

"Indeed, not! I will carry these marks to the grave!" Black Wolf assured her cheerfully. "I will have the other arm done to match during my next visit!"

"Oh, Da," Morning Star sighed.

"Now that you know, what do you think?" Black Wolf said, changing the subject.

It took Morning Star a moment to catch his drift.

"She is very nice. I did not expect to like her; she is . . . *different*, but she is nice. And I can see that she loves you and cares for you," Morning Star admitted.

"You know I would not hurt you if I could help it," Black Wolf said earnestly.

"I know," Morning Star nodded. "You do not hurt me. But Mama, although she would never admit it, is heartbroken."

Black Wolf was silent a moment, but his face became stony.

"It is hard to tell from my perspective, considering that she has refused me her affections for the last few years," Black Wolf stated.

"I am sure it has not been easy for you, Da," Morning Star told him. "I am not judging you. I want you to be happy."

"Willow brings me much happiness," Black Wolf said, his smile returning. "I cannot wait for you to meet our son, Oak . . . Black Oak."

"Yes, Da," Morning Star seemed somehow abashed at the existence of the child of her father's illicit union. Black Wolf sensed this as well.

"I am as proud of Oak as I am of all my children," Black Wolf announced. "I have behaved badly toward your mother, but in recent years there has been no other woman in my life except Willow, and that is the way it will stay. *Ack.* Women seem to value fidelity more than men do," he lamented. "You, Morning Star, are fortunate to have the rare mate who will spurn all others in your favor."

"*Da!*" Morning Star exclaimed, her mouth dropping open in embarrassed surprise.

I was taken aback by Black Wolf's announcement, as well. I began to wonder if perhaps his head injury might have affected his sensibilities.

"I was there when Tris told Aessa that he would have none but you," Black Wolf went on. "He said that he was paired with you and had vowed to always do his best by you. He meant to protect you from all harm, even — or most especially — any harm that he, himself, might inflict on you. It was then, to my shame, that I realized how badly I have treated your mother. While strict monogamy may not be typical amongst most beings, it does not mean that I should lie with any willing female like a stag during the rut. What was between your mother and I may be spoiled now, but I will not make the same mistake twice; I am changed now."

"I am glad, Da," Morning Star smiled though she still had tears in her eyes. "Truly, I am glad."

Morning Star then arose and came to me, where she slipped her arms around me as well as she could while Pony slept on my shoulder.

"I love you, Tris," Morning Star whispered to me.

I placed my free arm around her shoulder and kissed the top of her head.

"I love you, too, my sweet."

* * *

We enjoyed a delightful afternoon with Black Wolf, and when Oak was brought in Pony, now awake, was the one who captured the baby's interest, rather than Fox. Fox was far too active as he trotted from place to place around the room to much care about sitting and playing with an infant. Although Oak was significantly larger than Pony, they were nearly the same age and they were intrigued to at last meet a peer.

"Fox scarcely sits still," Willow Woman later noted as we ate our evening meal.

"Yes," Morning Star said with a laugh. "He hardly even comes to me to nurse anymore. He is a child who is constantly moving. Perhaps we should have named him Running Fox."

"He will slow down in time," Black Wolf said. "I remember it was not so many years ago when his mother was still running everywhere." Black Wolf's focus was divided between the ongoing discussions and patting his dogs, who were frantic for his attention after his long absence from them.

Slow Bear joined us, and the conversation turned to other things.

We again talked of relocating to the Lake Region.

"Do you recall it?" Slow Bear asked Black Wolf.

"I most certainly do!" Black Wolf sputtered. "That is where Ria's dimwitted brothers coerced us to bring down a woolly mammoth for them in exchange for allowing Tor to be paired with her. I also recall that as the mammoth breathed his last, he delivered the final blow and let loose his bowels . . . all over me! I would do anything for Tor and Ria, but I would have preferred to avoid that whole experience if I could."

Morning Star had not heard this story before, and she giggled at the mental image of the scene. But despite Black Wolf's less than pleasant incident, he had to agree that the Lake Region had many advantages. The nearby tundra was a wasteland during winter, but spring and fall it teemed with migrating animals, the lakes and streams provided much potable water, and the forests were largely untouched by either fire or man.

Gray Owl appeared with his healing kit in hand, and he nodded his greeting to us.

"Gray Owl, I would like to present to you my eldest daughter — and Tris's mate — Morning Star," Black Wolf said by way of introduction. "Morning Star has asked to see how I am mending. Would you mind if she watches while you change my bandage?"

Gray Owl stared at Morning Star a moment.

"Pleasant evening to you," he said. "Why, of course. Please feel free to observe. Black Wolf, I will need you to turn sideways so that the torchlight is shining on the proper side of your head."

Black Wolf obliged by shifting his body and then tilted his head, probably well-practiced by now, to the position Gray Owl required him to maintain throughout the procedure. Morning Star went to stand at Gray Owl's elbow as he carefully unwound the cured hides. Slow Bear knew what was expected, as well. He brought vessels of water and several small sections and strips of clean hides.

Gray Owl tossed the soiled bandages into the fire, where they threw up sparks as they landed. Morning Star leaned in to get a better look and immediately gasped.

"Not very pretty, is it?" Black Wolf said to her.

"Oh, Da!" Morning Star exclaimed softly. "Your poor head!"

I made no attempt to look. It was enough to have viewed what I had seen of it beforehand.

Gray Owl washed the injured area, applied a salve, and re-bandaged Black Wolf's head.

"Thank you for allowing me to watch, Gray Owl," Morning Star said. "And thank you for mending my Da."

Gray Owl smiled kindly at Morning Star.

"I am happy to be able to help," he replied simply.

"When will Da be well enough to go home?" Morning Star inquired.

Gray Owl shrugged and pondered her question.

"Your father has made great strides, but he should continue to gather his strength, and also to allow time for the swelling to continue to go down," Gray Owl replied. "Perhaps by the new moon or soon after?"

The new moon would be with us in about seven or eight days. I thought that Gray Owl might be a little overly optimistic, but then he knew much more about healing than I ever would. As it happened, however, Black Wolf did indeed begin to show dramatic signs of recovery, and within a few days after the new moon, Gray Owl told Black Wolf he was now well enough to travel, provided that he took pains not to overexert himself.

Although Black Wolf was not eager to leave Willow Woman and Oak, he was clearly anxious to return home and see to his family's winter preparations. Our fleeting summer moons were almost over, and it was imperative that we all attend to our long-neglected summer chores before it was too late.

When we finally bid our hosts farewell, Willow Woman clasped Black Wolf to her.

"Do not forget me," she requested earnestly. "Do not forget that no matter where I am, I will be thinking of you. I am yours and you are mine. Do not forget me!"

"As if I could ever!" Black Wolf responded, despondent to be leaving her. "I will be thinking of you, as well."

* * *

Slow Bear, Crow Feather, and Roe Buck again escorted us home. We moved at a leisurely pace to accommodate Black Wolf's slower step and frequently stopped to allow Black Wolf to rest. It seemed as though his endurance grew with each new day. As our journey progressed his spirits improved, and he delighted in showing things to Fox.

"Look at that living cloud!" Black Wolf said, lifting Fox from his perch on a sled and pointing skyward. "See how it changes shape and direction!"

"G'Puh, no cloud!" Fox exclaimed.

"You are too smart," Black Wolf laughed. "But it is a cloud of sorts. A cloud of birds. Every spring and fall they flock together to migrate to warmer or cooler places."

"*Migate?*" Fox questioned. I doubted he had ever heard this word before.

"That is when animals, birds too, gather together to travel to find more food. Those birds —" Black Wolf again motioned toward the flock as it flew in undulating patterns overhead — "they know that when winter comes they will have little to eat and drink, and then they fly away to a place where winter is less harsh so they can survive until they can return in the spring."

Fox seemed thoughtful.

"We *migate?*" he asked.

Fox's speech was not always very clear, and it took Black Wolf a moment to catch on to what he was saying. Black Wolf considered the question for a moment.

"Someday we might," Black Wolf replied.

"Da is certainly enjoying himself," Morning Star said to me in a low voice. "It is as though he knows he has had a close scrape with death and now life is all the dearer to him."

"I would not be surprised if that were so," I agreed quietly. "It is good to see him looking so much better. And Fox is enjoying his time with his G'Puh."

I then noticed movement in the distance. This was not the movement of the herd animals that grazed on the open grasslands, so far away that even the mammoths appeared to be little more than specks. These were men, men who were stalking game.

"Look," I pointed, "some men are on a hunt. I wonder if we might know them."

We all stopped and watched the developing scene. We were still close to the White River, which ran alongside us for several days' travel, all the way from the Fen of Falls down to the convergence of the River of the Bears, where the fall Gatherings took place. We had chosen to hike a path that ran farther inland so that we did not have to trek at the river's rocky shore.

The riverbanks could be extremely perilous, as I found last year when I fell into that treacherous river and nearly drowned. If my mammoth friend had not pulled me from the river, I never would have made it out on my own. I shuddered inwardly to recall that mad rush down the sluice of rocks, being battered against boulder after boulder, constantly dragged under the surface by the current and my own lack of buoyancy. Then the cow had stepped into the raging water, effectively blocking my way. She lifted me with her trunk and carried me to a safe locale, where I was gently deposited on the ground.

Most times a hunter cannot afford to think of his prey with undue sentiment, beyond doing his best to give the animal a swift death. Although men have hunted woolly mammoths since times untold, I have come to believe that at least some mammoths might have more compassion than some people.

"What are they doing?" Black Wolf asked. "One of them is bound to fall in the river!"

"Let us go downriver and wait along its bank," Slow Bear suggested. "If one of them falls in, we may be able to help fish him out."

"That is a good idea," Black Wolf agreed. "I see a few mammoths down there, but none of them is likely to come to their rescue as happened to Tris!"

We left the trail, but we were careful to pick a smooth route for the dogs and their sleds, slowly making our way toward the river. We would keep our dogs well away so they would not interfere with the hunt. As we came closer, I still was still befuddled as to the men's plan. I could see that they were standing atop a promontory of loose rock, and it looked to be a rather unsafe perch.

Then I noted the objects of their focus. They were just a little way from a spot where the river widened and the current moderated. A herd of mammoths had crossed there, but one lone infant was balking at following the others. Its mother remained close by, attempting to bolster the youngster's confidence by encouraging it to enter the water. In the meantime, the rest of the herd continued its way downstream, bellowing to the lagging comrades to catch up.

The calf seemed panicked at the sight of its herd moving farther away, and it cried out woefully, walking downstream as well as it tried to follow them. There, the river began to narrow, the current resuming its angry passage, where it was impossible for even an adult mammoth to cross. As the mother mammoth tried to push her baby back upstream to calmer waters, I saw that she had the same uneven tusks as my large furry friend.

"The mammoth! It is she!" I exclaimed.

"*Who?*" Morning Star questioned.

"That is the mammoth that has saved me . . . twice!" I told her.

"Oh!" Morning Star smiled and strained to look more closely at the heroic behemoth. "She is trying to get her baby to cross! It is so small; I wonder if it can make it."

"The calf must have crossed the river before," I started. "The mammoths have to move around a great deal so they have enough forage. They strip an area fairly quickly."

"Those men are prying at the rocks," Black Wolf observed.

Suddenly, it all became clear to me. The boulders tumbled down amongst the cow mammoth and her calf, and although the calf was not caught in the brunt of the cascade, its mother was buried to her knees.

"*No!*" I cried out.

I hastily removed my pack and cloak, throwing them down, and I began to run, still toting my spear, although I had not thought of using it. I was so accustomed to carrying my spear that I actually felt unbalanced if I ran without it.

"Tris! Stop!" Morning Star called after me, but I ran on, deaf to her entreaties, my dog Raena at my side.

The hunters quickly descended on the cow before she could attempt to free herself, and immediately began to slash at the backs of her hind legs, keeping clear of her thrashing head and swinging tusks.

"*No!*" I cried out again, still running at full speed.

My lungs were bursting with effort by the time I reached my friend.

"Stop! Stop! Please stop!" I begged the men, who stared at me incredulously as I stood there panting, with tears in my eyes.

They were strangers, men of The People, and they regarded me with some alarm, as though I had taken leave of my senses. They stood absolutely still, bloody knives in their hands. The calf bawled loudly, and its mother answered with sorrowful cries of her own.

Massive puddles of blood soaked the ground near the mammoth's hind end. I choked back a sob and approached her head, so feared and recently avoided by the hunters. Her eyes followed me as I drew closer and spread my arms around the nearest side of her massive neck. Her breathing was labored, and her voice was becoming weaker.

"I am so sorry," I tearfully told her. "I am too late to save you, as you have done for me."

She gave a low rumbling groan.

"I am so sorry," I said again. "But I promise to you I will make sure your baby makes it across the river and rejoins your herd."

The mammoth groaned once more, gave a few puffing breaths, and then her head sank down between her trapped forelegs. She did not move. I stood at her side as the spark of life left her eyes. I stroked her noble old head as the breeze tousled her long fur. I leaned my forehead against hers as tears continued to run down my cheeks.

Now that the mammoth was obviously deceased, the hunters joined me at her head.

"What is wrong?" one of them asked, appearing deeply concerned.

"Are you crazy?" Another shouted at me, clearly annoyed at my interference.

"Was this mammoth . . . *special* . . . to you?" inquired yet another, who seemed to catch on that I had some sort of attachment to the animal.

"Yes," I replied, wiping my eyes. "She was special."

"I am sorry," the first said. "We did not know she was your mammoth."

"She was not mine," I shook my head at the thought of owning a mammoth as one might own a dog. "But I thought of her as a friend." The angry man moved toward the infant, knife still in hand. "Please do not hurt the calf!" I called out.

The man halted in place and shrugged sullenly.

The group of hunters was obviously confused by my behavior, and I had to acknowledge that if I were in their place, I would be bewildered as well. They were a party of eight men, and while a few regarded me with sympathy, the rest appeared quite hostile.

"Black Wolf!" One of them muttered and I looked up to see that my traveling companions had caught up with me. Black Wolf was well-known amongst The People, both for his great size and his relationship with their Head Elder.

"Black Wolf!" the angry man started. "I implore you to tell this crazed Old One to get away from our kill!"

Black Wolf glared down at the man with a withering gaze.

"He is not crazed. And, as he is paired with my daughter, he is a member of my family," Black Wolf said calmly. "He is not looking for a share of your kill. He is mourning a creature that has acted kindly toward him. She saved him from drowning in this very river, and she probably saved me as well when we were attacked and she came to our aid. I was already knocked unconscious," Black Wolf said, gently touching his still-bandaged head. "But I am told that she bowled over one of our attackers and stomped the life out of him."

The men were silent as they absorbed this news. They looked at the mammoth with a new respect.

"Puh-Puh cry?" Fox asked, breaking the silence, his lower lip trembling.

I lifted Fox into my arms and hugged him.

"It is all right, little Fox," I told him. "Puh-Puh is sad, but it is all right to be sad sometimes."

Morning Star came closer, carrying Pony, to examine my mammoth friend. This was likely the only time she would ever have the opportunity to stand so near a mammoth that had attained such a venerated age. She was one of the largest mammoths I had ever seen, either bull or cow.

"Poor thing," Morning Star said of the mammoth as she draped an arm around me. "She was beautiful in her own way. I am so sorry, Tris. You must be heartbroken."

As Black Wolf continued to talk to the hunters, Slow Bear, Roe Buck, and Crow Feather were busily trying to keep the dogs away from the copious blood. When they finally gained the canines' attention, they commanded them to move off a short distance and sit. The dogs reluctantly obeyed.

"We did not know we would catch the cow in our trap," one hunter explained. "We thought we might catch the calf . . . we will be working on this creature for days to process all the meat."

I understood. Butchering an animal this large meant setting up smoking racks and curing batch after batch of meat until it was ready to transport, if they even had the means to take so much meat home. Plus, they would also be forced to fend off any interested predators that hoped to muscle their way in for a feast.

After a brief and somewhat contentious conference, one of the hunters approached Morning Star and me, where we still stood at the head of the mammoth.

"There is a tremendous amount of meat here. Why do you not take the choicest cuts?" he offered.

My stomach lurched at the thought. Unlike Binty's man-eating family, I did not feel up to actually consuming something or someone with whom I had felt a kinship.

"Many thanks for your kind generosity, but no," I replied.

Black Wolf approached us as well.

"I have convinced them that you are not insane," Black Wolf grinned. "But what will you do with the calf? You do not hope to take it home with us, do you?"

Looking across the river, I then noted the herd watching us. They were calling out to their fallen matriarch and her orphaned calf. The calf answered, but remained huddled by its mother.

"I must move the calf back to quieter waters," I said determinedly.

"But how, Tris?" Morning Star questioned. "That baby is bigger than you are!"

"The dogs!" I said suddenly.

I had seen our dogs actively shepherd children from place to place; perhaps they would be able to help me drive this calf upstream. The oversized infant might not like it, but if it did not rejoin its herd it would surely die. I explained my idea to our companions.

The stupefied hunters stood by and observed with interest as Black Wolf and I gathered Raena and the other dogs and took them over to the calf, as Morning

Star and the children waited with Slow Bear, Roe Buck, and Crow Feather.

The mammoth infant did not care for the dogs and it pressed even closer to its mother. The dogs began to bark at the calf, edging nearer with avid curiosity. Finally, it was too much for the calf and it broke away with a lumbering gait — but it was headed in the wrong direction. Black Wolf and I called out to the dogs to steer the calf back toward us.

The plan actually worked. The poor baby was thoroughly terrorized by the time we got it to the place where the other mammoths had made the crossing. The other members of the herd had retraced their steps back upstream, and they continued to watch from across the river.

"I wonder if some of them will come over and escort the calf back to the other side," Black Wolf mused.

"I was wondering the same thing," I admitted.

We waited. No mammoth came across to retrieve the little orphan.

"Perhaps they are afraid of the dogs," Black Wolf suggested.

"That may be so," I agreed. "Would you take them up the bank?"

Black Wolf nodded and he called the dogs to follow him, until they stood with the rest of my group, which lingered nearby.

Now that the baby was no longer constrained to a certain area by the dogs, it wanted to return to its mother. I tried to block its way, but it was steadfastly single-minded in its desire to reunite with its parent.

Finally, I stood at its head and pushed back on its body with all my might.

"Come on, little one," I said, pushing and shoving it toward the river. "We are going in the water. I know you do not like it, but you have to go back to your family!"

At last, some of the mammoths grasped what was going on. They came halfway out into the river and called to the baby. I managed to turn the calf around and kept driving it toward them, my shoulder at its woolly rump as I slogged through the thigh-deep rushing water.

I breathed a sigh of relief when we reached the waiting adults. It was somewhat unnerving to see them so close by, towering over me, but I had made a promise and I would see it through. The mammoths did not pause, but promptly turned and took the calf away. Before I knew it, I was alone in the river, surrounded by the swirling waters.

Chapter Thirteen

We left the raging river once more and resumed our trek along the inland path. Morning Star held my hand as we walked, glancing up at me from time to time with a worried expression on her face. I tried to smile at her reassuringly, but she did not appear to be totally convinced by my charade.

That night the sky was devoid of clouds and the still air was cool and crisp. Morning Star had taken care of cleaning and re-bandaging her father's head; Gray Owl had assigned this task to her for our journey homeward. Now she and I held our sleeping children on our laps as we snuggled under our cloaks around the fire, accompanied by our companions and our collective dogs. Most of the faithful canines were snoring after the long day on the trail, although they were easily startled to wakefulness by any stray sounds.

"Fall is almost upon us," Slow Bear noted. "It will be time to start work on the new Gathering hall soon."

"Where will it be erected?" I asked.

"At the edge of the forest by the old hall," Black Wolf informed me. "We will see the site on our way home."

We might have cut through the forest and vast plains to go home, which was the route we had used to reach the Fen of Falls. And actually, that was the shorter route; but we chose to follow one of the river trails so that we might show Morning Star and the children the stunningly beautiful late summer landscape, and also The People's great hall before it was abandoned.

River trails were sometimes chosen if you were not familiar with the territory and were in need of a guiding landmark; however, even though we were not in need of the river's guidance, I was glad to take this longer route, even if it extended our trip by a day or so. Morning Star took in the scenery with wonder alight in her eyes. She would turn to me and smile, squeezing my hand as if to say, *so this is what you were telling me about.*

"I understand that the new hall's floor has already been cleared," Roe Buck chimed in. "It was a prodigious project."

"Standing Oak would be so proud of Willow Woman," Slow Bear stated. "She has seen to everything he envisioned. And when Oak becomes a man, he will carry on her work."

I thought back on my conversation with Willow Woman in which she said she would reach forty winters of age in a few years. The men of The People took longer to mature than men of the Old Ones, who were considered fully-grown by the time they reached fifteen winters. Oak would not attain manhood until he was perhaps eighteen winters old. It occurred to me that it was extremely unlikely that Willow Woman would ever see her son inherit his role. No wonder she had told Black Wolf that she expected him to carry on with little Oak's training if anything should happen to her. At that time, she had been ailing. Now, Black Wolf was coming back from a perhaps even more serious brush with death. By my estimate, Black Wolf was only a few winters younger than Willow Woman; it was questionable that even he would live long enough to raise Oak to adulthood.

However, no one else seemed to be thinking such morbid thoughts. Perhaps it was the demise of my mammoth friend that had me in a melancholy mood. Just then, Fox shifted slightly in my arms and I looked down at him. As always, I was struck by his perfection. His rosy skin was splashed with freckles and his curling red-gold hair was just becoming long enough to reach his shoulders. Fox's lips were parted as he slept, and his eyes moved behind their lids. I wondered what his dreams showed him. Would he become a Dreamer someday? Fox and Pony, and all the other children in our combined families, would inherit the future. As parents, all we could do was our best to prepare them for that eventuality.

"Da, those are certainly some very fine boots," Morning Star was saying lightheartedly to her father.

"Indeed," Black Wolf agreed. "Willow made sure that I left her in good form, complete with a new suit of clothing and new boots."

"You do not think that they are too conspicuous?" Morning Star questioned.

This was her subtle way of asking if it was prudent to come home wearing such showy articles and thus rouse her mother's suspicions.

"If they raise any questions, it will be the perfect time to clear the air," Black Wolf stated. "Besides, do you not think your mother will ply you with countless queries as soon as you return?"

"I would be more surprised if she did not," Morning Star countered. "Unless the magnificence of your new outfit renders her speechless."

"Have you decided what you will tell her?" Black Wolf asked.

"I will answer her as simply as possible. That you were at the home of our Head Elder, under the care of her healer. And that you left to come home as soon as the healer said you had recovered well enough to make the trip." Morning Star paused in thought. "If Mama asks about the Head Elder, I will say that I was a little frightened of her at first, but she treated Tris and me with the utmost kindness and saw to our every need."

"I doubt she will be satisfied with so much simplicity," Black Wolf laughed. "But I leave that to you. Just do not feel you must lie to protect me; you will not betray me by telling the truth."

"Yes, Da," Morning Star nodded somberly.

The Dreamer IV ~ THE CAVE OF BONES

* * *

When we arrived at the Gathering hall the next day, clear skies still prevailed, and the sun's rays beamed brightly through the chimney holes in the great hall's roof. This was a stark contrast to the stormy weather that rolled through the last time I was here, when the wind shook the hall and flashes of lightning sent blazing white shafts of light down each chimney hole in the moments after every clap of thunder.

We walked through the empty rooms, Black Wolf pointing out various details to Morning Star. When we reached Willow Woman's chambers, he appeared to view them with nostalgia; after all, these now barren rooms were where he had first spent time with Willow Woman.

Then we ventured outdoors to inspect the grounds. This was a large area to cover. We walked through the field of yellowed grasses, often with Fox trotting alongside us, from one end of the huge parcel to the other. The enormous area had previously been stripped of trees around the original hall, not only for the construction of the building, but to provide the attendees with firewood. Now the nearest trees were some distance away. At each moon-long Gathering, the numerous attendees set up their lean-tos and shelters all around the hall. Not all stayed for the duration of the event, but even so, it must have been a tedious job to bring in enough wood to keep everyone reasonably warm and fed.

The workers who had cleared a place in the adjacent woods for the new hall had already left the area, leaving behind many large mounds of felled trees. Black Wolf and Slow Bear explained that another crew would eventually arrive to construct the new building.

Early evening was soon upon us, and we elected to spend the night in the great hall. Morning Star, the children, and I were given one of Willow Woman's rooms. I smiled to see my petite Morning Star reclined on a sleeping platform where I had once seen Willow Woman's massive form sprawled out.

"What is so amusing, Tris?" Morning Star said, noting my wry smile.

"I was just recalling that there was a time when we were invited into this room and Willow Woman was on that same platform. You present a . . . a much different view," I replied.

Morning Star laughed and then, remembering that the children were asleep, clapped her hand over her mouth to mute her giggles.

"I must say that Willow Woman is a lovely person, and while I admire her strength and spirit, I would not endeavor to imitate her unusual appearance," Morning Star said with a grin.

* * *

The next day we were readying to set out for home once more when I saw Black Wolf stop stowing his belongings in his pack and pause to look at one of the items. His wistful visage made me look closer and I noted that he held one of the figurines that had caused

Willow Woman so much angst. Black Wolf glanced up and grinned.

"See? She need not fret that I will ever forget her. I procured this trinket as a keepsake to cherish when I am not with her."

"You know she hates those figurines," I said.

"I do," Black Wolf replied, hastily packing it away. "But I have come to love them."

Our companions were still preparing to leave, so Black Wolf and I collected the dogs and harnessed two of them to the sleds, upon which we loaded most of our supplies, which consisted primarily of our lean-tos and foodstuffs.

The dogs were eager to leave. Their tails wagged, and the ones being hooked up to sleds happily licked our faces anytime we came within reach as we bent down to fasten the harnesses to their bodies.

"These dogs have done much to make the journey both easier and safer," I said to Black Wolf.

"They do, at that," Black Wolf agreed. "That is why I keep so many dogs. I have long encouraged your Puh to get more dogs as well, but he is adamant that he wants only one at a time."

"That is true, but I believe that is because his household is a bit more crowded than yours," I pointed out. "And it is becoming more crowded all the time."

"Well, as with the Gathering Hall, your Puh may just find that it is time to rebuild," Black Wolf said as began to lead the dogs to the pathway in front of the hall.

Morning Star came out and joined us, holding Pony in one arm as Fox trotted alongside her. I needed only to don my pack and pick up my spear and I was ready to leave, too.

"What a pleasant day," Slow Bear observed. "With weather like this, one could travel forever with hardly a care."

"Indeed," Black Wolf agreed. "We must enjoy it while we can. When winter sets in, warm sunny days like this will be but a memory."

"When we cross that big hill, we will be able to see the River of the Bears," Crow Feather said to Fox. "Would you like to see a bear?"

"Bear? Big bear?" Fox asked.

"From a distance, I hope," I piped up. I knew that Crow Feather was teasing Fox, but I had no desire for my toddler to meet with a bear up close.

When we reached the top of the hill, we stopped to enjoy the view and catch our breath. I scanned the surrounding area. The river stood out as a bright blue line against the late summer foliage that was just starting to turn color. From this vantage point, I could see the old Gathering hall and the spot opened for the new hall quite clearly.

"Black Wolf," I began, "is it just my perception, or will the new hall be much larger than the old one?"

"Oh, it will be," Black Wolf nodded. "I have discussed this with Willow. It has not been brought before The People yet, but we gradually want to introduce them to the idea that eventually all peoples will attend our meetings."

"*All peoples?*" I echoed.

I remembered what it was like when some of us Old Ones had gone to a meeting at Black Wolf's suggestion. He thought we should speak to the Head Elder because we were being raided by a band of thugs who were trying to force us off our lands; he thought we should ask for him to intercede on our behalf. This was before we knew that Standing Oak had passed from life and that his daughter Willow Woman had taken his place. Some of The People were sympathetic and supportive; others were outright belligerent. None of us knew Willow Woman at that time, but she handled the situation deftly and it ended well; nonetheless, it was obvious that many of The People were not ready to accept Old Ones in their midst.

"Yes, *all* peoples," Black Wolf reiterated. "It may not come to pass until our children come into power, but we will keep working toward that end." Black Wolf placed a weighty hand on my shoulder. "Our families have lived and worked side by side for many years. And look at you and Morning Star, you are of two different peoples, but you are happy together. It is proof that there is hope for all of us."

"I would like to think that is so," I agreed.

"Yes," Black Wolf went on. "Considering that we are already vying for the same resources, joining together and working together is the only way we will all survive. The winters are growing ever longer and ever harsher. More people keep moving into the area. The Wolf-men arrived here last year and although they did not stay, who is to say who else may arrive and choose to settle here?"

"But if we relocate to the Lake Region, will we not just carve out a new homeland for ourselves and live as we always have?" I asked.

"We will only put off the inevitable," Black Wolf stated with surety.

Morning Star and I exchanged glances.

"Bear?" Fox suddenly called out, pointing toward the river.

I saw a large gray rock near the river's edge.

"Do you know what a bear looks like?" I inquired of Fox.

"Big," Fox answered.

"Mostly, yes," I told him, "but that is not a bear."

Fox looked disappointed.

"No? No bear?" he asked.

"No, but see there? Do you know what that is?" I picked up Fox and motioned toward a fallow deer that was walking in a leisurely fashion across an open expanse of field.

"Deer! Deer with spots!" Fox responded.

"That is right!" I told him as we both grinned. "That is a fallow deer."

Fox was always so pleased when he could supply the right answer. We recommenced our hike as the trail took a long slow decline toward the River of the Bears.

* * *

We reached the family compound in four days. The weather had remained sunny and warm for the duration, but the nights were quite cool. Just the same, it was good to be home. The dogs seemed as pleased to be on familiar ground again as we were.

Our families gathered around us, first making sure that Slow Bear, Crow Feather, and Roe Buck were comfortably seated and provided with refreshments as the rest of us greeted our loved ones. Black Wolf's mate, Little Fawn, was working with Gran preparing food, looking taller than ever next to tiny Gran. She looked over at us as we embraced and traded pleasantries with our loved ones, and then Little Fawn spoke to Gran briefly, leaving her to finish the job. She smiled warmly at Morning Star and the children and me as she walked toward us, and gave us all a quick hug and kiss.

"You are well?" Little Fawn asked Morning Star.

"Yes, Mama. Very well," Morning Star nodded, smiling broadly. "And are you well?"

Little Fawn nodded absently, and moved away to proceed on to Black Wolf. She stopped in front of him and they looked searchingly at one another.

Black Wolf was still somewhat underweight. His hair was lacking his usual braids, since most of it had been cropped off. It would be some time before he could sport his customary spider hat again. The bruising was still fading at the side of his face, and although it was much improved, I realized that Black

Wolf's appearance was probably still shocking to those who had not seen him since he was clubbed.

"How is it with you, Little Fawn?" Black Wolf inquired, attempting to engage her politely.

Little Fawn ignored his question.

"You have been badly hurt?" she asked.

"I was, but I am much better now," Black Wolf smiled slightly. "I have come home so that we may be ready for winter. There is much work to do."

"You do not look able to work," Little Fawn said flatly. "You are so thin! Did they not feed you where you stayed?"

"I was fed anything I wanted to eat," Black Wolf said, losing his smile at both her tone and the insulting implication that his hosts had neglected him, especially considering that Slow Bear and the others were within hearing. "I was exceedingly well-cared-for while I was away; in fact, I did not have to lift a finger if I did not so desire. If I am thin, it is because my injury caused me to have prolonged nausea. I am over that now, and I am perfectly able to carry on with my duties at home."

Little Fawn was speechless for a few moments, as she must have realized that Black Wolf could have stayed where he was, in comfort and where he did not need to work unless the whim struck him. But in spite of that, he had made the long trip home so that he could be sure that his family was amply provisioned.

"I see," she said finally.

"We will talk later," Black Wolf said gently. "We need to have an understanding between us. I want us to at least be able to behave in a civil manner toward each other."

Little Fawn nodded. She then turned and walked away, entering their home without a backward glance. Morning Star and I exchanged glances.

"Poor Mama," Morning Star murmured to me. "She knows what is coming."

"Perhaps she does," I agreed quietly. "But she may find some comfort in knowing the truth and not being left to guess anymore."

Puh now joined us, peering up at Black Wolf with concern.

"How is it with you, old friend?" Puh asked.

"I am lucky," Black Wolf stated. "Gray Owl probably saved my life."

"Does your head still pain you?" Puh questioned.

"Only sometimes," Black Wolf said with a shrug. "Have I missed anything while I was away?"

"We have been harvesting and drying berries, herbs, and mushrooms," Puh replied. "Bror and I brought in a small boar earlier today, so we are looking forward to a good meal tonight."

"What of Aessa and little Binty?" Black Wolf inquired.

"Aessa is settling in well, and Binty is positively thriving." Puh smiled as he looked over at Binty, who was happily playing with the other children. "Now that we know he is unable to hear, we are trying to communicate with him with hand motions. He is a fast learner."

Fox was wriggling to be released from my grasp so he could run about with his playmates.

"Fox is going to be exhausted at the end of this day," Morning Star predicted. "He is going to collapse into bed."

Our evening sup was soon ready and, as it turned out, Fox was asleep before the end of the meal. Gran was seated beside me, and although she was quiet at first, she finally spoke.

"The journey went well?" Gran asked.

"Yes, mostly," I told her. "It would have been an idyllic trip except that my mammoth friend was killed. I tried to save her, but I was too late."

"I thought I had sensed a sadness in you," Gran said softly. "But you saved her baby again?"

"You saw that?" I nodded. "I returned the calf to the herd. I can only hope that one of the lactating mothers will adopt it. It is much too young to survive without that."

"You did your best," Gran patted my arm. "Life has a way of persevering when it must."

"I would like to think so," I agreed.

* * *

Later, Morning Star and I were cozily nestled in our bed. We had rolled onto our sides, but we were still coupled and pleasantly entangled. I lazily stroked the side of Morning Star's face as I waited for sleep to come.

"Tris," Morning Star began.

"Yes?" I said, eyes still closed.

"Thank you for taking the children and me on that trip. I know you were worried for our safety," she paused and kissed me. "But I so enjoyed it. And it made me appreciate all that you experience when you are away from us for long periods of time."

"I am just grateful that all went well. It was a good idea to bring all those dogs," I said, nuzzling her sleepily.

I was just beginning to doze when Morning Star spoke once more.

"Tris."

"Yes?"

"I love you."

"I love you." I tightened my embrace around Morning Star and counted myself so fortunate to have this woman. I felt sleep begin to descend upon me once more.

"Um . . . Tris . . . ."

"Yes?" I said in barely a whisper.

"I believe I am carrying another baby," Morning Star announced.

My eyes popped open.

"A baby? Another one? You are?" I stammered in my excitement.

"Are you happy?" Morning Star questioned a little tremulously.

I kissed her long and deeply.

"Of course I am happy! I have been waiting and wondering . . . ."

"Oh, are you not impatient! Pony is not yet a year old . . . ." Morning Star said, giggling. "We will have to start thinking on names for this child: if it is another dark-haired girl, perhaps we could call her Raven; if it is a boy he might be . . . ."

"How long have you been thinking about this?" I broke in lightheartedly.

"Oh, not long," Morning Star said. Her giggles dissolved as I kissed her again.

* * *

It is evening and multitudes of fireflies flicker in the background. My loved ones are gathered around the dancing flames in the fire pit, enveloping us in a glowing circle of light. I look into each face, trying to make sure we are all present, but the Dream only shows what it wants me to see . . . .

Author's Note

First, the obligatory disclaimer: all persons depicted in this book are fictional. Any resemblance between my characters and any person either living or dead is simply coincidental.

Next, the subtitle *The Cave of Bones* and the cave where Tris, Tor, and Black Wolf meet the less-than-hospitable family is based on the Goyet Caves in Belgium. These caves contained a wealth of ancient tools and bones, including fossilized bones belonging to at least five Neanderthals, dating to about 40,000 to 45,000 years ago. The group is known to include at least one woman and one child. The bones showed not only signs of being butchered, but of being smashed to harvest the marrow. Some of the bones were also used as tools.

It is difficult to say under what circumstances this episode of cannibalism had taken place. Was this the typical method they used to handle their deceased? In some primitive cultures cannibalism is considered to be a means for the beloved dead to remain with the living, by "incorporating" them into one's own body.

Also, one must keep in mind that during the last ice age, when permafrost existed in the ground on a year-round basis, digging a grave was no easy matter at any time of year. Perhaps some decided that they had to find an alternative to interment. After all, one would probably not want to just leave the deceased hanging around in the back corner of the cave. Taking them outside where the animals would get at the body wasn't likely to be an appealing option, either.

Could it be that those consumed were guilty of some heinous crime? Were they prisoners of some sort, or otherwise in disfavor with the clan? It's hard to conceive of such a thing, but is it possible that this clan was simply not sentimental about their dead?

Or was it simply a desperate state of affairs? Although the cave contained numerous bones of prey animals, particularly horses and reindeer, if the clan's hunters were killed or had become ill or disabled, starvation might not have been far behind. The Neanderthal people had heavy muscular bodies that required a high caloric intake to survive. Additionally, just living during an ice age climate when temperatures were ten to twenty degrees colder than they are now would require the consumption of quality high-fat foods, of which their fellow humans would be low on the list of available animals. People of that time period did not have a lot of body fat and would not have carried enough meat to sustain a clan for long. One of the reasons the Neanderthal were large-game hunters is that those were the animals that best fulfilled their dietary needs.

There is also the chance that it was some sort of ritualistic behavior; we can speculate, but we will probably never know the reasons behind this unusual practice.

I would like to point out that the medicinal remedies portrayed are based on what little we know of early man's healing methods. Often, ancients are believed to be primitive and subject to the whims of nature. While this is sometimes true, I think early humans' life skills would probably impress most of us. Many would not fare well in their world, but yet those people persevered through some of the most formidable times in history. Their skill as healers and their knowledge of nature's pharmacy would have varied from clan to clan, but make no mistake: in most cases it was probably quite impressive.

Some fossilized Neanderthal remains show definite signs of extreme injuries: head injuries that may have caused blindness or deafness, limb amputation, broken bones, etc. Often, there were also indications that individuals survived for a long time after being injured. These people could not have lived without a lot of "medical" intervention and care. Studies of Neanderthal dental calculus seem to confirm that they used a wide array of plant materials to ease or cure their ailments. It would not be surprising to someday find that they may have used substances like honey to heal wounds, as well.

Also, the Willow Woman figurines described in this novel — as you may have guessed — are based on the so-called *Venus Figurines* that were created during the Upper Paleolithic and have been found at locations over most of Eurasia.

I would also like to note that since we have little direct information about how people interacted with woolly mammoths (outside of hunting them), I have delved into what we know about modern pachyderms for both inspiration and data. Elephants are well-known for their empathy and intelligence. In many ways, their behavior is almost uncannily human. They are devoted to their fellow family members: comforting one another, attempting to care for the ill and injured, and grieving for their dead, even to the point of covering the deceased with dirt or branches.

While tamed elephants can develop loving relationships with humans, it is unlikely that most wild elephants would ever come to have a friendship with a person under normal circumstances. In rare situations, wild elephants have come to the aid of humans and even stood guard over them if they perceived that the human was hurt. Tris's bond with the herd matriarch was meant to portray one of those extraordinary and inexplicable connections between man and animal.

And finally, although I strive to make the books in this series as historically plausible as possible, theories change, and new discoveries render even the most current data obsolete with startling frequency. It's exciting to follow along, but ultimately, it can make it extremely challenging to write a book with historical accuracy that will stand up to the tests of time.

Before I close this note, I would like to thank my family and friends for their love and moral support as I labor to produce these books. ("Labor" seems a very apt term, since the writing, editing, and designing processes of each "baby" takes about nine months from typing the first words to receiving the finished books from the printer!) Very special thanks to my aunt Carol Beusee for her feedback on this and all the preceding novels.

Thank you, as well, dear Reader, for taking valuable time out of your life to read my humble books.

The next installation in The Dreamer saga will continue with *The Dreamer V ~ The Blood-Red Skies*. If all goes well, this next installment in Tris's adventures is due to be released in the summer of 2020.

With warmest regards;
E. A. Meigs

Index of European Ice Age Animals

Antelope (Saiga Antelope) These small antelope (24 to 36 inches tall at the shoulder weighing approximately 80 to 140 pounds) ranged over a good part of the northern hemisphere. They are exceptional in appearance due to their unusual muzzles, which feature a long, flexible snout that looks much like a truncated elephant's nose.

Aurochs (Extinct) Predecessor of domesticated cattle. Size varied between 61 to 71 inches at the shoulder, with weights of 1500 to 3300 pounds. Their horns could reach up to 31 inches in length. Sometimes aurochs is spelled "auroch", but from

my readings, I am lead to believe that but the "s" is often included even when the animal is referred to in singular form because it is an alternative form of spelling "ox" and isn't intended to indicate plurality.

Boar Wild boars are the plows of the animal world. They are built for digging. Their heads and massive

shoulders make up a good part of their bodies and their large, sharp tusks, which continue to grow throughout the life of the animal, are very effective at turning over soil. The largest adult male boars can reach weights of nearly 800 pounds and attain a shoulder height of 49 inches. Sows (females) are much smaller and they lack the mane and thick shoulder/back "shield" of the boars. Their tusks are also of a more modest size. The coloring of their coats varies from anything between white and black, but most tend to run towards darker shades.

Brown Bear

(Eurasian Brown Bear) Although this bear is called a "brown bear" its color can range from black to a tawny light brown. Males average 550 to 650 pounds but very large specimens can exceed

1000 pounds. Females weigh 330 to 550 pounds. During pre-history, the brown bear did consume some plant matter, but it was generally carnivorous.

Cave Bear (Extinct) This was a very large, stout bear. The average male weighed in at 880 to 1100 pounds.

Females averaged a little over half that (495 to 550 pounds). Despite their size, bone analysis and other indicators suggest that cave bears were primarily herbivores.

 Cave Lion (Extinct) (European Cave Lion) These efficient feline predators were some of the largest known cats in animal history. Based on skeletal

remains, it is speculated that the males may have reached 11 ½ feet in length from nose to tip of the tail, and weighed over 880 pounds.

Chamois A medium-sized goat/antelope. They are 28-31 inches tall at the shoulder and range in weight from 55-132 pounds. Besides being a fine source of meat, their hides were used to make garments.

Crow (Carrion Crow) A large black bird, approximately 18 to 21 inches in length with a large, heavy beak that is well adapted to catching and eating small prey such as mice, frogs, insects, etc., and scavenging off the kills of other animals.

Elk (Eurasian Elk) ("moose" in North America) A medium-sized elk/moose, now extinct in many parts of Europe. They average from just over 600 to just over 1000 pounds, with shoulder heights at 5.6 - 6.9 feet.

Fallow Deer A medium-sized deer, about 30 to 37 inches at shoulder height and weighing 66 pounds (small doe) to 220 pounds (large buck), although unusually large bucks may tip the scales at 330 pounds. Their winter coats are brown, but they are

freckled with white dots on their backs and sides during the summer.

Giant Deer (extinct) (Irish Elk) The giant deer was one of the largest deer ever to walk the earth. Commonly, it has mistakenly been called an Irish elk, although it was neither exclusive to Ireland nor an elk.

This huge deer averaged nearly 7 feet in height at the shoulder and carried antlers with a spread that could span 12 feet. They are estimated to have weighed nearly 1200 to just over 1300 pounds but larger individuals could have reached upwards of 1500 pounds.

Horse The Eurasian Ice Age horse came in many different varieties.

They were more than likely the size of modern ponies and appeared in all colors, spots and stripes. They may have resembled the Przewalski's horse that still exist today or the now-extinct Tarpan horse.

Ibex (Alpine Ibex) A moderate-sized, dun-colored mountain goat. The bucks' horns sometimes reach 39 inches in length. The does' horns may grow to a length of nearly 14 inches. Similarly, bucks achieve a much larger body size (35 to 40 inches at the withers and weighing from 150 to over 250 pounds) than the does (29 to 33 inches at the withers and 37 to just over 70 pounds).

Lynx (Eurasian Lynx) The biggest of all species of lynx. Approximately 24 to 30 inches at the shoulder, and including its short tail, it may be 31 to 51 inches in body length. The largest males weighed nearly 100 pounds, but the typical lynx will run between 18 (very small female)

and 66 pounds (good-sized male).

Marten (European Pine Marten) A small, weasel-like animal with dark brown fur, often with blond markings or a blond bib on its chest.

At a little less than 3 ½ pounds and about 21 inches in length, the marten was hunted for its beautiful, silky fur.

Mink (European Mink) A small mink,

even the largest is just under 20 inches in length and only about 1¾ pounds. They have been prized for their dense, luxurious winter coats.

Porcupine (Old World Porcupine) This rodent wears an impressive coat of quills, some of which may be up to 14 inches in length (Crested Porcupine). These species of porcupines come in a variety of sizes: the smallest adults run from 11inches to 34 inches long, and may weigh between 3.3 to 60 pounds.

Red Deer (European Red Deer) Another very large species of deer. The buck weighs in at 350 to 550 pounds (48 inches at the shoulder) and does run 260 to 370 pounds (45 inches at the shoulder). These deer, unsurprisingly, are known for their

reddish coats. During autumn, the males often have a short mane on the backs of their necks.

Red Fox The biggest of the fox species, the adult ranges from 14 to 20 inches tall at the shoulder and weigh from 5 to nearly 40 pounds. These animals were often harvested for their fine fur.

Reindeer (Also known as caribou) This important game animal consists of several different subspecies and varied in size from 120 to 550 pounds. Color varied as well, but all subspecies shared many of the same basic characteristics, such as a fairly

impressive set of antlers (in most reindeer, both the bucks and the does grow antlers) and a two-layered coat of fur, featuring a woolly undercoat that thickens dramatically each winter and an overcoat of longer, coarse, hollow hairs.

Roe Deer (Western Roe Deer) This small deer averages just over two feet to two feet, 6 inches at the withers, and a mere 33 to 77 pounds. Nonetheless, they were an important source of meat for prehistoric humans.

Sheep The actual breed(s) of ancient sheep that roamed Ice-Age Europe are unknown, but it is recognized that sheep were hunted and eaten by early man. It is possible that the Mouflon (shown in image) is the modern

day link to prehistoric sheep. The Mouflon have a shoulder height of less than 3 feet and weigh from 75 to 110 pounds.

Snow Leopard This beautiful cat is well adapted to life in a cold, mountainous habitat. It has a stout build and long, dense fur that varies in color from white to pale gray, with dark gray to black spotted markings. It is about 24 inches at the shoulder with a weight of 60 to 120  pounds, although larger males have been noted at 165 pounds. Their fur was considered to be very desirable and they have long been hunted for their pelts.

Vulture (Eurasian Griffin Vulture) This large scavenging bird may have a wingspan of over 9 feet and weigh as much as 33 pounds, although most individuals range from 14 to 25 pounds. It is known that early men consumed the meat of vultures.

Wisent (European Bison) An impressive animal, the wisent is the heaviest land animal that still resides in modern day Europe. Fully grown specimens range from 5 to 6 ½ feet at the shoulder and weigh 660 (small female) to more than 2000 pounds (large male). The wisent was an important source of food and hides for prehistoric humans.

Wolf (Eurasian Wolf) These are the largest of the European or Asian wolves. Their sizes vary greatly from 70 to 212 pounds. Although their coats could be black, white, or even reddish, by far the most common color was a grey/buff and white combination of medium length, dense fur.

Wood Grouse (Western Capercaillie) This Eurasian bird is the largest of the grouse species, weighing as much as 15 pounds. The cocks have an average weight of 9 pounds and a wingspan of 36 to 48 inches. The hen is considerably more modest in size, with a weight of  approximately 4 pounds and a wingspan of 28 inches.

 Woolly Mammoth (Extinct) This large mammal lived in Eurasia and North America, and was similar in size to today's African Elephants, but with considerably longer tusks, a shorter tail, and much smaller  ears. The males of this huge species could attain heights of up to 11 feet at the withers and weigh over 12,000 pounds. Females were somewhat smaller, although still impressive in size at up to 9½ feet at the shoulder and weights up to nearly 9000 pounds. Their hairy hides came in a wide range of colors that could be anything from blond to quite dark. They were protected from the extreme Ice Age weather conditions by a double fur coat that consisted of a short, dense, woolly undercoat and strands of long outer guard hairs.

Woolly Rhinoceros (Extinct) Looking much like a modern rhinoceros in a heavy fur coat, the woolly rhinoceros sported two horns on its long snout and carried its thick body on short, stout legs.

This animal averaged about 4000 to 6000 pounds, with a shoulder height of about 6½ feet. The larger front horn that grew from the woolly rhinoceros' nose could reach lengths of 24 inches.

About the Author
E.A. Meigs

I was raised on Cape Cod (Brewster, Massachusetts, USA) at a time when the Cape was still a rural area made up of woodlands, marshes, beaches, streams, and ponds. There, my life was divided between the land and sea. My father was a commercial fisherman, backyard boat builder, and an outdoorsman; so I had an early introduction to boats, working in the commercial fishing industry and spending lots of time in the local fields and forests. When I wasn't on a boat or roaming around the great outdoors, chances are I was reading or writing. I have been a compulsive writer literally since I could first put words on paper, producing my first full length novel at ten years old. Even at that age, my goal in life was to someday find a way to combine my love of nature, the outdoors, and writing.

After raising a family and embarking on a long and varied career that included many years working on and around boats and in the commercial fishing industry; a stint with Florida Fish & Wildlife in a small field office; and other jobs that actually allowed me to use my writing skills, I awoke one day with *The Dreamer* in my head. I began writing the novel with the intention of producing just one book, but as the story progressed it became apparent that the plot would require much more than one volume to tell the tale.

I have two wonderful adult daughters and nine delightful grandchildren. I am an avid camper and I strive to get out hiking as often as possible, daily, when my schedule allows.